# Satin

a stitch in time

# Satin

## a stitch in time

payal dhar

HARPER

First published in India in 2011 by Harper
An imprint of HarperCollins *Publishers*
Building 10, Tower A, 4th Floor, DLF Cyber City, Phase II,
Gurugram Haryana – 122002, India
www.harpercollins.co.in

2 4 6 8 10 9 7 5 3



P-ISBN: 978-93-5029-063-7
E-ISBN: 9789-35-136-043-8



Typeset in CG Omega 10.5/14.2
InoSoft Systems

Printed and bound at
MicroPrints India, New Delhi

*It was a* khamosh raat.
*All was calm, all was bright.*

# Contents



## Part 1

## Part 2

# Note to the Text: The Calendar and Clock

The world described in this book uses a different calendar, though many of its principles are similar to the calendar we are acquainted with. For example, they do have years, months, weeks and days, but they work differently.

A year (*sahal*) consists of five months (*mand*). A month has seven weeks (*hav*) of ten days (*roz*) each. This means a month corresponds to seventy days, and a year has 350 days (355 in Flame Festival years—more on that later). Though there exist names for the terms 'year', 'month', 'week' and 'day' (also hours, minutes, etc.) in Samanya (the common language of the world), we will be using the English terms in order to keep it simple.

The five months are called Bahar, Yaz, Riyen, Aki and Baridi, corresponding to the spring, summer, rainy, autumn and winter seasons. This five-month system is followed for four years consecutively; every fifth year, there are five extra days added in order to keep the seasonal cycle constant. These five days comprise the Flame Festival, and they are a period of celebrations. They are also considered auspicious.

A day is divided into twenty hours. An hour has 100 minutes, each comprising 100 seconds. Which is to say, this world uses a decimal system of time. Thus, half-past fourteen would be fourteen hours and fifty minutes, and called just 14.5 hours or 14.5 o'clock. It can also be written as just 14.5 for short.

*Please remember, however, that the absolute length of a day remains the same as ours.* That is to say, the same period of time (a day) is divided into twenty hours there and twenty-four here. Therefore, one hour in the world of Satin would correspond to one hour and twelve minutes in our world. This also means that their minutes and seconds are shorter than ours. (Work that out yourself.) Regular bedtime would be about 18 o'clock and wake-up time between 4 and 5 o'clock approximately. Remember that 10 o'clock is midday.

# Part 1

# 1

Though nobody believed her, Marik Fahe was really walking away when it happened. She was so angry that her head was pounding and a red mist invaded the edges of her vision. But she was still walking away.

A few dry leaves and dirt swirled in her wake as she stormed past. And even though the hot, dry summer afternoon was still, a magical breeze fuelled the dust into a tiny tornado that went unnoticed. The pain in Fahe's head rose to a crescendo and she clenched her fists tight, till something exploded inside her head.

A moment later, someone screamed.

'Fire!'

The sound of running feet was all around her. Fahe stared with her mouth open and her heart sinking.

'Oh, perfect!' she said out loud.

## Defiance

Far, far away in the Kuzerazi mountains, like Fahe, El'Karich Keas had problems of his own. He sat at his favourite spot behind his house, uncaring of the cold wind that buffeted him from behind. He pulled his overcoat closer around him and thought about his mother.

From his vantage point, Keas could see the mountain roads winding down towards the tiny village of Karich, the place of his mother's birth, from where he got his name. It was odd, he thought, that all his life he had carried the name, but he hadn't really known her and only felt a vague indifference towards her. It was even odder that right then he had the distinct feeling that he was missing her.

He looked down at his hand, which clutched a letter written on thick, creamy paper, embossed with a logo of a silver-blue flame encased in a five-pointed star in the top right-hand corner. It was addressed to him in neat calligraphy. It crumpled in his hands as he clenched his fist.

Sounds of traffic reached him from the road, muted by the distance. Most of it was headed into the town of Saje, and the bus station—with its newly acquired electronic displays—had a long line of buses waiting to enter. People were returning home from work at the end of the day. Some way to his left, a little distance below him, he saw two children skipping down the purple heather-clad mountainside towards the bus station. As Keas watched, one of them slipped and landed on her bottom, looking startled. The other one laughed and pulled her up. Keas smiled. He knew them. He knew just about everyone in the town of Saje. And, of course, more people knew him too. Though that had more to do with who his father was.

They were well into the summer month of Yaz. Dusk came late this time of the year in the Kuzerazi Low Lands, but the shadows were already lengthening, forming mysterious shapes in familiar places. Keas leaned back on his elbows. The thought of leaving Saje was wrenching. He had grown up in these mountains; they were part of him. And he was pretty certain that, given the circumstances, once he stepped out there would be no coming back.

Like almost every child in the world, Keas dreamt of being a mage. But for children in Kuzerazi, this remained a secret dream. For, Kuzerans despised and mistrusted mages. They resigned themselves to the fact that their children usually always coveted magic, but by the time they were in their teens, most of them grew out of that yearning, realizing that to yearn for such pagan powers was wrong. The Flame was to be revered, not exploited to draw power from. That was sacrilege.

Keas wondered what it was that made him different. To despise something as strongly as Kuzerans felt about mages and magic seemed wrong to Keas. But these were dangerous thoughts, and he was wise enough to keep them to himself. His father was a disciplinarian. He did not tolerate dissent. He knew of only one person who had ever matched wills with his father and won, and that was his mother.

She had been a travelling bard, and had been unable and unwilling to settle into the sedentary life that living with Keas's father brought. And so she had left when Keas was a few months old, seeking to follow her dream of gathering and telling stories. Thus, he had never known her, and this was the first time that he missed her. *She would have understood what it meant to make your own way*.

Keas felt something vibrating in his pocket. It was the alarm on his comm handset, reminding him to set off for home for dinner. He put the letter away and stood up to make his way down the narrow path.

Back home, he hung his coat up, washed and walked down the corridor to the kitchen. The house was warm, courtesy the wire-mesh baskets of crushed baskel leaves coated in mud and soaked in a weak water-reed sap solution that hung in every room. The combination gave off heat, but no smoke, and cost nothing in electricity. Another of his father's discoveries. He might have made a lot of money selling that idea, but no—that wasn't his way.

Keas greeted his father and took his place at the table. He ate his bowl of meat and vegetable curry silently, without tasting it. He didn't even notice that they were having drip breads today instead of plain ones. Every now and then, he watched his father.

Win ate with his eyes not on his bowl of food or on the dripping buttered bread in his hand but straight in front of him. His forehead was creased in intense concentration, like it always was when he was deep in thought or doing something important.

When, Keas wondered, looking at him through hooded eyes, had his father stopped being his hero? Ever since he'd learnt to walk and talk, Win had involved Keas in his work as a herbalist and apothecary. He took the young boy to the forest to gather plants, taught him to identify them by smell and touch, as well as sight. He let him watch him make potions, preserves and concentrates. In time, he let him stir, measure and bottle. It helped that Keas seemed to have a natural talent too.

Keas was five when he learnt that letters put together made words, and since then had regularly read to his father. They were mostly books on plants and potions and healing. At first, they made no sense to the child. Then, one day, sitting by the river with some friends, he discovered otherwise. Fooling around like ten-year-olds generally do, one of them had fallen into the water. He came up, sputtering, some strange tendrils hanging from his mouth. He spat them out, but in under a minute he was feeling strange. Moments later, he had passed out.

While the others had panicked, Keas had reached into the water, pulled out a thick stem, broken it and held it under the unconscious boy's nose till he came to. He couldn't tell how he had recognized the symptoms or known the cure. Instead of being filled with a sense of pride and fulfilment at having saved a life, that was when Keas began to see how he was different from other children. He never had toys or books like them. He never got money to go to the theatre or spend on sweets. His father never played with him or talked to him about ordinary things.

Ever since Keas turned fourteen—some two weeks ago—his father had been asking him to make up his mind if he wanted to leave school to apprentice with him. Everyone assumed he would agree sooner rather than later. Win took few apprentices—though they came in droves from all over to learn from him, from the towns and villages of Kuzerazi, and even from the east, from across the mountains—and Keas was envied for having that privilege by birth. But it was a privilege he didn't want.

Kuzerazan apothecaries were famed the world over for their natural healing with plants, and El'Idrin Win one of the most famous. Practitioners of modern medicines in the east, known as physicians, were often derisive of them, but Win's knowledge and wisdom were much sought after, and not just in Kuzerazi. People from the Nizrah plains and Far Darom were referred to him as well, sometimes by physicians themselves. Even mages had approached him, it was said. He had seven other apothecaries and three herbalists working under him, not to mention two apprentices.

His selfless devotion to his work had earned him the respect of the community. His humble home and lifestyle spoke of his single-minded determination to serve people, save lives. Of course, with skill and fame of that magnitude, it was impossible not to have detractors. There *were* people who questioned him—in some circles, Win's reputation was controversial because people thought he made use of eastern magic to achieve the results he did.

In general, though, everyone admired Win. But his son hated him. Keas hated his overbearing personality. He hated being *Win's* son. He hated not having a choice in his own life. He hated his father for thinking that anything he decided was all right with Keas.

Yet, with his ticket to freedom in his pocket, the boy was filled with dread.

Fahe tapped the pencil on her worksheet. With her quick mind, she ought to have raced through the numeracy problems, but she was preoccupied. When her brother Yavi had called her early that morning, informing her that she would be having a bodyguard, it was indication enough that this was to be a bad day. A Really Bad Day.

Then Inos, her closest friend (*former friend*, Fahe reminded herself), had announced that she was leaving Koda at the end of the summer. She was travelling to Far Darom with her parents to continue her studies there and learn about the family trade. She didn't know when she would be back.

And then there was the incident with the fire at her triangles game.

The only silver lining was that Mother was too busy to give her a hard time about it. That didn't mean she wasn't livid, though; in fact, her personal assistant had been waiting for Fahe with a very stern message when she got home from school. It was amazing how fast bad news travelled.

Fahe sighed and flung down her pencil. *To Mother, I am just the tool that keeps the title in the family,* she thought bitterly. *As for Inos—the Flame consume her! I am going away to the Academy, so why should I care if she leaves? And, finally, now that I'm fourteen, I can't compete with the juniors anyway, so they can ban me for all I care. In short, to repeat myself: I. Don't. Care.*

'Don't care about what?' said a pleasant voice behind her, as someone slapped a bag on the table and sat down next to her.

'Go away, Yanik,' said Fahe rudely, embarrassed that she had spoken about loud. 'Go and cuddle up with your pretty Sera, why don't you?'

Yanik pulled up a chair next to her. 'You know,' he said, 'there are certain things fourteen-year-olds mustn't say to adults. Including their brothers. That was one of them.'

'What do you want, brother?' said Fahe sarcastically. 'How may I be of service to you?'

'What's this I hear about some trouble at the game?' Yanik asked. 'There was something about a fire. Please tell me you had nothing to do with it.'

Like her brothers, Fahe had been playing for the junior trianglers of Koda with some distinction for the past few years. Both boys had played till they were no longer allowed to play in the mixed junior league and their education at the Academy had taken up too much of their time.

'Mind your own business.'

'Yes, yes,' said Yanik, settling in more comfortably on the chair. 'I heard about it from Sera.'

'Lovely,' said Fahe. Sera was Yanik's partner and she was a teacher in Fahe's school. 'That means she's already grassed on me and you know very well what happened. Why are you asking me then? Just stay out of my life.'

'Trouble is, whether you admit it or not, I am part of your life,' Yanik said patiently. 'Now, please tell me why you set fire to the triangles shed.'

Fahe looked at him. His face was sunburnt and the permanent scar from a particularly bad case of teenage acne made him look very young. He hated that, and was trying to grow a beard. Right now, he looked like a teenage boy trying desperately to look older. His dark reddish-brown hair was clipped unfashionably short, combed and pinned back neatly. Light-brown eyes regarded her with concern. Fahe knew that she was supposed to be a spitting image of him—though she didn't have a beard, of course—and she wasn't sure it was much of a compliment.

She crumpled the edge of her worksheet moodily, without replying. She knew she was behaving like a ten-year-old.

'You've not been suspended from school, have you?' Yanik asked quietly.

She had already had two suspensions that year. A third would mean her invitation to the Academy would be withheld pending a hearing. What was worse, at fourteen-plus, under juvenile criminal laws, she could be arrested and detained. A Marik with a criminal record... Fahe didn't want to contemplate what sort of reaction that would have in the family.

'No,' she said quietly.

'What happened exactly? Look, do you want to tell me now or do you want me to find out by asking people?'

Fahe glared at him. 'You wouldn't dare.'

'Try me,' Yanik said, mirroring her stubbornness.

'All *right*!' Fahe said, flinging herself out of her chair. 'I had a fight with Inos and was angry. I mean, *really* angry. Then I was sent off from the game for an unintentional foul... and sort of accidentally set fire to the games shed.'

'The Flame consume you!' cried Yanik, standing up as well. 'What is the *matter* with you?'

Over the years, Fahe had been showing some erratic powers, which made it all the more important that she go to the Academy as soon as she was old enough and get proper guidance. Lately, she hadn't been very good with keeping her anger in check, which often resulted in unfortunate incidents in her vicinity.

The Mariks had always been only moderately talented mages. However, the family was also one of the patrons of the Academy of the Flame at Koda. Which meant that unlike other prospective initiates who applied in hordes every year, Mariks only needed to be born to be assured of a place.

'I'm not so Flaming perfect like you and Yavi, all right!' burst out Fahe.

'Mind your language,' said Yanik, his tone stern.

'Why? You were just swearing!'

'That's... different. Do you realize what you've done? You're old enough to have a sense of accountability. Don't you ever think of consequences *before* you do anything?'

'Why do you care?' shouted Fahe. 'You can take your stupid triangles and stick it...'

'Fahe!' Yanik grabbed her shoulder. Her face was red with anger. 'Enough!'

Keas's conversation with his father wasn't going all that well either, though it had started innocently enough.

'Very quiet today?' his father said to him as they ate. 'Something the matter?'

'Not... er...' Keas cleared his throat. His voice still went squeaky without warning. He searched for a more grown-up pitch. 'Not hungry.'

'Trouble at school?'

He shook his head. 'No trouble.'

He knew he had to tell him. Sooner rather than later. Now.

He gathered his courage.

'Father,' he said tentatively.

Win turned his head. 'Yes?'

'I... er, I've been thinking. You know, of the future. Of my future.'

'Good. About time.'

'And, I, er, have... have decided—with your permission, of course—now that I am fourteen, I should be allowed to leave school and, er, pursue a... a direction.'

'Keas, I will be happy and honoured to have you as my apprentice,' Win said. 'However, I would like to make the formal announcement next month at...'

'No, Father,' said Keas. 'I... I didn't mean that.'

'Oh,' said Win, taken aback. 'Then what did you mean?'

'I don't want to be an apothecary. Or a herbalist,' said Keas in a rush. 'I... I want to make my own choice.'

Win's face took on a reddish tinge, contrasting oddly with his dark hair. Keas knew he was trying to control his rage. 'I see,' he said tightly. 'And what choice is that?'

'I have decided,' he said. Now that he had said it once, it was easier. 'I don't want to be an apothecary.'

'Are you mad, boy?' his father thundered. 'People come from the ends of the world to avail of the opportunity you have because you were born in this house.'

'Accident of birth does not make me a prisoner, Father,' said Keas warming to the subject.

'What sort of nonsense is this? All right, if you feel it's too early for you to leave school, so be it. You're young yet, and there's time.'

'But Father, you've never asked me what *I* wanted.'

'You are just a boy. You don't know what you want!'

'I am a person,' said Keas, starting to lose his composure. 'With a mind of my own.'

'You are nothing but a silly child!' said Win. 'Choice? You want a choice, right? Well, your *choice* was made the day you came into this world. You would do well to remember that, and be thankful for it.'

'But Father, that is not right! You always said that knowledge is the most powerful of weapons. I want knowledge. In other things.'

'For you, there are no other things. The sooner you understand that the better. Ten generations of your family have been apothecaries. You will be one too. So will your children. It is in your blood. You do not fight blood and tradition.'

This talk of tradition always incensed Keas. What was the point of having the ability to reason if your choices were already made for you? 'Then it's time to change that,' he said boldly. He took a deep breath and added: 'I want to be a mage.'

The silence in the room was thunderous. The blood drained from his father's face.

'What... utter... *nonsense*!' his father gasped. 'El'Karich Keas, have you been bitten by a rabid dog?'

'I am serious,' said Keas. He pulled the letter from his pocket. 'I sent my application and have an invitation to be an initiate at the Academy at Koda.'

'You are Kuzerazan!' Win said, raising his voice in anger. 'Have some *respect*.'

'Being Kuzerazan is no crime,' cried Keas, deliberately misunderstanding.

'You are not going,' said his father firmly.

'You can't stop me,' countered Keas.

'I will lock you in your room if I have to! Hear this, Keas, the day you leave Saje, you stop being my son.'

'I don't want to be *your son*!' said Keas, shouting as well. 'That's all I've been my whole life! I want to be my own person. I want to decide my own path.'

'You are a fool,' said Win. 'But at this age, all boys are fools. I am prepared to forgive you.' Pushing away his bowl of half-eaten curry and plate of breads, Win stood up. 'This conversation never happened. Good night.'

Marik Yanik was frustrated. There were eleven years between him and his sister, and sometimes he felt more like a father than brother. Father *and* mother, to be honest. In the six years since he had left the Academy as a trained mage, he had spent a significant part of his time being a de facto parent to Fahe.

His marrying Sera a year ago had made things worse. Fahe had just become difficult and erratic. He had moved out of the family home—for not only was it Fahe's by rights, his mother had not been pleased with his decision. Sera was much older than him, which was fine, and she might even have overlooked the fact that she had a child from an earlier relationship. But that she was a commoner had been the very last straw. According to Mother, marriages were for making political or business alliances. By that measure, Yanik's was useless.

Their mother, Prefect of Marik, had considered her duty done after she had produced a daughter to inherit the title, a daughter she never really noticed except when she needed her for strategic reasons. As for their father—Yanik never stopped wondering how he had managed to get himself elected to the city council in between lying in a drug-induced stupor at one of his 'poet parties' (everyone knew that that was just a polite euphemism for his group of pot-bellied middle-aged rich friends who dabbled in illegal drugs) and avoiding Mother by disappearing for days on end. Since he wasn't Mother's official consort any more, he hardly ever went to Marik either. In fact, Yanik couldn't remember when he had last seen his mother and father in the same room, let alone talking to each other.

Fahe had been little more than a baby when he had gone off to the Academy, and he only saw her when he came home for the holidays. Yet, he hoped he had somehow managed to be there for her whenever she needed him. When she was younger, it was obvious she completely worshipped her older brothers, but things were different now.

*She won't come running to me with a bruise on her knee like she used to seven years ago.*

He sighed. He loved his sister, but she was so difficult to like.

'Listen, it's just two weeks, all right?' he said reasonably. 'Grit your teeth through it. I promise you, things will be different at the Academy.'

Fahe turned away. Her anger seemed spent all of a sudden.

'Believe me, the Academy is nothing like you can ever have imagined,' Yanik went on. 'And I think it will do you good to get away and live with different people—people of your own age. The discipline also teaches us to control ourselves. I was as much of a hothead as you are, but one year as an initiate significantly altered that.'

Fahe shook her head, staring down at the floor. 'You don't understand, Yanik,' she said quietly.

'I don't understand what?'

There was a long silence as Fahe stood perfectly still.

'What's wrong?' Yanik prompted.

Fahe shook her head. 'Nothing. Maybe I am wrong.'

'Oh, don't be silly. Just... could you *please* stay out of trouble? Do it for me.'

She stared at the floor sullenly.

Yanik sighed. He knew what he was going to do. Sera wouldn't be best pleased, but he'd deal with that later. 'Tell you what—you come and stay with Sera and me for a while.

Till this thing blows over. Mother is leaving for Marik today, and Father... well, Father will distract himself, no doubt.'

'All right,' said Fahe with not very good grace.

'Always welcome.'

It was Fahe's turn to sigh. Being nasty all the time was so tiring.

# 2

Keas was up before dawn. He packed his canvas satchel with a change of clothes, a new notebook and some pencils, his favourite book, his birth certificate and the letter from the Academy. After a moment's thought, he took out the last two items and put them in his trousers' pocket. His comm device lay untouched on his table. He wouldn't be taking it.

*What about money?* he thought.

He counted the tokens in the pocket of his school uniform, and discovered he probably had enough for a couple of meals, and just about enough for his train ticket to Koda. He needed more—there would be toll tax to pay at the borders, and other things. He knew where the household money was kept, of course, and wrestled with his conscience about whether taking that would be stealing.

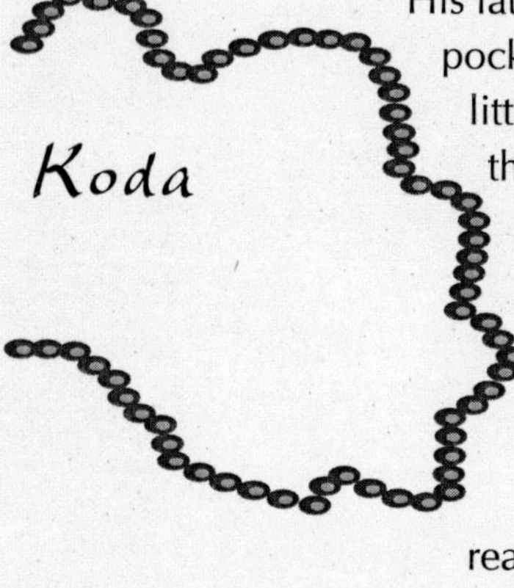


His father didn't believe in giving him pocket money, though he did put a little aside for him every month in the bank. Keas was given tokens for his trip to school and his lunch every day, and he usually managed to save a bit from there.

*Well, part of the household money is for me, after all,* he reasoned finally. *When I'm gone, they won't need to spend on me any more.*

He emptied the ceramic pot on the kitchen shelf, but there wasn't much. He decided he wouldn't spend anything on food till he got his ticket. He found some bread and cheese, which would suffice till then.

That done, he dressed for his departure. Linen undershirt, his dark school trousers and his thickest shirt, which he pulled over his head, yanking the criss-crossed laces closed and tucking the edges inside. A dark sweater, thick socks and his hand-stitched animal-hide boots. Keas was very proud of them—not many kids his age could boast of boots.

He tucked his trousers carefully into the boots and laced them up. He picked up his overcoat and his satchel. He realized he would have to ditch the overcoat and some of the woollens somewhere along the way. That far east, it would be too warm.

The planning and execution of his departure, effected as silently as possible, had enabled him to push anything that he was feeling into the background. But by the time he stumbled out of the house, his vision was blurred.

Motor caravans of merchants and buses lined up every day at dawn at the town centre of Saje. Keas looked around for a familiar face. If he could get a lift from someone, he could save on the fare to the Kuzerazi–Nizrah border.

But he found that, like him, there were a number of travellers looking for a free ride.

'Good morning, friend,' someone called to him. A dark man, probably from Nizrah or further south-east. 'Looking for a ride to the borders?'

'Yes. Yes, I am,' said Keas. 'You got place?'

'That depends. How many?'

'Just me.'

He regarded the boy evenly. 'Twenty-five rens.'

Keas's heart sank. He couldn't afford that. 'No, thanks.' He turned away.

'Hey, friend. Come back. Twenty. All right? Twenty.'

Keas was young, but he was no fool. He realized what was happening. 'I might as well take a bus. I can give you seven.'

'Ten and it's a deal.'

Ten it was.

Keas settled himself between sacks of vegetables and crates of fowl. He found some extra sacks and spread them on the floor. Hunger was beginning to gnaw at his stomach. That, combined with the unease and excitement of the adventure, kept him from feeling anything else.

'I'll have a nap,' he told himself. 'Then I'll eat my bread and cheese. Maybe I can keep some for later.'

He shut his eyes and waited for the motor to move. With luck, he would be at the border in a couple of hours, maybe three. The formalities at the border would take another hour at the most. He would be on the Trans-Nizrah Rail to Koda by noon.

Fahe had always known she would have a bodyguard when she went to the Academy, but that had been so far off that she had never given it much thought. Yanik and Yavi had had their bodyguards, Karev and Rindan respectively, for so long that Fahe couldn't remember a time when they hadn't been around. Karev and Zurel, who was going to be her bodyguard, were half-siblings, and Rindan their uncle. Both Karev and Rindan were in fact more than just bodyguards—they were trusted friends and companions, and they had an almost magical quality of blending into the background most of the time. She wondered what Zurel would be like.

'So you're going to have a permanent tail now, is that it?' Inos had said cuttingly when Fahe told her. 'Surely even blue-bloods like you deserve their privacy? Now everything you do is going to go straight back to your brothers or your parents.'

'It doesn't work like that!' Fahe had retorted, not sure why she was defending a stranger to her best friend. 'She's not a spy.'

'Then what is she? What does it work like? Are you going to tell me some rubbish about complete trust and lifelong devotion?'

'Why do you care anyway? You'll be gone next month and you never have to see me again. What difference does it make to you?'

'Don't blame it all on me. You're going away to the Academy too.'

'At least I'll still be in Koda.'

The conversation played back in Fahe's mind as she stood outside the massive gates of the Koda Academy of the Flame. The five-pointed-star logo along with its stylized flame was worked into the iron grille of the gates. A ceremonial guardhouse stood at each side, but they were unoccupied. Instead, there were two cameras mounted on the gateposts, one of which whirred towards Fahe as she came closer.

The Academy grounds were vast, and a network of roads and landscaped lawns lay between Fahe and the complex of buildings in the far horizon. She had been inside before, of course, attending Yavi and Yanik's anointing ceremonies, but she had never been to the interiors of the immense property. The living and academic quarters were deep inside—you couldn't even see them from the gates. Fahe wondered what it would be like living there. It was like a little town in itself, she had heard, with its own shops and theatres and what not.

*Oh well, I'll find out soon enough*, she thought.

There was an automated self-service ticket counter at Besnal, but Keas was too scared of making a fool of himself. It wasn't that Saje had been completely backward, but there had been a sleepy casualness about it. Besnal was quite different—it was a modern-day town, complete with wide roads and fancy motors. Keas was familiar with Besnal, but he had never crossed the border to Nizrah. He already felt apprehensive about what it would be like when he got to Koda.

The surly woman behind the ticket booth at Besnal Rail Stop stared at Keas when he asked for a ticket on the next train to Koda. He had looked up the timetable and knew there was one in less than an hour.

'Well?' she demanded.

'Sorry?' said Keas, awkwardly clutching his satchel as well as a bundle made out of his overcoat and sweater. He was already sweating in his heavy shirt and trousers.

'What kind of ticket do you want? Seater or sleeper?' she asked impatiently. She looked him up and down in a manner that was exceedingly judgemental, if only Keas could figure out what she was judging.

'Er... seater,' he said, 'I guess.' He assumed a seater would be cheaper than a sleeper. He noticed a chart behind the woman, with a list of prices by distance, and yes, seaters were by far cheaper.

'Reserved or unreserved?' she asked with an air of doing Keas a great favour.

Another quick glance at the price chart. 'Unreserved.'

She tapped away expertly at her computer terminal, asking Keas for his name and age. He gave his name as Karich Keas; the 'El' would give him away as Kuzerazan, and for some reason, he didn't want that.

'You will need to pay a toll of twenty rens at Koda,' she informed him. 'You have the option of paying it now if you like, and I'll give you a receipt. Saves you the trouble later, but your choice.'

'All right,' said Keas. He paid for his ticket and the toll, his heart sinking at how it depleted his finances.

When the train pulled in, he was surprised to find the unreserved carriage empty. Just to be sure he was in the right place, he got off and took another look at the big letters that said 'Unreserved'. He took a seat by the window and put his things away on the overhead rack.

A middle-aged couple with a small child clambered on, and he felt ridiculously relieved. He smiled at them and nodded a greeting, but they stared back at him. Blushing, Keas looked away. Maybe smiling at strangers was not something you did as a matter of course outside of Kuzerazi.

An alarm went off, making Keas jump. The doors hissed shut slowly as a disembodied voice over the public address system said again and again, 'Engaging lock. Please stand clear.' There was a sort of vulgar sucking sound which Keas assumed was the lock engaging, and the train started to move.

The breeze from the open window felt cool to Keas's sweaty face, and he leaned back, closing his eyes. He didn't realize it as the day caught up with him and he dozed off.

Marik Yavi, the younger son of the Prefect of Marik, took off his mage's cape and draped it on the seat next to him. The waterlogged banks of the palm-lined backwaters rolled back steadily as the train pulled out of Marik, and Yavi was thankful for his air-conditioned carriage. Travelling in the day across the summer Nizrah landscape was not his idea of recreation.

Yavi always liked a good puzzle, but even odder than the things his late grandfather had bequeathed him was the fact that he had left him anything at all. It was no secret that he disapproved of Yavi because he was adopted, and often muttered things that sounded suspiciously like 'bad blood' when he was around.

Though nobody would admit it, when Grandfather Avin (Mother's father) died some months back, everyone was really quite relieved. There were no two ways about it—he was incredibly difficult. Especially difficult to like. He was opinionated and didn't know the meaning of tact. Thankfully, he had wanted little to do with the children. He was pretty much a recluse, forever writing, and he barely emerged from his study. When Yavi and his siblings had to go and see him every summer on their annual visits to Marik, he hemmed and hawed at them, insulted Yavi and handed them some money. It took about five minutes altogether.

Mother always thought Grandfather's writing was the ramblings of a senile mind, but Yavi—who could never resist anything made of paper and bound into a book—had spent a considerable amount of time since his teenage years snooping around in Marik, trying to figure out what Grandfather was writing. And now that the entire collection had literally fallen into his lap, it was a cruel joke that he had absolutely no idea what it was all about.

*He probably did it on purpose,* thought Yavi. *Left me with an unsolvable puzzle so I could finally convince myself that I am the idiot he always thought I was.* This realization made him even more irritable.

It was a small private carriage reserved for the Marik family when they travelled. All of the seats stretched out into comfortable bunks if required. His bodyguard Rindan paced its length restlessly. The third occupant was Zurel, a serious-faced woman in the same Marik guards' uniform as Rindan, and she was pacing the carriage in the opposite direction.

'Will you two please sit down,' Yavi snapped.

Rindan sat without a word, but with a small, sympathetic smile. He had some notion of what was going on in Yavi's mind.

'Yes, sir,' said Zurel, perching awkwardly on the seat opposite Yavi.

'And none of that sir business,' said Yavi severely.

She nodded to acknowledge, but Yavi's sour mood dipped further at the realization that their carefree childhood friendship was now just a faraway memory.

He flipped through a collection of bound fabric samples on his lap. They were all different sizes and various colours, and all silky, satin cloths. *Why has Grandfather left me books of cloth samples?* he asked himself for the hundredth time. *The Flame consume him!*

He gave up on the cloth and picked up an old, battered diary. *And what is it in his diaries that he needed years putting it together?* He riffled through the pages aimlessly. It was just a collection of cursory notes in chronological order, mostly to do with his travels in Kuzerazi:

—

63 Baridi: Reached Fezar. Varda coming later. Komas reports Lake House testing in order.
64 Baridi: Made progress. Helped with testing.
67 Baridi: Lake House ready for occupation. Varda in town.
Flame Festival, Day 1: Commence moving into Lake House.
2 Bahar: Komas's birthday.

—

And so on. About a dozen journals filled with such mind-numbingly boring details in Grandfather's neat hand. In fact, Yavi would have dismissed the diaries and cloth pieces as rubbish had it not been for the sealed note that had been handed to him by the lawyer. It hadn't said much. Just: *The key is in Satin.*

The only conclusion Yavi could draw from it was that it referred to the cloth samples. Did that mean there *was* a mystery to solve or was it Grandfather's idea of a joke? He was deep in thought, when a banging on the door of his carriage startled him.

Keas had no idea how long it had been when he woke with a jump to feel something moving next to him. To his surprise, there was a group of three boys—teenagers, maybe a few years older than him. One of them was watching him with amused eyes as the two others were going through his things.

'Hey!' Keas jumped up in indignation. 'That's mine!'

The boy who had been watching him suddenly grabbed him by the front of his shirt and hurled him across the seat into the aisle. Keas went sprawling, hitting his head hard. His vision spun, but he scrambled for a hold to pull himself up. A vicious kick to his side threw him to the floor, and another kick straight into his diaphragm winded him.

Someone spoke in a foreign dialect and then pulled Keas up roughly. Impatient hands felt about his pockets and then said something in a disgusted voice. He was pushed again, and this time, Keas broke his fall by hanging on to one of the seats.

He didn't pause to think. Instead, he ran. The moving, lurching train, coupled with his aching side and the fact that he couldn't seem to see out of one eye, made progress difficult, but Keas didn't stop. He stumbled on and on, till he fell against a dead end.

A handle... Keas gripped it with relief, but when he turned it, it only rattled ineffectually.

He heard laughter behind him and realized that he hadn't gone all that far. He wondered what had happened to the family in his carriage as he banged his fists on the door, crying out for someone to help him.

*I should have never left home*, he thought as he slumped helplessly against the door, his palms weakly slapping the surface. Remorse and pain battled for dominance as Keas collapsed, sobbing, on the floor.

*Father was right, I am a fool. This is my punishment for defying him*. That was his last thought as he suddenly fell forward. The chill in the air hit him as his head banged against someone's legs. Through one eye, he saw a pair of sandal-clad feet and a thin silver chain around one ankle.

He grasped the ankle. 'Help,' he sobbed one last time and passed out.

When Keas came to, he was stretched out on a comfortable bunk, covered with a blanket. Something cool was pressed to one side of his face, and when he tried to sit up, his side hurt.

There was a man sitting next to him on the bunk; he gently pushed him back.

'Easy now,' he said. He was speaking in the standard Samanya of Nizrah, also commonly spoken and understood in Kuzerazi, and Keas was fluent in it. But this man had a hard accent he had to strain to follow. 'You'll be all right. Try not to move for a bit.'

'These yours?' asked another voice. Keas turned his head to find a woman dressed in some sort of uniform. She was holding his overcoat and sweater.

He nodded.

'I caught one of them,' she informed him. 'I handed him over to the guard, but I think the other two got away. There was a stop, and they jumped off.'

Keas nodded again, bewildered and overwhelmed. 'Thank... you,' he croaked, and then cried out as a sharp pain pierced his upper arm.

The man next to him said, 'Don't worry, just an injection. For your pain.'

He helped Keas sit up, and for the first time, he saw that he was in a much grander carriage now. The windows appeared to be sealed shut, the seats plush and comfortable. A carpet covered the floor and the air was refreshingly cool.

He blushed to find three pairs of eyes curiously regarding him. The man next to him stood and closed what seemed to be a physician's kit on the table by the side. Keas was used to noticing things about people. This man must have been in his early twenties, rather striking to look at. He was brown-skinned, darker than he was—they all seemed Nizrahis by their skin colour. The man had brownish hair tied back and blue-grey eyes. Keas assumed he was from one of the noble families of the plains that he had heard so much about. There was something in the way he carried himself and the way everyone else was waiting for him to speak that seemed to indicate he must be in charge.

But then, Keas reasoned, would a noble dress in ordinary cotton trousers and simple shirt? Though he had ornaments in his hair. And would he talk to him like he was an equal? It confused him.

The man spoke finally.

'What's your name?' he asked.

Keas told him.

'Do you know what happened?' the man asked.

'I... I... no,' said Keas. 'I was sleeping, and I woke to find some boys ransacking my things.'

'Train gangs,' said the woman who had retrieved his things. Keas studied her. She was about the same age as the man. She was darker, and her hair was very strange—cropped really short. Her eyes were dark too, almost black.

'T... there was a family,' said Keas, 'in my carriage. Are they all right?'

The woman shrugged. 'There was no one there when I looked.'

There was another man standing behind her, with a clear resemblance to her. He too wore the same pink-and-grey uniform she had on, and had the same clipped hair.

But before anyone else could speak, the door at the far end of the carriage rattled open and a woman in black stepped inside. There was a bag slung over one shoulder and a handheld computer in her hand.

'Good day, Mage Yavi,' she said, addressing the handsome man. 'May I see your tickets, please?'

Keas's mouth fell open. He was a *mage*!

'And you, young man?' the ticket checker was asking him, making Keas fall back to reality with a thud.

'My ticket!' cried Keas in dismay, remembering. 'It was in my bag.'

The mage put a hand on Keas's shoulder, and the boy flinched.

'He was attacked and his things were stolen,' the mage explained. 'I am willing to take responsibility for him.'

'That is very good of you, sir,' said the rail official, 'but I still need to verify he's authorized to be on the train. What's your name, boy?'

'Karich Keas,' said Keas, his heart hammering. 'Are you going to throw me out?'

'Don't be silly,' said the ticket checker, not unkindly. 'Yes, I have your name here. Do you have anything to prove your identity?'

'I have this... and this.' He handed her his birth certificate and the letter from the Academy, thanking the spirits that he had had them on his person and the boys hadn't taken them.

'Birth certificates don't really prove much,' the checker murmured as she put the piece of card on the seat beside her and started on the letter. She read it for a long time. The birth certificate fluttered to the floor and the woman who had rescued his things picked it up and handed it back to Keas.

'Please,' said Keas desperately. 'Please believe me. I...'

The ticket checker looked up. 'I believe you,' she said. 'A Kuzerazan on his way to the Academy. Never thought I'd live to see that.' She turned to the mage. 'His ticket is for an unreserved seater, toll paid.'

Yavi nodded. 'I will pay the balance.'

'I will pay you back,' said Keas, overcome with gratitude. He was so grateful that he could cry. He didn't notice the young woman in the pink-and-grey uniform watching him carefully.

# 3

Yanik had a prayer for the conveniences of modern technology as he stood barefoot on a damp patch of land, waiting for the porters to finish loading the last van with supplies for Marik. Dressed casually in calf-length trousers, a loose shirt, a wide-brimmed hat and leather sandals, he looked like an ordinary person in his mid-twenties but for the silver chain around his left ankle that told of a privileged descent. And on his right hand was the Flamestone ring of mages.

There was a touchscreen tablet cradled in his left arm. At a quick glance, you could see that its screen was in the shape of a five-pointed star, but a closer look showed a system of intricate runas filling it. The pattern pulsed with magic and it made the air around Yanik glow bluish-purple. Every now and then, he would reach across with his right hand to add a slight modification. Beads of sweat stood out on his forehead, but his concentration was complete as he powered the conveyor belt that dragged the boxes up into the van. His magic was rooted in earth and water, and it was the contact with both—by standing on damp mud—that kept him going. Even then, it was taxing—the machine running the conveyor system had broken down, and they were on a tight schedule.

Yanik sighed with relief as the supervisor gave him the signal to stop. The glow around him disappeared and his pentaster's display went blank. He stepped on to the bricked path, wiping his forehead with a large handkerchief. He couldn't imagine what it must have been like in the old days, when such tasks were routinely done with magic. The time wasn't far, he mused, when magic would be merely ornamental and mages little more than performers.

A basin of water stood ready for him to wash his feet in, and just as he was pulling his sandals back on, one of the Marik motors pulled in through the gates. A hand waved at him as it passed by—it was Yavi.

As the older son of the House of Marik, and a city council member of Koda, Yanik was always terribly conscious of the proprieties. And it irked him a little that he hadn't the easy grace and charm of his brother, or even the reckless confidence of his sister. *Yavi should have been the older one,* he thought.

There was no trace of jealousy because it was so plainly the truth. For, Yavi wore his nobility easily. He was charming and gracious, his good looks helping a great deal. He liked people, dealt with them well. He was a born leader. Yanik, on the other hand, had to fight his natural shyness every step of the way to struggle to fulfil a role thrust upon him. He was the estate adviser to his mother, a job that required him to make many public appearances, travel, meet people. In short, everything he hated.

He sighed. He wished things were simpler, especially now, with the baby coming. He pushed himself to his feet and prepared to gather his things. He had things to discuss with Yavi, including asking him to recommend a physician of his choice for Sera.

Yavi grimaced in distaste as a bead of sweat ran down between his shoulder blades, momentarily regretting having put his cape back on. He had shrugged off Rindan's offer to carry in his luggage and asked him to take Zurel and Keas to the guards' quarters instead. Having abandoned the brick walkway that continued from the drive, he was now struggling up the garden, carrying two cases and his computer bag.

The prefecture of Marik was, of course, owned by the family, but the house in Koda was their primary residence. That was where the children had grown up. Mother had to spend a good bit of time in Koda, and Father, of course, being a council member at Koda, had to have a base in the city. They had had the house built a few years before their oldest child Yanik was born.

Yavi's favourite saraca trees were flowering, and it pleased him to find that the stone bench that was his personal spot in the garden was covered with the sweet-smelling scarlet blossoms. It always brought back a certain memory of when he was a teenager, back from the Academy for the holidays. He stepped on the brick-paved path that cut across the garden, leading to the family shrine. He took a little detour to pay his respects and then walked towards the house.

An assortment of servants came running up to divest him of his burdens, but Yavi shook his head, smiling wryly, before any of them could get close enough. It was a relief to be back from Marik. Being waited upon hand and foot and putting up with the constant obsequious attentions wherever he went had been a severe strain. Not that it was much better back home in Koda, but it was far more casual, and the absence of an extended family around him afforded at least some semblance of privacy. Also, he didn't have to walk on eggshells to avoid a 'family diplomatic incident' by doing—or, worse, not doing—something.

His navy-blue mage's cape swirled around his thighs in the warm breeze. It was made of linen, with a heavy edging to make it fall in sleek folds over his arms and across his back, down to his knees. The edges were held together in front by loops over three gilt-edged wooden buttons. Though it was light, he was still glad to enter the cool confines of the house, away from the summer heat.

The main hall was open from two sides, affording a cross-ventilation that kept the place pleasant even during the hottest part of the day. The open archway at the other end led out to a small, shaded courtyard, across from which was the main house. A large wide-mouthed stone cauldron took up the centre of the hall. It was filled with water, and rose petals floated on it. Around it was an intricate design, hand-drawn with coloured rice paste. A wind chime made up of a collection of tiny bells hung from the ceiling. It moved in the breeze, giving out a soft tinkling music that was almost ethereal.

Yavi inhaled the familiar fragrance of rose and the burning incense wafting from the stand in the corner of the hall—the smell of home, he thought. Putting his things down, he bent to take off his sandals and slot them into the shoe rack. He loved the house, and it saddened him to think that one day he would have to move out.

The redstone floor was cool under his feet as he crossed over to the covered courtyard and across with just his computer case and made his way to the kitchen to ask for something cold to drink. But he only got as far as the dining room when a voice stopped him. It was Yanik.

They greeted each other. 'Is it as bad as they say in Marik?' Yanik asked.

Yavi grimaced. 'Yes,' he said after a slight hesitation, 'and it could get worse. The mood is restless. The tourist season was cut short by the storms, and jobs will be in short supply soon.'

Yanik sighed. 'It has been pretty bleak anyway this year.'

'That much was obvious,' Yavi agreed. 'And now, after the storms, everything is... well, you know.'

'And so it comes back to the same thing. We need money. I'm meeting someone tomorrow who is interested in investing, but I don't like what he is proposing. However, I don't see that we have much of a choice.'

Yavi glanced at him. 'This is not your fault. It was not your decision to go ahead with the...'

Yanik stopped him with a raised hand. 'It doesn't matter.'

'It does,' said Yavi firmly. 'Mother chose to go against your advice, and now you are expected to take the fall for her mistake.'

Yanik didn't say anything, and Yavi coloured faintly at his outburst. Since they were young boys, they had had an unspoken pact that parental dissent was only to be silently acknowledged.

'I have something to ask you,' said Yanik, changing the subject.

'You want to fob your job off on me?' said Yavi seriously. 'The answer is no.'

Yanik smiled. 'Believe me, if I could, I'd have done it long back. No, it's Sera. We only found out yesterday, and no one knows yet. She's pregnant, and we wondered if you'd recommend a physician.'

Yavi laughed. 'That is the best news I have had all month. And, yes, of course.'

'Thank you.'

'You're welcome. And congratulations.'

They made their way upstairs, greeting their housekeeper Hadia, asking him if he would send up some refreshments.

'Now tell me about your trip,' Yanik said, when they were settled. 'Did you find anything interesting in Grandfather's things?'

Yavi pursed his lips. 'Not really. I can't think why he left his things to me.'

'He probably thought they'd be of interest to you. You are the only literary person in the family, and it's no secret you've been curious about his work for years.'

Yavi snorted. 'Family? Grandfather hardly even looked at me when he was alive. He told me once that he never had and never would consider me family.'

'Grandfather was eccentric,' said Yanik. 'Don't forget, Mother appointed you to stand in in case Fahe came into the title before she was old enough. Not me.'

'Well, Grandfather accused me of using drugs and magic to confound her!'

'What?' Yanik started to laugh.

Yavi looked at him, and then he smiled too. 'Well, yes, he was a little odd, I suppose.'

'So what exactly did he leave you?'

'It's a little odd,' said Yavi. 'There was a good-sized iron chest with my name on it. It had some diaries and some bound volumes of cloth samples.'

'Cloth?' said Yanik, laughing. 'Seriously?'

'Yes,' said Yavi. 'The journals document his travels to Kuzerazi. He went on a couple of expeditions, it seems.'

'Was he looking for something?'

'I don't know,' said Yavi. 'They don't really say much. They're ordinary personal diaries, talking very briefly about travel and things. And there's a letter that says something about the key being in the satin.'

'Maybe he was looking for trade opportunities, and that's what the cloth samples were for?'

'Could be,' admitted Yavi, and he couldn't help feeling a bit disappointed. 'I was hoping for deep, dark secrets from Kuzerazi, though, and not possible business opportunities.' He was lost in thought for a while. Then he shook his head vigorously. 'It can't just be that, Yanik. Grandfather spent years and years of his life working, writing, doing the Flame knows what. The result of that can't be logging his travels and collecting cloth!'

'Maybe that's why he left you his things,' said Yanik, grinning. 'To torment you with a non-existent and unsolvable mystery.'

'Unsolvable?' said Yavi with a derisive grunt. The familiar irritation that threatened to overcome his better judgement whenever he thought about Grandfather's legacy was raising its head again. 'I will go to Kuzerazi if I have to, but I *will* get to the bottom of this.' *If there is anything to get to the bottom of.*

But he pushed that thought down.

Yanik had been eleven and Yavi almost nine when Fahe was born, both boys old enough to sense the tension at home. At least Yanik—with the maturity of the older sibling—was aware of it, and Yavi, used to taking cues from his older brother, latched on to his unease.

Yanik was also old enough to know what the birth of a sister meant with regard to the title, though perhaps not realize all the implications of it. All of a sudden, Cousin Kedra and her family became strangers. Comings and goings between their house and Uncle Tachi's ceased without warning, which to the young boy was a welcome relief from having to spend time with the spoilt and temperamental Kedra.

The first time Yanik had got a hint that things were perhaps not as they should be was when Fahe was just over a year old, and they were spending the Flame Festival holidays at the ancestral home in Marik. On the last evening of the five-day revelry, in a house filled with people, the little girl vanished. When she was nowhere to be found, panic ensued.

It culminated in an ugly showdown between Tachi and his sister Vadi, Yanik's mother, who accused Tachi of having Fahe kidnapped. That was when it hit Yanik that Fahe's arrival had meant that the title had been snatched from Kedra. Before Fahe was born, she had been the oldest female child in the generation, but Fahe now took priority because her link was direct.

But what Mother was saying made no sense to Yanik—that if Uncle Tachi thought getting Fahe out of the way cleared the path for Kedra to inherit, he was making a very big mistake.

'Know this, Tachi,' his mother had hissed angrily at his uncle. 'If anything happens to Fahe, Kedra will not be the one to inherit. So, if you have any semblance of propriety, any respect for this family, for Marik, you *will* make sure that Fahe survives. Otherwise, you will destroy us both.'

Uncle Tachi had gone white at Mother's words, but before he could say anything, Grandfather Avin had interrupted to tell both his children to shut up, that they were fools if they thought the future of Marik was confined to their daughters. It was around the same time that a commotion had ensued in the dining hall that signalled the discovery of Fahe, curled up and fast asleep with the cat under the table, hidden from view by the long, hanging tablecloth.

Yanik remembered feeling a numbing relief that she was safe; yet, his enduring memory was of Uncle Tachi's shocked countenance as he had staggered back and fallen on the sofa, and Mother's expression of disbelief as they stared at Grandfather. Yanik never figured out what Grandfather had meant, and it was only many years later that he understood what Mother was trying to say.

The other thing Yanik remembered from that night was that Mother never went to Fahe after she was found. Fahe's nurse was sacked, and Hadia, who used to look after the two boys at that time, was given custody of the little girl as well.

Yanik didn't understand what was going on, but he understood that he would have to look out for his sister. He had padded across the nursery in the dead of the night, unable to sleep, and stood at the foot of Fahe's crib, clutching the rail, consumed by the loneliness of a child who blunders helplessly into a world of grown-up intrigue. The cold sweat that covered him had made him shiver in the overpowering humidity of a Marik pre-summer season, and he was filled with a dread that left his limbs weak.

# 4

# Letters and Runas

The four o'clock alarm ripped through Keas's head. He sat up with a yell. For a horrible moment, he didn't know where he was. Then he remembered—the kind mage had told him he could stay in the guards' quarters till he went to the Academy, and he had been given a place in the dormitory.

He pulled his pod's curtain aside. The dormitory was a hubbub of activity. Keas picked up his things and slithered down the wooden ladder. He showered and changed into a fresh set of clothes someone had given him. One of the younger guards told him there was a laundry room at the back if he wanted to wash his things, and Keas decided to do that later. His bruise was much better today.

He spent his morning sprawled on the grass, watching the guards train on the hard, rubberized cement practice yard.

'Come and join us,' said one, poking him with a wooden stick.

Keas laughed and rolled away. But he thought about it. Maybe they'd let him train as a guard if the Academy didn't work out. He watched the young woman Zurel who had travelled with them. She was practising some complex martial technique using a pair of giant forks. There was a grizzled older man with her, who barked instructions and seemed exceedingly displeased at whatever she did.

Zurel didn't talk much, but Keas had found a sort of gruff kindness about her. The previous day, he had felt awkward and out of place, and she had kept an eye on him and told him about things he could do to help out. Now, watching her with the ill-tempered older man, Keas burnt with anger on her behalf. He thought she was rather good. The man was trying to get her to retreat off the edge of the court, but she held him off.

The sun was high by the time he was satisfied. He went off without a word, leaving Zurel to clear up their equipment.

'Want some help?' Keas called.

'Sure, thanks,' she called back.

'He was rather hard on you,' he said, bending to open the weapon cases as she started to dismantle the weapons.

'Oh, Father is always like that.'

'That's your father?'

'Yes. Well, no. Not really. He's my mentor. He trained me. So I get to call him Father.'

She didn't say anything more. Keas stole a glance at her. She was taller than him, with skin like smooth chocolate. Her hair was dark brown, cut very short. Her face was devoid of any expression, but her eyes, a couple of coal-black buttons, were sharp. She bent and deftly started taking the bidents apart, and Keas couldn't help noticing the muscle tone through the white training suit she wore. He knew for sure that if he met her in a dark alley, he would run for his life.

'How do you become a guard?' he asked.

'By being born in the right family,' she said blandly.

'What do you mean?'

'My clan has been in the service of the Mariks for many years. Some of us are chosen to train as guards when we are small children.'

'How old were you when you started training?' Keas asked.

'Five,' was Zurel's surprising answer.

Keas's eyes nearly popped out. 'Really?' Then his face fell. 'So there's no chance I could train as one.'

She turned to look at him then, her eyes pinning him. He almost stepped back. 'You are a Kuzerazan. You left your home to be a mage. Now you want to be a guard?'

Keas blushed. 'I... I mean, if... you know, if it doesn't work out.'

She continued to stare at him, till Keas started to get uncomfortable. He looked away, and then looked back to find her smiling faintly.

'When I was your age, I wanted to be a mage,' she said, the smile widening.

Two letters arrived for Yavi that morning, both with the Academy logo. One had his name and address computer-printed; the other was addressed by hand. A hand that he recognized and that sent his pulse racing. He slid his finger under the flap and tore the envelope open, running his eyes greedily over the single sheet of text that emerged:

> My dear Yavi,
>
> By now you must have got the letter about the position. I hope you won't do anything foolish. Think it over carefully and do what your heart and your mind tell you to do. I know you have wanted this more than

anything else, and I hope you will not let insignificant history affect your decision...

Yavi frowned. What decision? What position? His eyes swept to the unopened letter. He guessed the answer lay there. He went back to the letter in his hand and read through the rest quickly. It finished with:

... and it would be wonderful working with you. You know that.

Yours,
Kariad

Yavi stared at the familiar signature for a long time, a tumult of emotions swirling in him. He knew now what the official Academy letter was about, and if he was right, it was unbelievable. It was his dream coming true. But that neat, slanting hand held him equally captive—Disciple Kariad. Whom he had worked so hard to put out of his mind for four long years.

Slowly, he turned to the other envelope.

When Fahe heard from Hadia that Yavi was back, she went looking for him. She had to admit, she was curious about what Grandfather had left him. She found him in the garden, sitting cross-legged on the grass amidst a collection of old books. The saraca flowers floated down towards him, a few even in his hair, but he was oblivious to them, or to the noises around him. His eyes were almost closed, his fingers moving as he drew intricate patterns inside the translucent pentaster that hung in air. When he drew in air, his magic transformed the symbols into a colour depending on his control. They were usually a blue-tinged white, for Yavi's magic was skilled.

Pure white indicated perfect skill, while pitch black denoted pure strength. Fahe watched silently, leaning against a tree. She knew that his near-white skill annoyed him, even though it was the envy of mages thrice his age. Yavi, ever the perfectionist, aspired for the ultimate balance of skill and strength—which would split his magic into the seven colours of the visible spectrum of light. But Fahe had never yet seen magic of that sort.

Yavi was a word mage. He had no control over the elements, but could direct his magic to demystify text, symbol, code—in short, any sort of literal or graphical representation. He could draw not only on solid surfaces like paper, stone, whiteboard, a computer or even on the ground, but also in air, as he was doing now. That was his preferred method, even though it was more difficult. Fahe watched her brother with fascination. It made no sense to her, but she had always enjoyed watching him work.

There was an exclamation of frustration from him, and the ethereal motif before him faded. He noticed Fahe finally.

'What are you doing here?' he said.

'Nothing,' said Fahe automatically.

'Weren't you at Yanik's?'

Fahe shrugged. 'Well, I decided to come back.'

Yavi frowned. 'Why?'

She shrugged again. 'It's just... well, Sera seemed a bit off and distracted, and I thought maybe I'd best leave.' She wrinkled her nose. 'You know, a year ago, I wouldn't have cared, and I'd have still stayed.'

'It's called growing up,' said Yavi drily as he gathered his things together.

'Are these Grandfather's things?' asked Fahe. She knelt and examined a book of cloth pieces.

'Yes.'

'What are they?' She ran her hand across a smooth, satiny cloth.

'Pieces of fabric from Kuzerazi,' said Yavi. 'Cut, mounted and bound into books. I was trying to see if they can be read, if they hold any secrets.'

Fahe flipped through the book. 'What do these numbers mean? It's like a little code on every piece of cloth.'

'Show me... yes, you're right. Interesting. Wonder what it refers to.'

'What did you mean when you said it holds secrets? Did you mean magical Kuzerazan secrets?'

Yavi looked startled. 'What makes you say that?'

'I find it so hard to believe that the Kuzerazans don't believe in magic. I bet they do and just don't tell us, and Grandfather stumbled upon their secret.'

Yavi smiled. 'Maybe you should ask Keas about magic in Kuzerazi.'

'Who's Keas?'

Members of the Brei clan had been in service of Marik for so long that no one really remembered how it all began. Some sections of the family had in fact been settled in Marik for generations—to the point that some had even taken on Marik names and formed nuclear families, leaving behind the commune-type existence of the Far Darom clans.

Zurel was surprised to see Fahe. So different now from the fierce little chubby child of long ago. She was just fourteen, but already about as tall as Zurel. It was a relief to find that she was physically fit and was fairly well-tutored in self-defence. It was one of Zurel's tasks to make sure Fahe was able to take care of herself. She had good reflexes and the fluidity of movement of a natural athlete.

Unfortunately, Fahe also had the sullen countenance of many teenagers that Zurel had encountered, and regarded her new bodyguard with deep suspicion and a dislike only restrained by good manners. Zurel wasn't sure what she had done to earn that disapproval, but this was something she had known to expect. The sudden arrival of a virtual shadow couldn't be the most pleasant of experiences for anybody, and Zurel herself was quite sure she would have hated such an intrusive presence in her life when she had been fourteen.

She learnt that Fahe had lately started going for a run early every morning, and it was also clear that she intended to use these outings to figure out exactly how far she could push her bodyguard. Zurel was half irritated and half amused, especially when she realized that a five-masaaf run at the crack of dawn actually bothered Fahe much more than it did her.

'You intend to tail me everywhere?' Fahe finally broke the silence as they cooled down that first day.

'Whenever you leave the Marik House premises, I will be with you,' said Zurel.

'Don't you need a life or something? Hobbies?' Fahe's tone was almost mocking.

'I manage,' said Zurel evenly.

'Well, I am going to the bathroom now. Do you want to follow me there?'

'That will not be necessary,' replied Zurel, refusing to rise to the bait.

'Disciple Kariad,' said Yavi, bowing his head respectfully and placing a hand on his chest.

'Mage Yavi,' said the slight figure before him, a smile in her voice. She rose with the help of a single forearm crutch and deftly manoeuvred her way around the desk to come closer.

She stopped for a moment, looking up at Yavi, and then grasped his shoulders with one hand and pulled him into a warm hug. It was only when they were seated and Kariad was pouring jasmine tea for them that Yavi finally gathered his nerve to study his former scholarly guide and mentor.

The badly cut shoulder-length hair, unadorned face, the shapeless, dull grey clothing of Academy—that was exactly how Yavi had last seen her about four years back. Her skin was smooth, almost ageless, she had a small pointed chin, and the corners of her mouth were turned up in what seemed like a permanent smile. The eyes were a light blue, and they spoke of deep intelligence. She made Yavi feel once again like a gawky teenager who didn't know what to do with his arms and legs.

'You studied to be a physician, I hear,' said Kariad, handing him a mug.

'Yes, I did,' said Yavi. 'Thank you.' He raised his mug, 'To your health.'

'And to reforging old alliances,' said Kariad, raising hers.

Yavi felt the colour rising in his cheeks. Kariad smiled.

'I was referring to working with you again,' she said.

'I... ah... I know.'

'So, have you sent in your acceptance?'

'Not yet,' replied Yavi. 'You see, my young sister is to be an initiate this year. I am not sure if she will be altogether comfortable having me as an instructor.'

'Yavi, if you turn down the offer, you will not get another one. You know the Academy will consider it a snub.'

'I know that,' said Yavi, 'and you know better than anyone else that teaching at the Academy is all that I've ever wanted to do. But I do not want to make a formal acceptance before I have spoken to Fahe.'

Kariad set her mug down and linked her hands together in front of her. She looked up and studied Yavi. 'Is that all?'

He tried to hold her gaze, but couldn't. He looked away. 'Yes.'

Kariad sighed, shaking her head. 'You are still a terrible liar. I meant what I said in my letter—don't let our history affect your decision.'

'I'm hardly the ideal role model for young initiates,' said Yavi, trying not to blush.

Kariad laughed. 'And what does that make me?'

'I didn't mean it to come out like that,' said Yavi, shifting uncomfortably.

Kariad leaned forward and touched Yavi's arm lightly. 'Look, you were not the first and definitely not the last Academy scholar to sleep with your mentor. It does not make you a criminal. We won't argue the ethics of it, but as you can see, I am not apologizing for it. We're adults, Yavi, and the question is, are we going to be able to leave history where it belongs—in the past?'

Yavi noted the use of the pronoun 'we', but was aware that it referred to him. He knew she was right. He cleared his throat and changed the subject.

'I... in fact, came to talk to you about something else.'

'Yes?'

'Pagan magic. What do you know about it?'

Kariad frowned. 'As far as the Academy believes, it's unnatural. It cannot exist. Only Flame magic is true magic. Why?'

'That's the textbook opinion,' said Yavi. 'What do *you* believe?'

'I keep an open mind. I mostly believe it to be impossible because I can't figure out how it could work. But I'm open to being convinced otherwise. Why the sudden interest?'

Yavi told her about his grandfather's legacy. 'I've been struggling to make some sense of what he was trying to tell me for some time now. Despite what the letter says, I've tried everything possible within my skill and have gleaned absolutely nothing from these cloth pieces. The only option I have left to consider is outside the realm of Flame magic.'

Kariad digested that in silence. 'Have you ever considered that the cloth is just... ordinary cloth, the journals plain, boring travel logs, and the letter a friendly business tip?'

'I... yes, of course. Er... but, well, you see, my grandfather did spend extended amounts of time in Kuzerazi, and he *was* a mage. Even if there's a little chance he might have stumbled on to something...' Yavi trailed off. He felt foolish suddenly. Kariad was probably right and he was looking for mysteries where none existed. *Maybe this was what Grandfather intended—to let me make a fool of myself,* he thought.

He also realized he had sounded very arrogant insisting that since he hadn't found anything, nothing existed.

Kariad was flipping through the fabric samples Yavi had brought along. This one had a collection of dull-brown satin pieces of different sizes. 'Have you showed this to anyone else?'

Yavi shook his head. 'I wasn't sure whom to trust.'

'Good. Going around talking of pagan magic is not sensible,' agreed Kariad. 'So you want me to take a look?'

'If you have the time or inclination.'

'Of course I do,' said Kariad with a laugh. 'What else can you tell me about your grandfather?'

'Nothing much. I wasn't close to him. But I do know he spent the last decade or so of his life shut inside a room, writing away.'

Kariad scratched an eyebrow thoughtfully. 'Ten years is a long time. What was he writing?'

Yavi shrugged. 'I have no idea. Compiling these diaries, I presume, because there was nothing else.'

He watched in silence as Kariad put one of the cloth samples into a scanner, wishing he had thought of that himself. He told her about the numbers on each sample Fahe had noticed as they waited for the images to come up on the screen.

'Curious,' said Kariad, leaning forward. She pointed with a stylus. 'See that here... there seems to be a mistake in the weave. It looks like a tiny triangle woven into the design. Hmm... I wonder... Yavi, would you scan the others?'

# 5

## Surprises and Shocks

'Don't you want that?' asked Fahe, pointing to a glass that appeared to contain something deliciously cool, given the beads of condensation running down it.

Yavi was on the floor, his back against the wall and his outstretched legs nearly reaching the balcony railing. The computer on his lap had wires trailing from it along the floor and into the room behind. A stack of paper files and some discs lay next to him. A low stool had a plate of biscuits and a glass.

'Get your own,' said Yavi, swatting her hand away.

'What are you doing?' asked Fahe, leaning against the railing.

'Work.'

'Grandfather's stuff?'

'Yes.'

'Did you find out anything more?'

'Why the sudden interest?' asked Yavi, looking at her curiously. 'And how come you're hanging around at home all day?'

Fahe shrugged. 'Not like I have a great many things to do right now. School's as good as done. No triangles either.'

'What do you mean nothing to do? These are your last days of freedom. Go out with friends.'

'Don't want to,' said Fahe.

'What? Don't want to be seen in public with your bodyguard?' said Yavi, teasing.

'It's not that.'

'I know it's a little embarrassing at first, but you'll get used to her. After the first few weeks, I forgot Rindan was around.'

'I said it's nothing to do with her!'

Yavi nodded. 'Are you getting along with her?'

'She's not really a bundle of laughs.'

'She's supposed to keep you safe, not entertained.'

'Oh, hilarious,' said Fahe, rolling her eyes.

Yavi gave her a piercing look that made her squirm. 'Tell me, when I left for Marik, you and Inos were thick as thieves. I'd have thought you'd want to spend all your waking hours with each other.'

'Mind your own Flaming business, Marik Yavi!' said Fahe, glaring at him.

Yavi raised his eyebrows. Fahe looked away.

'Friends fight,' said Yavi. 'But you're going to the Academy soon—you haven't much time to make up.'

'Can we not talk about Inos?' said Fahe, teeth gritted.

'All right,' said Yavi, holding up his hands in surrender. 'Do you want to hear about what I did today?'

'What?'

'I went to see my old teacher at the Academy, Disciple Kariad. She's agreed to help me with my puzzle.'

'Did she find anything?'

'She did, in fact. Come and see this.' He showed her a series of images of the scanned cloth. 'See, all of them seem to have a little defect. They are of different shapes or sizes, and we have no idea what they mean—if they are indeed mistakes or done on purpose.'

'Did you ask her about the numbers?'

'Yes. She doesn't know what they might be, though.'

'Hmm,' said Fahe. 'Sorry, but this seems pretty lame. It's like you're purposely looking for something.'

This was a little too close to what Yavi sometimes wondered, so he nudged the subject along.

'I also asked her about pagan magic.'

Fahe brightened. 'Ooh, that sounds more interesting. What did she say?'

'The general consensus is that Flame magic is the only kind of magic,' said Yavi. 'But she agreed to try and find out more for me.'

'But why can't other types of magic exist? There are different kinds already, right, like yours and Yanik's?'

'Magic is either literal or elemental. Literal magic or word magic works on written or drawn systems. It is selfish magic—I can only use it to do things for myself. Natural or elemental magic works with nature—wind, earth, water, fire, and so on—the elements. Like Yanik's magic. But it's all sourced from the Flame.'

'Hmm,' said Fahe, intrigued. 'So you think the cloths are also magical objects?'

'They could be. Oh, and Fahe, don't discuss all this with anyone, will you?'

'Who do I have to talk to?' said Fahe gloomily.

'I was thinking of travelling to Kuzerazi if... oh, the Flame take that dog! What is she up to now?'

They watched from the first floor balcony as Buttons, Fahe's dog, flattened herself on the grass behind a flower bush. She was an odd-looking dog of questionable intelligence and origins. As a guard dog, she was quite useless, though she showed a remarkable propensity to learn silly tricks. The garden path curved right where she was hiding, and from their position they could see Yanik striding down it, taking on his portable comm device. Fahe giggled.

'Shh!' she said to Yavi. 'It's a new trick she's learnt. Watch.'

Yanik disconnected his call and looked up, seeing his siblings. He smiled and waved as he turned the corner. With a joyful bark, Buttons jumped out. Startled, Yanik gave a sort of yelp and leapt into the air, his scarlet mage's cape billowing around him, the comm slipping out of his hand and clattering to the ground. He put a hand on his chest.

'Idiot!' said Yanik. 'You nearly gave me a heart attack!'

Buttons was delighted with Yanik's response, especially when he bent to retrieve his comm, placing her paws on his knees and licking his face enthusiastically.

'Oh, get away!' said Yanik, pushing at her, and then giving up and kneeling to pat her.

Fahe and Yavi grinned, leaning over the railing, watching Yanik trying to extricate himself from Buttons' ministrations.

'Poor Yanik,' said Yavi.

'Oh, ha ha,' said Fahe. 'Did you notice the beard he's trying to grow? Says it'll make him look older.'

'What beard?' asked Yavi.

'I never said he was being successful. But I've been really polite about it. He can be so touchy.'

'Right now, I'm sure he is,' said Yavi.

'Why right now?'

'I meant with the baby coming.'

Fahe frowned. 'What baby?'

Yavi stared at her. 'You don't... I mean, he hasn't told you?'

'Who hasn't told you what?' asked Yanik, appearing on the balcony.

Fahe whipped around and glared at him for an instant, then she stormed out.

'What was that about?' asked Yanik, startled.

Yavi raised his hands in surrender for the second time in a short span of time. 'You haven't told Fahe about Sera's pregnancy?'

Yanik said a bad word.

Fahe ran through the gardens. She hadn't even bothered to put on her shoes. Buttons gambolled after her, delighted at this unexpected new game.

Yanik... *her* Yanik. First Sera and Sera's daughter. And now a new baby! It was just too much to take in.

'Buttons! Come here!' called Fahe, refusing to think further about Yanik and his forthcoming offspring.

Buttons stopped, gave an excited yelp and plunged through the bushes. Fahe made a sound of frustration as she ran across to the path that led up to the guards' quarters, calling after her dog.

'Buttons!' shouted Fahe angrily. 'Are you deaf? Oh!'

She pulled up short to see a strange boy sitting on the bench by the practice yard in front of the guards' quarters. He was rather odd to look at. His skin was pale, though it was red and blotchy, like he was really embarrassed or angry. He had jet-black curls, which made him look paler than he really was. But what she found really startling about him were his piercing green eyes and the way he looked at her—all intent and serious.

'Who in the Flame are you?' Fahe challenged.

'I...' began the boy, but Buttons ran to him and jumped up, putting her paws on his knees, and he stopped and scratched her head.

'Buttons!' cried Fahe. 'Come *here*!'

Buttons gave Fahe a quizzical look, but as the boy made a sort of clicking noise in his throat, she turned back and jumped on him again.

It made Fahe inexplicably furious. Buttons's preference of a stranger's company was simply too much for her.

'*Buttons*!' she yelled.

'Why don't you let her be?' the boy said. 'She doesn't want to go to you.'

'How dare you tell me what to do!' cried Fahe, incensed. 'BUTTONS!' She was so angry that she was seeing stars—and when Fahe got angry, she lost control.

There was a yelp from Buttons, followed by a howl. She rolled to the ground and twisted her body around to lick her back. There was a tiny patch of skin visible through singed hair.

The boy jumped down beside the dog, bending to look at the wound.

'Next time, pick on someone who can fight back!' he yelled.

'Get away from my dog!' Fahe shouted back, giving him a shove.

'*Your* dog?' The boy laughed mirthlessly. 'People like you don't deserve...'

'Enough!' A firm voice cut in. 'Keas, get some cold water for the dog.'

Fahe was shaking now, but her anger was spent. She felt weak at the thought that her out-of-control magic had hurt Buttons. She looked down at her shaking hands, but try as she might, she couldn't still them.

Zurel looked curiously at her. 'Are you all right?'

Fahe couldn't reply. She had hurt Buttons. And Yanik was going to have a baby. He would no longer have any time for her. And Inos was leaving.

'Fahe?' asked Zurel again.

But Fahe didn't hear her. She didn't even notice the shock on Keas's face as he realized who he had been shouting at. Buttons seemed to have suffered no lasting damage despite her initial howling, and she was quite happy after Keas washed the burn with cold water. As Fahe turned and fled into the gardens, back towards the house, with as much dignity as she could muster, a confused and morose Buttons trotted after her.

So that was Keas, thought Fahe. And he would go to the Academy with her. She already hated him.

# 6

## Unexpected Help

Fahe jogged along the running track around the Lake Park at a leisurely pace. The early morning runs were beginning to become a ritual, and she didn't mind it. Running was a pretty boring sport, but now that she no longer had triangles practice, she did like the physical exertion.

It was early and still cool enough to be outdoors. The park was more or less empty apart from the occasional jogger or morning walker. She checked her pedometer and decided on one last lap before heading home.

Fahe had also largely given up trying tricks on Zurel. She realized that the older woman was far stronger and fitter than she was, and trying to outdo her physically would only result in embarrassing herself. When Fahe upped her pace and Zurel matched it, she didn't even notice it. It looked like Yavi was right, Fahe thought to herself. She might actually get used to having a tail for the rest of her life.

Keas still preyed on her mind and the thought of him made her burn with anger. She had seen him hanging around near the guards' quarters when she and Zurel did their daily practices. She'd caught him staring at her a few times, though he'd looked away guiltily each time she caught his eye and glared. Fahe found that hard to believe that he was really Kuzerazan and was going to the Academy.

She had made up her mind to ignore him, but she was still curious about him. Zurel also said that he had some sort of strong natural magic that gave him an affinity with plants and animals. Which would explain why Buttons was nuts about him. Fahe understood this wasn't Buttons's fault, though that didn't stop her from feeling betrayed, and she disliked Keas all the more for it.

Just as they were nearing the end of their run and Fahe's thoughts were running to a large breakfast, a figure jumped out at her from the trees that lined the running track. Startled, Fahe stumbled, and even before she could catch herself and regain her balance, Zurel was between them.

Fahe didn't see exactly what happened, it was so fast, but when she recovered, she found Zurel poised threateningly over an indignant figure sprawled on the ground.

'Rehin!' exclaimed Fahe, recognizing her old friend.

'What was that for?' cried Rehin in an injured voice, pushing himself slowly off the ground and dusting himself.

Zurel's face was cold and devoid of expression. 'My apologies, Scholar Rehin,' she said in a tone about as far from apologetic as possible. 'But you should know better than to approach like that.'

'It was just a joke,' said the boy.

Zurel said nothing.

'You can't go around attacking my friends!' said Fahe, suddenly angry.

Zurel's eyes shifted to her, a flicker of surprise in them. Fahe blushed. Telling your bodyguard off in public—that was absolutely not done. She had never ever seen Yanik and Karev or Yavi and Rindan argue seriously.

Rehin broke the tension by raising a hand in apology. 'All right, that was probably a bit over the top. I'm sorry.'

He was looking at Fahe, who had no option but to nod.

'Well, I just spotted you and came over to greet you. You're joining us at the Academy this year, I hear.'

'Yes,' said Fahe, 'but I hear you scholars don't want to have much to do with us lowly initiates.'

'Ah, well,' he said, grinning.

They fell into step, exchanging news and talking of the Marik Commemorative Day coming up that weekend. They had been good friends in school and they'd played triangles together. He was a couple of years older and had left the junior trianglers two years ago, when he joined the Academy. But Fahe kept running into him off and on during social occasions.

Rehin was a Shenara, a family from the governorate of Muradia. Even though Marik was a small province, it was significant. It shared a border with Muradia, the commercial hub of the Nizrah Union. Muradia was one of the larger administrative units, and the Shenaras one of its most influential traders. Many people in Muradia had their eyes on Marik, whose mainstay was tourism. It was no secret that the Shenaras were willing to go to great lengths to acquire Marik and make use of its network of backwaters that led deep inland. Marik, on its part, was not averse to some sort of alliance with Shenara, especially now that they were desperately in need of funds to rebuild after the summer storms. But if the backwaters were taken up with trading vessels, what would happen to the quiet, leisurely houseboat stays that were the biggest tourist attractions in Marik?

At one time, the families had hoped for a marriage alliance between Rehin's older sister Rihal and either Yanik or Yavi, which might also have brought to an end a long-running feud between the families. But then Yanik had settled down with Sera, and Yavi had categorically stated that he would like to be left out of any such arrangements. Once it had been a matter of great amusement to the older Marik siblings to tell Fahe that it would soon be her turn to be pursued by Rehin, especially as they were already friends.

When he was not bound to Marik duties, Yavi worked at the Narra Surgery down at the Koda city centre. As one of the junior physicians during the afternoon shift, he hardly ever got to see patients. Most of his time was spent assisting one of the senior physicians, and he tried not to mind that too much, knowing that he had yet to figure out if this was going to be his main profession. And now, with the Academy offer, things were even more in limbo.

He was surprised, therefore, when he was paged to attend to a patient that afternoon. Pulling his overall straight and picking up his personal tablet, he entered the examination room to find a middle-aged woman waiting for him.

'Mage Yavi, I presume?' she said in a brisk voice.

Her accent spoke of an education, which her well-worn clothes and slightly shabby appearance seemed to belie. Also, the tone in which she spoke made it clear that she was used to commanding and being heard.

'Yes, I...' began Yavi, but stopped in surprise as she rose and crossed the room towards him.

'Disciple Kariad sent me,' she interrupted. 'I haven't much time. You wanted to know about pagan magic, and I thought this was the safest place to make contact.'

Yavi's eyes automatically went to the CCTV camera affixed to one corner of the room.

The woman smiled. 'I fixed it, but it won't stay offline forever.'

'How did you...' began Yavi, amazed. He had no head for electronics.

'Never mind that now,' she said quickly. She thrust a computer disc at him. 'I put together whatever I could find that might be useful for now. Go through it first, and then we will talk again. Now, the disc is encrypted, but you're a word mage, right?'

'Yes, I'll manage,' said Yavi.

'Good. The contents are meant for one-time viewing and cannot be copied. It will automatically seal itself after you access it the first time, and then you will be left with a coaster.' She grinned suddenly, showing a row of even teeth.

Yavi suddenly realized that she was younger than what he had assumed at first. The creases on her face were a result of a lot of time spent outdoors, not age—she couldn't have been older than the mid-thirties.

She looked at her watch. 'Well, the cameras will be coming back online in less than thirty seconds or so. Go out and come back in after one minute.'

'I... but... how do I...'

'We'll talk again,' she said, pushing him towards the exit.

Yavi had no choice but to obey. He let himself out using the physicians' entrance, and in exactly a minute he walked back in. But the mysterious woman was gone.

Yavi realized he didn't even know her name, and he had no idea how he was supposed to get in touch with her.

Fahe figured that running into Rehin had been a good thing. Her mood improved vastly. Rehin promised to tell her a bit about what to expect in the early days of the Academy, and since it was unlikely they'd get much of a chance to talk about it during the Marik Commemorative Day festivities, they made plans to meet later in the day.

Despite Marik's modest status, its commemorative day event was a sought-after social occasion, even though Fahe classified it as a complete bore. Some of the most powerful people from the Nizrah region, including mages, and other parts of the world gathered under one roof. It even merited a mention in her school history book, according to which, 'political affiliations were forged, marriage alliances proposed, and business deals inked.' Fahe translated that as people trying to impress each other, attempting to get other people to part with money for their half-baked causes, and throwing their sons and daughters around like cattle traders.

Her good mood was soured somewhat when she remembered that this year she would have to host the early morning triangles game along with her brothers. It was not even a real game. Usually, it started off well, but as the day grew hotter, people wandered off, till even the umpires—generally Yanik and Yavi—retired to fan themselves under the picnic umbrellas. At least she was not required to dress up and attend the banquet in the evening, thought Fahe, and tried to take solace from that fact.

Yavi called the mysterious woman Grey in his mind. He suspected that her colourlessness was carefully calculated to present a nondescript appearance. And when he read all that she had compiled for him, he could see why that might have been important.

Breaking the disc's encryption had been a simple matter. It had information about what could broadly be called pagan magic, which Grey had juxtaposed against the broad history of the world, explaining how and why alternative magic might have evolved.

Magic, it was widely believed, came from the sacred Flame. This referred to the eternal blue flames that burnt in the half a dozen venerated Shrines, one of which was in the Academy at Koda. Though humans were able to harness this magic, it was a matter of considerable skill and discipline. Ancient disciples of the Flame had long ago devised a system of symbols, consisting of a pentaster and its incorporated runas, that helped them tap the Flame's power and use it in different ways. Some people were able to perform literal magic, while others used their affinity to the elements to direct magic in different ways. Thus, while the Flame was revered by all humankind as being the giver of life, for mages it held a special meaning.

Learning runas to use magic had once upon a time been an elite pursuit. Five of the sacred Flames had been privately owned; the sixth was in the Kuzerazi region and more or less inaccessible. The five eastern owners had coveted power and riches in exchange for allowing people access to the Flame. Thus, for the privileged, proximity to the Flame was easily bought, affording them the opportunity to learn magic. In time, institutions known as Academies sprang up around them, the one at Koda in the present day being the most renowned.

Since magic and its control were completely in the hands of the elite, mages became some of the most powerful people in the world. They controlled everything—from money to the government to trade to public opinion. And the common people—non-mages—found themselves existing only to serve the needs of mages, often little better than slaves. They lived in squalid conditions, crime was rampant, they were barely able to feed and clothe themselves.

After almost a hundred years of oppression and simmering discontent, non-mages engineered an uprising. This had happened some two centuries ago, and was known as the Velvet Night Resistance. In fact, it was originally referred to as the Resistance of the Velvet Knights, but given its covert nature and the fact that meetings took place under the cover of darkness, the movement soon came to be called the Velvet Night. The resistors had carried a small patch of velvet, which was a metaphor for equality with the upper classes, suggesting that all humans were equal.

When the mages attempted to squash the rebellion, they found themselves vastly outnumbered. At this time, the Nizrah plains and Far Darom were not structured as they currently were. The region was divided into independent, often warring, states. Yet, the Velvets had organized well, united in their search for justice. It was a bloody battle, where the might of the mages was unprepared for the spirit of the common people.

However, despite having the numbers and the element of surprise, the Velvets were never going to win. The mages had far too much power and technology at their disposal. They also had the resources to petition the Kuzerazans for help.

Kuzerazi, an independent and self-contained region that comprised almost the whole of the far western mountain ranges, had a proud history of democratic governance. And while they also revered the Flame, they had always steered clear of using it for magic, believing that to be evil and against nature.

But as it happened, the class disparity in the rest of the world went against the Kuzerazans' socialist ideals, and they agreed to join the revolt, but on the side of the Velvets. From an uprising it now became a war, the War of the Nations, as it was eventually called.

With this unprecedented turn of events thanks to the Kuzerazans, a truce was called, and the mages and Velvets came to an agreement. As the War of the Nations came to a close, a massive process of rebuilding and reorganization followed, in which the Kuzerazans were forgotten. Parts of the Nizrah region broke away to form smaller, independent provinces, and later on the Nizrah Union was formed as a group of largely independent administrative units brought under a broad regulatory system. The south-eastern clans had broken away to form their own state, Far Darom, which was loosely associated with the Union. All heads of the Nizrah provinces, variously called prefects and governors, sat on the Union Council at Koda, the capital of the Union itself. The rest of the council was made up of elected representatives.

Meanwhile, a body known as the Pentastra was formed, consisting of five mages that represented everything magical in the area, including regulating the learning and teaching of magic. Subsequently, the Academies became institutions of public learning, even though there were still seats reserved for patrons' families.

However, discontents on both sides remained: mages who felt that magic was the birthright of an elite few, and some of the Velvets who opposed everything that conventional mages stood for, including allegiance to the Flame. Rumour had it that the more fundamentalist parts of the Velvet Night had retreated underground following the War and had experimented and developed their own systems and techniques of magic. This was broadly referred to as 'pagan magic', though no one knew exactly what it was.

All this was, of course, mostly common knowledge that every schoolchild was taught. However, Grey's research was a little more exciting, touching upon how, apart from the Velvets, plenty of 'legitimate' mages too took an interest in alternative forms of magic for academic purposes. But what interested Yavi most of all was her brief note on what she called Kuzerazan magic.

The term itself was an oxymoron. The very fact of being Kuzerazan came with the denial of magic. The history that Nizrahi children were taught was derisive of the westerners' choice to deny themselves the power of the Flame. But according to Grey, historians had missed—or chosen to ignore—a fine point. The Kuzerazans had always been adamant about not exploiting the Flame for magic, but they had never said anything about any other kind of magical source.

There is no evidence to suggest that the westerners did *not* develop a magic of their own. But this much is clear: Kuzerazan magic, if it existed, was different from ours. Some artefacts similar to runas have been discovered by archaeologists. These have typically been engravings on stones and barks, but little is known of their antecedents. They might possibly have been smuggled to Kuzerazi from the east. The few treatises and documents that have been recovered are now the property of the Hyran Monastery Archives and closed to the public.

My own studies have led me to believe that Kuzerazan magic did exist at some point, but for some reason died out. There is no indication that magic is used as a matter of course in Kuzerazi in the present day. This brings us to the interesting question as to why they would turn their backs on it, denounce it. The only rational answer that suggests itself is that it died out because they were either unable to harness it or control it effectively.

# 7

# A Banquet

The Marik banquet had always been the Brei guards' nightmare, even though most years it passed without event, unless one counted extricating the odd drunk dignitary from the swimming pool. With parts of the house and grounds thrown open to some of the most well-known names in that part of the world and their families, not to mention their own guards in some cases, it had them all on edge, especially the bodyguards, who were on unofficial duty. Because the family couldn't possibly be seen trailing bodyguards in their own home in front of guests, Karev, Rindan, Zurel and their extended family were mingling with the guests, dressed casually, but keeping a beady eye on proceedings. Already Rindan and Kara—Cousin Kedra's bodyguard—had broken up a fight between a couple of twelve-year-olds.

Fahe found herself bored out of her mind. There were plenty of people her age, some she had gone to school with. A group of teenage girls next to her huddled together, speaking in what she only assumed was some sort of code—something about pre-ordering their 'Animators'—with half their attention focused on a group of boys some distance away, who appeared to be similarly occupied.

'You know how to kill,' she muttered to Zurel as she passed her on her way back from getting another drink. 'Kill me now.'

Zurel's mouth twitched in an approximation of a smile. 'Sorry. Outside the scope of my job profile.'

'Useless,' said Fahe, rolling her eyes as she went back to the group of young people she had been sitting with, realizing that this was the first normal conversation she had had with Zurel.

As Fahe sat back down, one of the girls got up to approach the group of boys. The boys scattered immediately, leaving one lone individual standing. This was accompanied by laughter on both sides. Fahe took advantage of the flurry of movement to slip away again. A sense of foreboding settled on her. This was school all over again, and she suddenly had a sense that the Academy would likely be just the same.

Fahe had never really found her place among her peers. She had struggled to find things in common with other boys and girls her age. Even triangles had just been a way to keep herself occupied, a habit rather than a hobby. But she had always found herself surrounded by people and she had got used to being around them without belonging. It partly had to do with who she was, and partly that she had excelled both academically and in sports, at least until things had started going wrong the past few years. But, even in crowds, she had always felt isolated. It had bothered her sometimes, and sometimes it was lonely, but she had managed and mostly been quite happy.

She had always assumed that at the Academy she would finally fit in. Where her fellow initiates would accept her for who she was. Where she would find other people who thought like her, were like her. But now she doubted it. At least these past years she had had Inos. Inos, who was conspicuous by her absence now.

Fahe wondered how much of what had happened with her friend was making her so restless. She couldn't bear to think about the fact that Inos had already left. It made her feel physically sick, and for a moment she stopped and leaned against a tree.

When she had composed herself, she found that she had strayed into the Grove, the Marik House fruit orchard. It was quiet because she'd left the crowds far behind, and there was no sound other than the birds calling and the wind rustling the leaves. It was cool in the shade of the mango trees, and Fahe eased herself to the ground, closing her eyes, thankful for the tranquillity. She automatically put out her hand to pat Buttons before realizing that she wasn't there. She had been confined to the guards' quarters for the day because she tended to get overexcited with too many people around.

Fahe swore under her breath. She would have liked Buttons's company right then. A wet nose pressed into your hand took care of a lot of problems. She would miss her terribly at the Academy. Initiates were allowed to take pets along, but dogs needed to live in the kennels and Buttons steadfastly refused to get along with other dogs.

And then there was Yanik and Sera's baby.

Fahe couldn't stop the tears that started rolling down her face without warning. There was no one here to see if she did cry. But she knew that it wasn't Buttons she was crying for.

It was probably years of triangles honing her reflexes to a fine degree that helped her notice a small movement from the corner of her vision. There was a reddish spark, and she instinctively dived flat to the ground. But the burning, blurry object bore down upon her. It hit her on the side of her head. A burning sensation, and then excruciating pain followed. Fahe cried out, even as she heard footsteps running towards her and Zurel's voice calling her name. She fought to hold on to consciousness, but the pain was too much and she blacked out.

Defy the Spirit of the Flame and know it's Wrath
Tell your Brother

'What does it mean?' asked Fahe, holding a poultice to the side of her face and feeling the burning sensation fading.

'That someone doesn't like what I'm doing,' said Yavi grimly.

'If you're conducting research on pagan magic, discretion is of utmost importance,' said Rindan, disapproval dripping from his voice.

'I have been discreet,' snapped Yavi, but he seemed preoccupied with the note. He frowned. 'This doesn't make sense.'

'What doesn't?' asked Fahe.

'This note. "Wrath" is not a word I would use in everyday conversation.'

'So, it was someone who went to a fancy school, you mean?'

'Well, yes, it would indicate someone educated. But then look at the capitalization. It's all over the place. And it should be i-t-s, not i-t-apostrophe-s...' He looked up at Fahe. 'You said you saw magic?'

'Yes, reddish.'

'That's raw magic. Someone not very skilled.'

'Like?'

'I don't know, Fahe,' said Yavi irritably. He pushed her head to one side to examine her injury again.

'How many people know you are studying pagan magic?' asked Rindan.

'Kariad,' said Yavi, looking sharply at him. 'And perish the thought. There is absolutely no way she could have betrayed me. A few other people, but they're all trustworthy. Oh, wait a minute, there's also Grey.'

'Pardon?' said Rindan.

'The woman Kariad sent,' said Yavi.

'What kind of name is Grey?' asked Fahe, but Yavi was lost in thought.

The rooftop of the guards' quarters afforded a generous view of the open terrace adjoining the Marik House banquet hall. Bedecked in lights and flowers, it twinkled like an exotic jewel in the dark, moonless night. Food and drink stalls were set up along the sides of the terrace and tables dotted the remaining area and the lawns. It teemed with activity as guests lined up for dinner and drinks. Strains of lively music reached the watchers up on the rooftop, and part of the dance floor was visible from where they stood, still quite busy.

Fahe watched quietly, sitting on the edge of the roof, her knees drawn up under her chin. Buttons was stretched out lazily next to her and Zurel was on the other side of the dog. Some of the other off-duty guards were present, talking in low voices or just watching the party in progress. Keas hung back, curious but too polite to openly stare. He was a little awkward with Fahe, and she completely ignored him.

Fahe was considered too young to attend the banquet, though she knew fully well that once she started attending the Academy she would be expected to take part in all such social events. *My last year of freedom*, she thought, with a slight tinge of sadness. She sighed and produced a tiny pair of folding binoculars. Zurel raised her eyebrows.

'What?' asked Fahe, noting the look.

'Nothing,' said Zurel.

'You're going to tell me to put this away, right?'

'Put what away?' asked Zurel, eyebrows still raised, but a polite, puzzled look on her face.

Fahe stared at her, confused at first, and then started to laugh. She shook her head. She might begin to like Zurel if she wasn't careful.

'Oh, look, there's your brother,' she said to Zurel, as she noticed Karev. 'Oh...' She trailed off as she saw Yanik next to him, arm-in-arm with Sera. She was saying something and Yanik's face was turned, looking at her, smiling widely. Karev was smiling politely at her other side too, but Fahe knew that his eyes would be darting all over the place. Watching Yanik and Sera, looking so happy, was hard. Fahe looked away.

There were plenty of people she recognized. There were Uncle Tachi and Aunt Amel, and they seemed to be in a serious conversation with a group of boring-looking, overdressed people. Their daughter Kedra stood between them. Fahe stared at her for a long time, wondering for the millionth time why she couldn't have been born a boy so that Cousin Kedra would have got her life's wish to be the next Prefect of Marik.

She looked like someone about to inherit a title. Fahe assumed she was beautiful, and despite Yanik's stories about how she had been a bully as a child, she was really quite pleasant. She carried herself with poise and confidence—quite like Yavi in public—something that Fahe never imagined she would be able to pull off. She hated being heir to a title she neither wanted nor imagined she'd ever be ready to take on—and here was Kedra, who seemed to be born for it.

Fahe was neither stupid nor too young to know that the situation in Marik was restless after the summer's storms had ravaged parts of the countryside. She also knew that Mother had made some bad choices, going against the advice of Uncle Tachi, and now that a significant part of the infrastructure had to be rebuilt, there was little money coming in. Mother had conveniently made no attempt to deny the rumour that it was Yanik's misjudgement, since he was the estate adviser. But it wasn't as though there weren't people lining up to invest in Marik. The Shenaras, for instance, had always been keen. But everyone had their own agenda, and if Marik had to survive as a tourist destination, they would have to tread very carefully.

Fahe was quite startled when, in the middle of her dark thoughts about the Shenara family, she spotted the younger daughter Rihal going up to Yavi. She saw him turn as she touched his arm and greet her. They talked for a bit, till Rihal nodded towards the banquet hall and they went off, presumably in the direction of the dance floor.

If Fahe knew anything about the older Shenara siblings, it was that they never did anything without an ulterior motive. She wished she could be a fly on the wall.

'Mage Rihal,' Yavi said, dropping his eyes, a hand on his chest in greeting. 'It is good to see you.'

'Likewise, Mage Yavi,' she said. 'You're looking well.'

'As are you,' Yavi replied. 'I was sorry to hear about your mother?'

'Thank you,' said Rihal, a moment of grief crossing her expression. 'And I offer my condolences about your grandfather.'

'Thank you,' it was Yavi's turn to say.

There were a few moments of silence, and then she gestured questioningly towards the dance floor.

'Of course,' said Yavi, allowing himself to be led away.

Yavi, like all Mariks, more or less distrusted the Shenaras. Rihal had been a year senior to him at the Academy, but a severe illness had robbed her of a year. When they were anointed as mages, it was the same ceremony. Both Yavi and Rihal were Blue Cape mages, a status accorded only to the most exceptional and skilled. Rihal had resented sharing the honour with Yavi, not least because he was younger, but also because he was clearly more skilled.

But then it appeared that time had mellowed the bruised ego. Rihal had followed an older brother and sister into their family's highly successful business, while Yavi had immersed himself in further studies. Indeed, it was now Yavi's turn to be slightly resentful, if anything. For, while she had a fleet of merchant vessels under her management, he wasn't even sure what to do with himself.

Yavi studied her surreptitiously as they moved to the music. Her face was tanned by the long hours spent in the sun, and the effect of the wide-set grey-green eyes and the head of curly hair was unusually pleasant. She had gained some weight since the austere Academy years, and if the cut and handwork of her gown were anything to go by, life was certainly treating her well.

While Yavi did not take personal vanity to be a bad thing, and spent considerable time and effort over how he looked, he did hate formal gowns with a vengeance. It was a warm night and he could feel beads of sweat running down his back, under the heavy brocade work on his shoulders. The swirling folds of the skirt felt oppressive. His hair ornaments felt heavy and he wished he had just tied up his hair in a simple ponytail. He felt clumsy next to the cool, collected Rihal, and hoped he wasn't showing it.

'I heard that Marik took some damage in the early summer storms,' Rihal said, raising her voice to be heard over the music.

'You heard right.'

She sighed. 'Nature can be cruel. I lost an entire ship. The loss can be borne, but the fifty-three lives—that can never be replaced.'

'I am so sorry,' said Yavi, shocked. 'I had no idea.'

'Yes, well, times are bad.'

'So they are.'

'Pardon my inquisitiveness, but I hear that some areas of Marik took a significant hit. Is that true?'

'It is true,' said Yavi. 'It's no secret. Fortunately, though, we did not sustain much loss of life, but it will take time to rebuild.'

'The loss of livelihood takes its own toll,' said Rihal softly. 'Jobs must not be easy to come by.'

Yavi sighed. 'It's a chicken-and-egg scenario.'

'You do know that Marik could take advantage of its strategic location?'

'How do you mean?' Yavi asked neutrally.

'It's hardly a subject to be discussed over one dance,' said Rihal. 'But you know very well that my family has always considered Marik a potentially attractive place to invest in for various reasons. I am no different, but I see other possibilities too.'

'You should be talking to my brother about this,' said Yavi.

'I do not mention this in a purely business sense,' said Rihal.

'Would you care to elaborate?' asked Yavi, curious.

'Of course, I am a businesswoman, and I am ready to put my money where my mouth is, but—and I've been giving it a lot of thought—we could build something lasting. Something that would outlive a mere business contract. Marik is small, but it has promise. If we could put aside our past differences, we could benefit from each other's strengths. For all time.'

'I... am not sure what you mean,' said Yavi, mostly untruthfully.

'All right, if you want me to speak plainly... If you and I were to marry, Yavi, not only would we forge a lasting relationship between our two powerful families, but we could find an answer to Marik's troubles and make a significant difference to Shenara. And what's more, we would both benefit equally from the prosperity.'

Yavi was only mildly surprised at being so openly propositioned—he was quite used to it. What astonished him was that it was coming from Rihal.

She misunderstood his silence.

'And think of the future, Yavi. The next generation. With our skill as mages and our intellect, our children would also be heirs to a vast business enterprise and have a stake in Marik.'

'You do know I'm an adopted son, don't you?' said Yavi, when he had found his voice. 'According to our inheritance laws, while *I* get all the privileges of the ruling family, my children don't. So my daughters will never be considered eligible for the title, and no child of mine would have a stake of any sort, as you put it, in the Marik family's fortunes. In any case, I do have a sister and an older brother.'

Rihal was surprised. 'You are adopted? I didn't know that.'

Yavi shrugged. 'It isn't a secret, but I've not shouted it from the rooftops. Look, Rihal, I appreciate your proposition, and certainly, I am more than flattered. But you do see, don't you, that I will have to decline?'

Rihal spread her hands in defeat. 'No offence taken, Mage Yavi.'

# 8

## Breaking and Entering

Two days after the banquet, when Fahe was stretched out on the window seat in the library at home, reading, she heard raised voices coming from down the hall. She sat up—that sounded like Yanik. But Yanik didn't raise his voice, not ever.

Fahe pushed aside the curtain at the doorway and poked her head out. Someone was shouting in Mother's study and, yes, it was Yanik. Fahe's mouth fell open. He was not only incensed, he was yelling at *Mother*.

'I do not believe that my own mother could have done something like this!'

Fahe edged out into the corridor to hear better. She stopped a few steps from Mother's study. The door was ajar and she could hear everything clearly.

'Try not to be so naïve, Yanik,' said Mother. 'This is your future daughter we could be talking about.'

'My future offspring is my business,' said Yanik. 'You have no right telling Sera to name the child for Marik.'

Fahe gasped. Mother had never really thought very highly of Sera, but to ask someone to name their child for a place other than its mother's home was a bit audacious. Even for Mother.

'I have a right to protect the future of Marik in any way I see fit. Your daughter would be second in line for the title. I don't see what is so unreasonable in offering her the name of Marik.'

'It is not your right to offer it. Her name would have no bearing on her right to the title in any case.'

'Lower your voice, Yanik. The staff will hear.'

'Is that all you are concerned about?' said Yanik, his voice louder than before. 'That the staff will hear? Do you think they are stupid, and we are all stupid? That you are so concerned about the future of Marik that you will do nothing to change the inheritance law that treats your own son as less than equal?'

Fahe frowned. What did that mean?

'That's enough. Don't talk about things you don't understand.'

'I think I understand very well. You don't care about Marik, Mother, or me or anyone else. You only care about yourself and about making yourself look good. A Marik heir with a common name is beneath you. Also, naming a granddaughter for Marik is as good as crowing to Uncle Tachi's that Kedra is pushed back another notch on the title line, isn't it?'

'Why are you such a child, Yanik?'

'Thank you for your vote of confidence, Mother. Now hear this: until Sera receives an apology from you, I am not setting foot in this house again. You are not welcome in our house either. Goodbye.'

He thundered out of the study and came face-to-face with Fahe. His face was white and he was shaking. He didn't say anything and didn't stop, but when he passed her, he placed a brief hand on her shoulder.

Fahe followed him with her eyes. Yanik was always there for her when she needed him, and right now there was nothing she could do for him. She was still angry with him. But how could she be angry with him when he must be hurting so much? She had a horrible thought—what if she was just like Mother?

Grey listened with a frown as Yavi told her about Fahe's accident on the banquet day.

'Well, whoever they were, they didn't hear it from me,' she said.

'I wasn't implying that,' Yavi hastened to add.

'I saw the scans Kariad forwarded. She mentioned that your grandfather travelled to Fezar in Kuzerazi. Is that a town?'

Yavi shook his head. 'I think it's a private estate. It's a name I got from his personal journal.'

'Does it say anything about the Fezar Weaving Mill?'

'Weaving mill? The sort that makes fabric?'

'That's what weaving mills make, yes.'

Yavi was too disappointed to be embarrassed. 'You mean there *is* a mill? The textiles samples... So Grandfather was talking about a business deal, after all.'

'You can't do business with a defunct company. The Fezar Weaving Mill shut down over forty years ago. What do his journals say about it?'

'Sorry, what?' said Yavi. 'The mill shut down? Then why did he have the samples?'

'I don't know.'

'There are no references to the mill that I have found.' He frowned. 'There is something odd about the journals, though.'

Grey leaned forward expectantly. 'Odd?'

'Well, the dates, they're random. I mean, some of the entries aren't chronological. I hadn't noticed that at first, but I spotted it later on when... Look at this section.'

—

13 Yaz: Lake House breakdown. Fixed.

45 Baridi: Quick visit to Marik with Komas.

15 Yaz: Fezar. Rain. Lake House inaccessible.

16 Yaz: Lake House up.

18 Yaz: Trying Varda's idea.

59 Aki: Old Fezar Festival. Incognito.

20 Yaz: Birthday celebrations at Fezar (Varda).

—

'Why would anyone keep a journal where the dates are all mixed up?' asked Grey.

Yavi shrugged. 'I haven't an explanation. And it's not all mixed up. Just in phases.'

'Maybe your grandfather just wanted to confuse people who sneaked into his personal diaries?'

'Oh, very likely. He was rather eccentric, but I do find it hard to imagine he spent years working on just mixing up the dates of his journals...'

'Are Komas and Varda people?'

'Varda was his friend who travelled with him. Komas was the owner of Fezar at that time.'

'Any idea what Varda's idea was that they were trying?'

Yavi shrugged. 'Not a clue. Nor why they talk of the Lake House suffering a breakdown or being back up.'

'What do you know about these Fezars?'

'There's precious little on the Infonet about the place or the family.'

'Yes, I noticed,' said Grey. 'Do you think I could see the journals? I could...' she coughed delicately. 'I mean, I don't mean to imply you're lacking as a word mage, but I do have experience in, well, let's say, subjects that you don't.'

'Are you...' said Yavi hesitantly, 'a... follower of pagan faith, then?'

Grey looked back at him for a few seconds, motionless, leaving Yavi convinced that he had said something horribly wrong. Then, to his mortification, she threw her head back and laughed heartily.

Yavi found his face turning hot with embarrassment as Grey touched his arm, shaking her head, trying to compose herself.

'I am sorry,' she said. 'I did not mean to offend you.'

'You didn't...' started Yavi, but, as was becoming a habit in their conversations, she interrupted him.

'Yes, I did. I saw it in your face. Tell me, Yavi, do you know of the philosophy of agnosticism?'

'Vaguely,' said Yavi, frowning. 'When the truth can neither be proved nor disproved.'

'Simplistic, but close enough. Metaphysical reality—like whether the Flame really is the fount of magic, what happens to human beings when they die, and so on—is often ambiguous. It cannot be conclusively proved one way or the other. Therefore, I choose not to believe one way or the other. I keep an open mind.'

This woman and her complex ideas were making Yavi's head ache, but not in a way that he wanted relief from. In a few short days, she had filled his mind with so many new thoughts that his years at the Academy hadn't been able to.

It was the sort of frenzied mental activity that Yavi lived for when he had something new to chew upon.

'I believe that I keep an open mind too,' said Yavi slowly.

Grey smiled. 'Open it too wide, and you have all sorts of people stuffing things into it. Then it becomes a problem too. You're very young, Yavi, and very recently moulded by the Academy. If there's one thing the Academy teaches us very well, it's to close our minds.'

'I beg to differ,' said Yavi stiffly.

'I never graduated,' Grey went on, like he had never spoken. 'I was asked to leave because I asked too many uncomfortable questions. The Academy calls for unquestioned subservience to the Flame. I couldn't find that in myself. I needed proof that my magic is indeed sourced from the Flame and, apparently that is not something I could demand from my instructors. I have not to this day found an answer. I'm still looking.

'See, you may label things you do not understand as "pagan", but have you ever stopped to ask yourself whether everything you hold as sacred *is* really gospel? What makes your beliefs truer than the beliefs of those you call pagan followers?'

Yavi blinked. 'I... I guess I never thought of it that way.'

'It's not your fault,' Grey said. 'That is not the way the Academy teaches us to think.'

Yavi shifted. 'I'm not sure I'm comfortable with what you're implying,' he said. 'The Academy isn't the hotbed of suppression you make it out to be.'

'Of course not. Did I imply that? Then I apologize. The Academy years teach us the self-discipline without which it would be impossible to harness magic. Nor can we learn the runa-and-pentaster system through a do-it-yourself correspondence course. If that were the case, every second person would be able to harness magic and be a mage.'

'I want to know more,' said Yavi. 'About pagan... I mean, the theory of agnosticism. I think the key to my grandfather's secrets lies in it. Maybe he discovered some secrets of Kuzerazan magic, and the diaries are some sort of code that I haven't been able to crack.'

Grey seemed lost in thought, so Yavi felt compelled to continue in his own defence: 'You probably feel it's a ridiculous conclusion to leap to, but I know for certain that my grandfather had secrets, especially related to his travels to Kuzerazi. He never spoke of it to anyone in the family. And while I can accept that what I know of Flame magic is too limited to understand what the journals say, it is significant that a skilled mage like Kariad hasn't been able to read anything between the lines either.'

'I don't have access to much information about Kuzerazan magic,' said Grey, 'but I know where we could try.' She gave him an upraising look. 'If you're up for an adventure.'

'The Hyran Monastery?'

'Yes.'

'But you said it isn't accessible to the general public. And what about the mystical Monks who guard the Hyran Archives?'

'Mystical?' Grey said derisively. 'They're just disbanded combat mages who are caretakers of the Archives. I doubt there's a single Monk younger than seventy, and I bet they're blind and deaf to boot. And that collection is supposed to be the biggest archive of ancient manuscripts. Dating back to before the War of the Nations. It's been a while since I have sneaked inside. Would love to do it again.'

'*Sneak* inside?'

Grey winked.

Yavi struggled with himself, but curiosity won. He nodded. 'You... er... won't mention this to Kariad, will you?'

'I won't if you won't.'

'Is Kariad also a... what do you call yourself?'

'Agnostic? Liberal?' offered Grey. She shrugged. 'She believes in the Flame and its powers, but she respects alternative thought. And anyway, if you are a disciple, you do not question openly.'

'How do you know each other?'

'We were scholars together at the Academy. She is also a distant cousin.'

Yavi nodded. 'I see. And are there many liberals around?'

Grey shrugged. 'It's not like we have a cult,' she said with a quick smile. 'I do belong to a small group, but that's only to share information and talk. It gets lonely being a rebel. But you have to realize, Yavi, this is a quagmire. For every one of us liberals, there are at least two fanatics out there who believe that subservience to the Flame should be unquestioned, and any other way is treason. On the other hand, there are still underground Velvets around who completely denounce the Flame.'

'Velvets?' asked Yavi, eyebrows raised. 'You really mean Velvet Night followers from the War of the Nations?'

'Well, their ideology has changed, of course. Common people are no longer oppressed, so it isn't social order that they object to. They're just interested in their own brands of magic, as far as I know.'

Yavi nodded. This was no different from what her notes said.

Grey looked at her watch and stood up. 'I must go now. I will see you at midnight at the two-masaaf milestone outside the north gate of Koda. If you're not there fifteen minutes past midnight, I'll assume you're not coming.'

Yavi left his motorcar in the parking lot of the amusement park just outside the northern city limits of Koda around midnight, intending to walk down to where he was supposed to meet Grey. He had about half an hour to cover the two masaafs, and tried to swallow his guilt about having given Rindan the slip. He wasn't sure what sort of outrageous plan Grey had, but he didn't think he should drag his bodyguard into it. Not to mention the fact that Rindan would have completely disapproved of it, and if he thought it was too dangerous, he would think nothing of forcibly restraining Yavi.

Yavi had remembered to dress in black. He had removed his ankle chain and mage's ring. His head was covered with a cloth cap, and he wore a pair of glasses in an approximation of a disguise. He had also borrowed a friend's motorcar.

He kept to the shadows inside the tree line along the highway that ran through the middle of the Nizrah plains. It was quiet at that time of the night and, apart from the odd motorcar, there was no traffic on the road. He was quite beginning to enjoy the walk in the cool night when a shadowy figure emerged from the trees in front of him.

'Yavi?' it called in a loud whisper.

It was Grey, and a startled Yavi nearly died with relief. She led him to a small clearing, where a map was spread on the grass, weighed down by rocks on each corner. A dark backpack lay beside it, along with an old-fashioned wicker basket lined with a cushion in which reposed a mangy-looking cat.

'Say hello to Scrap,' she said, waving towards the cat. 'He'll help us out with the motion sensors.'

'Motion sensors?' repeated Yavi uncomfortably. 'Ri-ight.'

Grey knelt beside the map and drew a quick five-pointed star on the grass with a piece of rock. She made a little squiggle inside it and the area around the map lit up with a soft glow.

'The Monastery is about a ten-minute walk that way,' she said, pointing in a direction away from the road. 'There's a little dirt road that leads up to it from the highway—you'd have seen the turning if you had walked ahead—but we'll just cut through the woods. They have a perimeter wall, but scaling that will be quite easy. Now, once inside, there'll be the large library building towards the back, and the Monks' living quarters closer to the front of the property. As far as security goes, they have motion-sensitive lights and alarms, and CCTV, coupled with a few token patrolling guards in front of the Archives.'

'You sound like you know the place pretty well,' said Yavi, trying not to sound disapproving.

'Been inside a few times,' said Grey matter-of-factly. 'When I've needed to look up something not otherwise accessible. Now, the thing is, I can fix the CCTV problem, though I can't do much about the motion sensors. But I do have a way of getting around it. It's going to be pretty dark in there and there may not be time to use magic, so we'll have to make do with these.'

'What are they?' asked Yavi as she handed him a pair of glasses with straps.

'Night-vision goggles. I have torches for when we are inside the library.'

'Oh,' said Yavi. 'I... er, I got some equipment too.' He lowered his own backpack and opened it. Grey watched with raised eyebrows as he divested it of its contents. 'I don't know what you call these things, but I got it from the guards—they use it in their training.'

Grey picked up a dart gun with a sort of winch attachment.

'It'll easily embed in a brick or wooden wall, unrolling the cable and pulling it up. And see these hooks? We can use them to climb up. And this...'

'Sorry to disappoint you, but all we'll need is my tablet computer and a manual lock-pick kit,' said Grey, smiling. 'Oh, and I have this handheld scanner, to scan pages.'

'I see,' said Yavi, blushing. 'All right.'

'We're not exactly breaking in. As in, not in the robbing sense of it. We just want to look at a few books.'

'I'm not sure I have my morality issues sorted,' said Yavi, 'but I'm trying not to think about it.'

'Well, let's go. Now, remember to do as I say, and no questions asked. Got that?'

'All right.'

'These are combat mages, Yavi. Know what they are?'

'Of course.'

Combat mages, also known as Monks, were an old cult dating back to the War of the Nations. They trained as combat specialists and lived extremely austere lives, dedicating themselves to magic and the martial arts, spending their entire lifespan in the study and practice of their skill. Back then, they had been the mages who were trained to fight, but about a decade before Yavi was born, the Monks were officially disbanded as mages were no longer required to be martial. The Hyran mages were the last of the cult left.

'Good,' said Grey, 'because if anything happened to you, Kariad would have my hide.' She seemed to have forgotten her earlier dismissal of the Monks.

They left Yavi's backpack and the cat's basket in the clearing. Grey slung a shoulder bag across herself, which carried her tablet and the lock-picks, and she gave Yavi her own backpack to carry. Scrap travelled on her shoulder. They crept as quietly as possible through the trees, the night-vision goggles casting everything in a greenish soup around them.

The perimeter wall was about seven feet high and concrete. Grey told him it was topped with jagged glass pieces.

'There are sacks inside that backpack. Take them out,' she said. Then she showed him how they were going to pad the top of the wall with the sacks. 'This area is a CCTV blindspot,' she went on. 'I can remotely access the controls and turn them off, but I want to keep that for as late as I can because it'll only be a matter of time before they discover the glitch and turn them back on. We need to be inside the library before that happens.'

She lifted up Scrap and chucked him on top of the wall. He made a low, indignant sort of sound, but disappeared on the other side.

'Ready?' she whispered. 'Don't linger over the sacks. The glass will eventually cut through.'

She heaved herself up easily and swung over to the other side. Yavi followed, startled to find himself landing on some rather uncomfortable bushes. He thought they had made an inordinate amount of noise, but all was silent around them. A clump of trees obscured the view partially, but Yavi could see a low, squat building straight ahead from where they were, and a much larger one to the left, set further back. There was no sign of the patrols Grey had mentioned. If he were to hazard a guess, he would say the place was deserted.

He felt a touch on his arm.

'There will be guards posted near the main entrance of the Archive building,' Grey whispered, 'so we need to use the side entrance. For that, we'll have to cross over to the other side of the Monks' quarters. What we'll do is make a dash for the side of the building straight up ahead.' She pointed to the smaller building right in front of them. 'There's a camera at that corner over there that could pick us up, so we'll have to go when it's turning away. Flatten yourself against the building and stay there till I join you. As long as we're directly under the cameras, we're safe. Ready?'

Yavi nodded, his heart thumping with excitement. This was just like sneaking out of the Academy after curfew.

They waited for the camera at the corner of the quarters to turn away from them, and then, bending low, Yavi ran swiftly across the open lawn. It was uneven and the grass badly cut. He nearly tripped, but made it to the other side long before the camera had started its circuit back. Grey joined him soon after, with Scrap on her shoulder, and they slowly and carefully crept along the side of the building.

Like the previous night, it was partially cloudy, dark and moonless. Yavi still had trouble believing that there were people around them, till they passed under an open window and the sound of soft snores reached them. Someone coughed, and Grey and Yavi froze. But nothing moved and they made their slow and steady way across to the other side of the guards' quarters.

They reached the other side of the building, and Grey stopped and pulled her goggles off. She got her computer out.

'Now for the tricky part,' she said. 'We need to go across the empty space between this building and the Archives, and there are too many cameras. So I'll disable them. The Archives are also surrounded by motion sensors. But Scrap here will go along and set them off for us. Once they see it's a cat, they'll need to reset the system, and it usually takes a couple of minutes for them to come back online. That's our window.'

As she spoke, she tapped away on her computer.

'It seems almost too easy,' said Yavi.

'Be thankful, they have old systems here. There. Done.' She put the computer away quickly, lifted the cat from her shoulder and peeked around the side of the building. 'Go, Scrappy. Shoo!'

Scrap streaked across the lawn, and suddenly a bright light came on. A man's voice called out and then laughed. In the stillness of the night, they heard the crunching of heavy boots on the ground, and in under half a minute, the light went off.

'Now!' said Grey, clasping a hand around Yavi's wrist.

As quietly and as fast as they could, they ran diagonally across the lawn, in the opposite direction from which Scrap had gone. They rounded a corner and were in front of a stout wooden door. As Grey got out her lock-picks, Yavi took a quick look at the building. It reminded him of his grandfather's house, the huge windows, with bars and shutters, the heavy doors...

All of a sudden, a loud, clanging noise ripped through the silent night. For the second time that night, Yavi thought he was having a heart attack.

Grey said a very bad word—something that was illegal in every province of the Nizrah Union as far as Yavi knew.

She turned to him. 'Run!' she said. 'Go around the building and use the cover of the bushes along the wall. Just run! Go now!'

'But...'

Shouts were heard now, and footsteps. 'Halt! We see you!' a female voice called out. Something streaked in their direction, and Yavi and Grey dived to the ground.

'RUN! NOW!' Grey yelled.

Yavi didn't think twice. He picked himself up and tore along the side of the building, diving into the bushes near the perimeter wall. Keeping low, he crawled along it till he was behind a cluster of trees. He sat still, panting. His clothes were ripped and he hurt all over. Lights blazed on all around the area now, and black-clad Monks had surrounded the Archive building.

Yavi knew that they would be searching the grounds—if not now, then soon. He shook himself. He couldn't help Grey by getting caught himself, he thought, and resumed his way along the wall, behind the cover of the shrubbery. Miraculously, he made it without being discovered, and it was only when he was safely on the other side did he stop to wonder if he should have stayed to help Grey.

But then, he couldn't imagine what would have happened if he had been caught. A Marik captured trying to break into a restricted building. He could just see the look on Mother's face.

'Oh, you coward!' he said aloud to himself, sinking to the ground. He groaned, leaning his head on his knees. 'You Flaming coward. She was trying to help *you*, and you left her there by herself.'

He was still leaning against the wall, and suddenly he heard a shout very close to him. A light, probably from a torch beam, shone above him.

The sacks! They had found the sacks, he realized. There was nothing else to do now. Scrambling up, he half stumbled and half ran into the forest, in the direction of the road. He had the presence of mind to stop and pick up his backpack, but he didn't stop running till he was within sighting distance of the car park.

He was an idiot to have agreed to this foolhardy adventure. *Grandfather was right—I am stupid. I bet if he were here to see me, he would be laughing till his head fell off!*

It was easy beating himself up over it. It was especially so because it kept him from thinking the one thought that had been at the back of his mind when he realized he had abandoned Grey to the Monks.

The Monks—they were trained to kill.

# 9

## Departure

Yavi was quite put out to find Kariad rather dismissive. He had called her and then arrived at her doorstep in the early hours of the morning, still very disturbed, and after she had finished laughing about the fact that he had christened her cousin Grey, she insisted that she would be fine.

'She's been in more tight spots than runas you've drawn,' said Kariad, making him a steaming cup of sweet tea. 'I'm not going to stay up nights worrying about her—the Flame knows, I've done it more times than I care to remember. She'll get out of it all right, she always does. She can take care of herself.'

'I've decided that I'm going to go to Fezar,' said Yavi.

'Oh? And what do you hope to find there?'

Yavi shrugged. 'I don't know, but I'm hoping there will be someone there Grandfather might have worked with. Someone who might know more. There might be some of his things left behind.' He paused. 'If I take up the Academy position, this might be my last chance for an adventure.'

Kariad looked him up and down. 'I wouldn't have put you down as the adventurous type,' she said drily. 'It seems more like something my dear cousin would do.' She frowned at him. 'It's not guilt about having left her that's making you take a reckless decision, is it?'

Yavi bristled. 'I'm not as docile as you think.'

'Oh, that's not what I meant. Just that, going off at half-cock like this will serve no purpose. You don't even know what you're looking for—if there's anything to find.'

'I won't know that till I go there, will I?'

'Have you considered the fact that a mage going into Kuzerazi seeking information on magic is *extremely* foolhardy?'

'I won't go as a mage,' said Yavi. 'I intend to contact the Fezars and tell them who I am. I will say I'm researching my grandfather's life for a biography. I'm sure there will be someone who remembers him. All I want is to talk to them. Maybe I could look around, perhaps explore the old mill, its records. The key is in the satin, after all.'

'Hm,' said Kariad. 'I suppose nothing ventured, nothing gained. Who will you take with you?'

'Rindan, I suppose. Why?'

Kariad shrugged. 'In my experience, researchers usually travel with a retinue—having an assistant, scribe, attendant, what have you, will add weight to your story.'

Yavi was not the only Marik contemplating travel plans the next day. Standing in line at the ticket booth at Koda's railway station, Fahe thought of her favourite fable when she had been a little girl, the one about the feather that tipped the scales. Not that she had understood the moral then. She had just found it hilariously funny that a fox and a mouse could be friends and they should have chosen to live together. When Mouse decided to move into a nice, warm hole in one of the houses that had come up at the edge of the forest, they had to find a way to divide their possessions equally. So Fox procured a set of scales and they decided that each one would get an equal share in weight. Which was all very well to start with, but in the end they were left with the feather that lined Mouse's bed, and whichever side they put the feather on, it tipped the balance.

She wasn't sure exactly what had tipped things for her over the past day. In all her life, she couldn't ever remember Yanik ever having lost his temper so completely. His fight with Mother the previous evening had shaken Fahe quite badly. It wasn't just the shock that Yanik *could* be pushed to such a display of anger. It was also that she couldn't understand why she was feeling so lousy about being mad at him in the first place. She didn't even know why exactly she was upset with him. To want to talk to him and not be able to was worse than anything else she could imagine. And then there was the call from Inos.

For Fahe, the best way to get her mind off things was to immerse herself in something intensely physical. And now, with no triangles practice to go to, running was the only way out. The previous evening, she had walked out towards the guards' quarters, intending to get Zurel and Buttons and take a trip down to the park. Maybe a little jog, followed by throwing sticks for Buttons (she only ran after them; she didn't know she was supposed to fetch them back, and Fahe had to follow her, pick up the sticks and throw them again) would be good.

Zurel came out of the guards' quarters when she saw Fahe approaching.

'You have a call back at the house,' she said. 'Want to take it in here?'

'A call for me?' Fahe was surprised. She followed Zurel into the recreation room of the guards' quarters, where there was a comm console. The display showed a code that she didn't recognize, but since it was configured to pick up the caller's identity from the common database, it did say that it was from a public booth.

Fahe picked up the handset and identified herself.

'Flame's heart! You took your time! Do you think I'm made of money?' cried a familiar voice.

'Inos!' said Fahe. She sat down with a bump on the bench behind her.

'Yes, remember me?'

'Where are you?'

'I'm in Krandish with my parents. It's a seaport in Far Darom.'

'I know where Krandish is,' said Fahe, fleetingly irritated. Inos could be such a know-it-all. 'How are you?'

'Great,' said Inos enthusiastically. 'I'm going to join the business academy here in a couple of years.

'Couple of years?' said Fahe. 'So... you'll be coming back?'

There was a silence. 'No. I don't think I can. If I stay here, I can get to know more about my parents' trade. It'll be good experience.'

'You could have done that from Koda, you know.'

'Why are you being like that, Fahe? Can't you just be happy for me?'

'Just like you were happy about my going to the Academy?' asked Fahe sarcastically.

'Right... you know what? I'm sorry I called. I just wanted to know if you were all right, and this is all the thanks I get.'

'Funny how you never actually got around to asking about me at all.'

'You're a horrible girl, Marik Fahe,' said Inos, her voice shaking. 'I can't imagine how I could ever have been friends with you.'

'And I don't know how anyone as selfish as you can expect *any*one to be friends with you!'

It couldn't have got much worse than that, but it did. When she stepped out, she found Buttons playing with Keas, both of them too preoccupied to notice her. Fahe didn't even attempt to call Buttons—she didn't think she could handle it if she chose to ignore her, but when she was halfway to the house, an ecstatic yapping reached her and Buttons's furry form hurled itself through the trees.

The dog's insane happiness helped to a certain degree, but as she tossed and turned that night, Fahe thought she would go mad if she stayed on a day longer. Yanik didn't have time for her with his new baby coming; besides things were awkward with him. Yavi was immersed in his own project. She had no friends. In a few weeks, she'd go to the Academy anyway. There was nothing left for her here. Even Buttons was happy enough without her.

She would go to Marik, she decided, and spend her last few weeks of freedom there.

Thus, the fag end of the rush hour the next morning found Fahe pushing her way through the thronging office crowd at Koda's railway stop. Just as she reached the escalators going down to the subway connecting the platforms, she felt a hand on her arm, and a relentless grip pulled her away.

'Hey!' yelled Fahe, swinging her elbow back hard in the direction of her attacker's midriff. Her cry was lost amidst the noise of the crowd, and all she got were a few glares. Her arm was immobilized by someone far stronger, and she found herself face-to-face with Zurel.

'Get off me!' cried Fahe.

'What do you think you're up to?' asked Zurel. With scant regard for the direction of flow of human traffic, Zurel more or less marched her towards the nearest exit, and only let go of her when they were outside. Fahe wrenched her arm back and walked away, enraged and defeated.

By the time she reached the park between the bus and railway stops, she had more or less composed herself. She sank down on a bench, throwing her bag down next to her. Her adventure was over, and she was a fool to have thought it would have worked. She couldn't remember a single time she had gone anywhere outside of her home unescorted.

There was a crunch of sandals on gravel, and a creak as the bench shifted as someone sat beside her. To her surprise, it was Yavi.

'Yanik sent me,' he said by way of a preamble.

'I don't want to talk of Yanik.'

He reached across and plucked the ticket from her hand. 'Marik? Not very imaginative of you. How would you like to come with me to Kuzerazi instead?'

'What do you think of Keas?' asked Yavi when they were on their way home in the motorcar. Zurel was driving, which was odd because Yavi never let anyone drive his motor, but he looked rather tired and drawn this morning. He was even walking with a slight limp, dragging himself like he hurt all over.

'The Kuzerazan boy?' Rindan asked, frowning. 'He's a quiet sort, but works hard. Why do you ask?'

Fahe turned from her seat in the front, curious. Yavi was staring into space. Rindan was looking somewhat displeased, which made her wonder if perhaps he was unhappy about the expedition to the west.

'I think I might want him to come along with us,' Yavi replied. 'Do you think he's reliable enough to keep quiet about it?'

'He can keep a secret,' said Zurel.

Yavi raised his eyebrows. 'How can you be so sure?'

'Trust me on this, Mage Yavi.'

'Why do you want to take *him*?' asked Fahe, not bothering to hide her displeasure.

'He's the only Kuzerazan we know,' said Yavi. 'None of us has ever been there. It might help to have a local along.' He addressed Rindan: 'I'll talk to him when we get back. And you, Zurel, need to stop referring to me as a mage. Where we are going, that would be especially inadvisable.'

'What's the plan, then?' Fahe asked. 'We go to Fezar to snoop around?'

Yavi winced. 'Not snoop. I hate that word. We are going to try and find out what Grandfather did when he was at Fezar.'

'How do you know they won't throw us out when we get there?' Fahe asked. 'Why should they tell us anything?'

Yavi closed his eyes like he was very tired—he certainly looked it. 'Those are good questions,' was the only thing he said.

Yavi occupied himself with frenzied activity to take his mind off Grey. It didn't help that all his attempts to reach the Fezar estate were in vain. In fact, leave aside contacting them, he found it quite impossible to get any information about them from the worldwide information network, more commonly called the Infonetwork, or from the communications system. It was almost like Fezar didn't exist, and apart from a little spot on a map he had dug up on the Infonet and a forty-five-year-old news snippet about the Fezar Weaving Mill ceasing operations, it was almost like it didn't.

That little voice in his head that popped up every now and then, telling him that Grandfather had just played a mean trick on him, was now louder than ever. In fact, right then, the voice sounded very much like Yanik, telling him he was chasing the proverbial rainbow.

'You can't prove a point to a dead man,' he said to Yavi, who was tapping his fingers impatiently on the table.

'It's not to him but to me that I'm proving a point,' said Yavi. 'He always made me feel like trash. Never missed a chance to tell me I was no good and I didn't belong in this family. He even insulted me in death—he left me a puzzle, a possibly unsolvable one, to mock me. So I'm getting to the bottom of this, whatever "this" is.'

'So we go,' said Fahe, who had been listening, but studiously ignoring Yanik, 'knowing fully well there could be nothing there to find? Just for the record, I think Grandfather was an ass.'

'I wouldn't put it in quite those words, but I agree, he was,' said Yanik.

'Thanks for the vote of confidence,' said Yavi to his siblings. 'And yes, we go.'

'Yessss!' said Fahe, punching the air. 'I really, really want to go to Kuzerazi.'

'So do I,' said Yavi. 'Fahe, go and find Keas at the guards' quarters and meet me in the annexe.'

'What?' said Fahe, making a face. 'You're seriously thinking of taking him? Well, go get him yourself!'

Yavi turned to her. 'I don't have time for your childish fights. I'm not asking you to be best friends, but if you're going to be part of my team on this expedition, I expect you to behave like... well, like you're not five years old.'

Fahe opened her mouth to protest, but Yavi waved her quiet. 'In a few weeks, both of you will be entering the Academy. Together. Think of this trip as a chance of working together to sort out your differences because, believe me, you'll have plenty of other things to worry about later.'

'Don't act like you're doing me a favour,' said Fahe sulkily.

'I'm not,' he admitted. 'In fact, you're doing me one. But if you're sensible, you might get something out of it yourself.' He toyed with the idea of telling her about his Academy job, which he had decided to accept. On the other hand, it could wait.

Fahe looked at him suspiciously. 'There's something you're not telling me, right?'

Yavi pretended not to hear. Fahe could be very sharp.

# Part 2

# 10

## Western Air

Keas closed his eyes, breathing deeply as the chilly mountain air whipped against his face. *The smell of home,* he said to himself. The thought was like a slap. He opened his eyes. This was not his home now. He had identification saying he was a Koda resident.

It was ironic that he was returning to Kuzerazi much earlier than he had anticipated, and that too as an outlander—that was what they called easterners here. He was still apprehensive about his decision to accompany Yavi. He wasn't sure what the mage wanted from him. He had said he would be the local connection, but the truth was, Keas didn't really know much about the High Lands area of the Kuzerazan region. His former hometown of Saje, and even Karich, had been in the northern Low Lands. It was true that he had visited Vaker—the city under whose jurisdiction the Fezar estate was—but he had been just six at that time. He had tried in vain to tell Yavi that he was as much an alien to the High Lands as the others. But he hadn't told anyone his real fear—that he would be too afraid to even raise his eyes for fear of being recognized.

The option of staying behind had at one point seemed rather attractive, but then he found that most people he knew and had grown to care about in his new hometown were going—Zurel, Rindan, Yavi. He would have preferred not to have the spoilt Fahe in the group, but staying behind alone at Koda—even though the other guards were good to him—had seemed as scary as returning to Kuzerazi.

Keas was also still shaken from his first experience of flying. Yavi had wanted to waste as little time on travel as he could, but there was no direct air link to Kuzerazi from Nizrah. So they had taken a flight as close to the border that he could manage. There, a friend of his former Academy mentor's had had a motorcar waiting for them, in which they had had to negotiate the long drive south-west to Vaker.

It had got progressively colder as they moved west and climbed higher, and none of the Nizrahis had been pleased about that. While they wrapped their coats and scarves more tightly around themselves, Keas smiled at the familiar bite in the air.

'Are you insane?' Fahe snapped at him. 'Shut that Flaming window!'

Keas smirked as he rolled up the window a tiny bit. Who knew, this might turn out to be fun after all.

Cold. It was so cold. That was the only thought in Fahe's head as she huddled miserably on the narrow street. Zurel and Rindan unloaded the motorcar, helped by Keas, as Yavi rang the bell by the gate. Vaker, her hurried research on the Infonet had told her, was one of the handful of cities in the High Lands, but by all accounts it looked like one could walk from one end of the 'city' to the other in under half an hour.

Fahe looked at her watch—which was useless because she had forgotten to set the local time—and figured that the reason she was feeling so spaced out was probably that it was two in the morning back home.

Visiting Kuzerazi had been a more exciting prospect than even going to the Academy. Fahe had never ever imagined she'd ever see it for herself. And if and when she was a mage, she would probably never *want* to see it. Of course, she had seen photos and paintings and read about it. About mountains obscured by clouds, the sun rising behind the ranges, snow-capped peaks, glaciers, the view of a river rushing down a valley, mountain slopes covered with flowers. In fact, Grandfather could have been smuggling drugs for all she cared—for her, this was going to be the chance of a lifetime.

Vaker had been visible as a twinkling collection of lights nestled in the side of the mountain from afar, but any hopes Fahe had had of seeing scenic vistas through the day had been dashed by gloomy and depressing weather. It had drizzled throughout their ride, and a dull mist seemed to obscure everything in the distance.

Yavi had arranged for them to put up at a tourists' homestay—the sign above Fahe's head said 'Blue Hill', and a small sign under it informed them: 'Rooms available'. She was too tired to notice much else when a woman with a yappy little dog answered the summons at the gate, introduced herself in a high-pitched voice as Lily and welcomed them inside.

The house was completely different from any other Fahe had been in. The floor was carpeted, and if the creaks on the stairs were anything to go by, the flooring was all wooden!

It was all rather cramped too, but it was comfortingly warm, and that was all that mattered.

It was well past midday by the time the travellers managed to stir themselves the next day. Fahe had been quite bewildered to open her eyes to something very different from her large, airy bedroom back in Koda. The tiny, crowded room was not only momentarily disorienting, but the curious flower-patterned walls and the heavy drapes at the window by her feet were quite unlike anything she had ever seen before. There was a device that appeared to warm the room—Zurel had said it was a radiator—but it was still cold when she threw off her heavy quilt. The bed was uncomfortably soft too, and when she tried to get out, she found that her entire body hurt from sleeping on it.

Zurel was amused to see her fingering the wall.

'Wallpaper,' she said.

'What do you mean?'

'Just what it sounds like. Patterned paper stuck to the walls.'

'Really?' said Fahe. She looked down at the carpeted floor under her bare feet. 'And the floor is actually wooden under this rug?'

'Carpet. Yes.'

'Is that practical?'

Zurel shrugged. 'Probably is, for this part of the world. And who am I to judge? My clan family in Far Darom lives in a house with paper walls.'

Fahe grimaced. 'Can't take two steps without bumping into something. And I'm hungry. What time is breakfast?'

'It's a quarter past midday,' said Zurel. She was sitting on a chair, reading, her feet propped up on her own bed. She seemed fresh and well rested—and probably fed too, thought Fahe sourly.

As it turned out, the landlady was happy to prepare a quick meal for them. Yavi was still bleary-eyed and Keas appeared a little tense. Only the two guards seemed to be their normal selves.

'It's the time lag that's making us feel lethargic and tired,' said Yavi between bites. 'But we'll all feel much better if we step out. I'd like to visit the public library.'

'Why?' asked Fahe.

'To find out whatever I can about Fezar. I've got what I could over the Infonet, but no contact information. I'm sure the library will have that, and maps, books on local history and all that sort of stuff. I'd like you to come with me. You too, Keas.'

'Yeah,' said Fahe, looking distastefully at Keas. He didn't seem particularly thrilled either.

'Rindan, could you and Zurel ask around and see if you can find out anything about the people who live there? They must need supplies—food, clothing, other essentials. Someone must know the family or the house staff. Any point of contact.'

'Sure,' said Rindan, and Zurel nodded. 'But I don't like the idea of us roaming around separated.'

Yavi thought for a moment. 'I promise you, we won't leave the library till you come for us. Does *that* make you feel better?'

'It'll have to do,' said Rindan evenly.

In the light of the day, the mountain-city of Vaker looked completely different. It was late afternoon by the time they left Lily's, but it wasn't dull and drizzly today. A pale sun was still high in the sky, and Lily had informed them that during the summer, it stayed light till well into the night, and markets and public institutions worked double shifts.

None of the outlanders had seen high mountains before. The low sprawling hills that were native to the Brei homeland in Far Darom were very different from the stately valleys and ranges of the western mountains. Being on the windward side of the valley, Vaker usually got rain towards the late afternoon each day, but today seemed especially clear by regular standards—almost as though in honour of the visitors.

It was a pleasant walk into town, and they stopped at the crest of the main road that dipped downhill to admire the view.

'Oh my,' said Zurel under her breath.

'Yes, it's quite something,' agreed Yavi.

'It's not just that. It reminds me of something. Someone I knew... someone who used to talk about this place. Promised to bring me here, if I chose it.'

'Ooh,' said Fahe. 'Tell us!'

Zurel gave her a look. 'No.'

'Why didn't you?' asked Yavi.

'Didn't what?' Zurel said.

'Choose to come here. Imagine what you missed.'

'It was this or that,' said Zurel with a sigh. 'It was just before taking my guardsmanship oath. I chose to be a guard.'

'Lucky me,' said Fahe drily.

'Why is the slope over there purple?' asked Rindan. 'I didn't know there was purple grass in Kuzerazi.'

'That's heather,' said Keas, speaking about the first time that afternoon. 'It's very soft underfoot—like walking on carpet. But the ground it grows on may also be boggy.' He pointed ahead, where the trees were denser as the mountain sloped down into the valley. 'And that, I'm guessing, is the famous Vaker Oak Forest.'

'You mean the prized Vaker oak used for furniture?' Yavi said.

Keas nodded. 'It's also got some rare medicinal plants. I've been... uh...'

Everyone looked at him, waiting for him to go on, but he just flushed and looked away. He had been jumpy and nervous since they'd entered Kuzerazi.

'Are you all right?' Yavi asked him.

Keas just went a deeper shade of red and refused to answer.

Vaker Town Square was easy to find, thanks to the map Lily had provided. Like the name suggested, it was a large open square barred to traffic except pedestrian. Shops and stalls framed it on all four sides, and most of them were decorated with streamers—blue and yellow flags strung on shiny silver ribbon. Confetti littered the ground as well.

'Festive,' said Yavi.

It certainly was. The centre of the square had a small children's play area, with a sandbox, swings and some other rides, and it was full of screaming, happy toddlers. Older children ran about freely, and the grown-ups seemed rather upbeat too. A trio of young people played a set of instruments, and a crowd had gathered around them. Vendors with portable stands were selling sweets and other eatables.

'It must be the Summer Rave,' said Keas, who was looking around, almost fearfully. 'Signals the end of the summer, the holidays.'

Fahe sniffed. 'And what's that smell? Makes me hungry again.'

'Cinnamon biscuits,' said Keas abruptly.

Yavi had stopped outside a shop that sold and repaired wireless electronic devices. 'Fahe, you and Keas go on ahead to the library. I'll join you in a bit.'

'Where are you off to?' Fahe asked.

He pointed towards the shop. 'My GPS doesn't seem to be working out here,' he said. 'Maybe they'll help me sort it out.'

'I'll come with you,' said Rindan.

They went in, and Zurel, who had the map, pointed to a tall, grey building visible behind the row of shops. 'If I'm right, that's the Town Hall. That's where Lily said the library is.'

'Hmmph,' said Fahe morosely.

Zurel walked slowly along the row of shops. Something about the crisp, fresh mountain air made her feel unusually cheerful despite the dull lethargy that gripped her limbs. She stopped outside a small snack shop. A red-and-white canopy extended over a glass door that said 'Please step in', and the array of eatables displayed in the window looked quite appetizing. Zurel pushed the door open and was momentarily startled as a bell jangled over her head.

There were three small tables with red-and-white patterned cloths. A refrigerated cabinet stood next to the till, packed with drinks. The main counter held packaged food items, and there was another cabinet with cakes and other savouries. A long table against the wall had a selection of jars and bottles, along with cutlery and paper napkins. There was a menu displayed on a large electronic board behind the cash counter, headed by the words 'Self-service'.

There was no one in the shop, though Zurel could see movement in the room behind. She glanced at the menu, curious about the alien food items. The cardamom tea intrigued her. Flavoured tea?

'May I help you?' A plump, middle-aged man with a wide smile stepped through. He was mostly bald, but had a brilliant black moustache.

Zurel smiled a greeting. 'I was wondering if a serving of your cardamom tea might help soothe my aching limbs.'

'A good choice,' the man said. 'Been walking, have you?'

'Not really. My friends and I arrived late last night from Nizrah. I guess I haven't yet shaken off the effects of the time lag.'

'Ah, say no more,' he said, waving a massive hand. 'Went to Nizrah last summer, so I know how you feel. Seat yourself. I'll get you your drink. How about some carrot cake to go with it?'

Carrot cake sounded in equal parts appalling and fascinating, so Zurel nodded as she took the seat next to the window.

As it turned out, she had no trouble drawing the friendly shop owner—his name was Bross—into conversation, especially when she told him that she was a research assistant helping her friend. And the carrot cake was excellent, though the cardamom tea wasn't.

'Yes, Vaker has changed quite a bit since the time your friend's granddad must have been here. This entire region has. It must be, what, forty years, you said?'

'About that,' admitted Zurel. 'Changed how?'

'Well, for one, this was hardly more than a village then, and it was quite remote. I was just a child, but my sisters and brother and I would come up here every summer to stay with our father's aunt. This shop belonged to her. At that time it was the biggest shop in Vaker, and it sold everything, from ice creams to shirt laces.'

'Any chance that your great-aunt mentioned running into a traveller from the east called Avin? Karis Avin?'

Bross pursed his lips and gave it some thought. Then he shook his head. 'If she did, I don't recall anything.'

'Well,' said Zurel, warming to her task, 'it's quite likely he didn't spend too much time here in town. It was Fezar that he really visited when he came to Kuzerazi.'

There was a perceptible change in Bross. 'Fezar? That's... interesting.'

'Why?' asked Zurel curiously.

'They keep to themselves. At least, they have in the last few decades.'

'Maybe that would explain why my friend hasn't been able to contact them yet.'

Bross shrugged. 'Probably. I'm not surprised.'

'But surely they can't be that reclusive,' Zurel persisted. 'They must be coming into town for food and other essentials? What's their line of business, do you know?'

'Nobody knows much about the Fezars,' said Bross after a pause.

'But what about the mill? I hear they manufactured cloth?'

'Before my time,' said Bross. 'All I know is that after the old man died, his niece inherited the estate, and I have never seen her in town. Nobody really knows what goes on up there since the mill shut. They don't seem to want anything to do with us, and the feeling is mutual. For all we know, there could just be caretakers living there.'

He pushed his chair back with a harsh, grating sound and stood. 'If you'll excuse me, I will make up your bill.' Halfway to the till, he turned around again. 'Can I give you some unsolicited but well-meant advice?'

'Be my guest,' said Zurel.

'It's not a good idea walking around asking about the Fezars. Ignorance breeds fear, and the locals fear the Fezars and what happens in that estate because they know nothing about the family. As outlanders, you'd just be marking yourselves out for trouble.'

Zurel nodded. 'Appreciate the warning.'

# 11

## Secrets

In a crowded Muradian public bar, two women and a man bent their heads together to talk. Even huddled across that tiny table in the corner, they had trouble making themselves heard over the raucous music and the conversation and laughter of the other patrons.

'The Hyran Monks have reported another break-in,' the man said.

'When was this?' one of the women asked.

'A couple of days back.'

'One of the intruders got away before anyone could get a good look,' the other woman said. She was older than the others. 'They said it was most likely a man.'

'What about the others?' the first woman asked. She turned her glass round and round with her fingers. The light caught her Flamestone ring, making it glint.

The man shrugged. 'We don't know.'

'Was it Sareka again?'

'We don't know,' he repeated. 'But what's interesting is, Marik Yavi left town quite hurriedly the next day.'

'Someone should talk to Kariad,' the woman with the Flamestone ring said. 'She'd know what is going on, with Sareka and maybe even Yavi.'

The older woman shook her head as she banged her glass down. 'Don't be silly, Rihal. I don't want her to know I'm taking an especial interest in her once favourite student.'

When Keas had been ten, he had run away to his grandmother's place in Karich after getting into trouble with his father. One day, he had gone into town for some sweets and was startled to find a notice in the window of the civil guards' station about him. Walking into Vaker had reminded Keas of that time, and he half-expected to come face-to-face with 'Missing' posters with his face plastered across them.

Thus, it was a relief of some sort to be safely ensconced in the library, trying to find information about the mysterious High Lands estate. The sensible part of his brain told him that as long he was poking around remote locations like Fezar, there was little chance of his being recognized, if indeed there were people looking for him.

Fahe muttered something next to him, and he turned to her.

'Nothing?' she said, mostly speaking to herself. 'How can there be nothing?'

'Maybe there's nothing to write about?' suggested Keas quietly.

They were seated at a terminal in the library, looking up the index. And as far as they could make out, local records about the Fezars stopped some thirty-eight years ago, when the previous owner of the estate, El'Fezar Komas, died. The land passed on to his heir—his niece, Manara—but there was nothing more. It was so intriguing that for a while Keas and Fahe forgot their problems with each other.

Fahe went to the librarian to ask how they could access old newspapers around that time, only to learn that there weren't any computer records dating that far back. If she was interested, the man suggested, they could take a look at the microfilm records.

It was a creaky, flickering, old machine and the microfilm cans dusty, but the results were interesting. It seemed that up until before Komas's death, the Fezars were quite active in the local community. Whether it was donating money to repair the main road, getting the play area in the Town Square built, or hosting annual sports and cultural events, they had been very visible. The mill had been a prosperous one. Nobody seemed to know why it had shut down some forty-five years ago, but it appeared that the workers were compensated adequately.

'He's the one!' said Fahe, excited, leaning in towards the grainy display, pointing to a middle-aged man waving to the crowd from a stage. 'I've seen this man in photographs in Grandfather's study. Fezar Komas. Or El'Fezar Komas, as you say out here.'

'And that must be his niece,' said Keas.

The photograph wasn't very clear, but as they progressed through the next few months, other images showed her constantly by her uncle's side. She was about the same height as him, and certainly quite striking to look at.

'She looks very familiar,' said Fahe, frowning. 'But I can't put my finger on it.'

The last photograph they found was of her entering the funeral shrine some weeks after Komas's death. It was a hurriedly taken shot from the side, and her head was bent, away from the camera. She seemed very young, in her early twenties, when the responsibility of the estate had passed on to her.

Fahe was about to move on, but Keas stopped her. He had been reading the accompanying report, and frowned. 'That's interesting.'

'What?'

'Komas disappeared and his body was never found. It says that he went for a walk and didn't return. "Search parties combed the estate, but were unable to find any trace of Komas. His walking stick and backpack containing waterproofs and a thermos with traces of cardamom tea were, however, recovered. The Vaker Civil Guards eventually pronounced him missing, presumed dead. A spokesperson said in a statement that given current weather conditions it is highly unlikely a man of his age and health would still be alive."'

'I can read,' snapped Fahe. 'Through it doesn't really mean anything. Unless he reappeared later.' But they went through the next few months with no further mention of the Fezars.

Keas stretched as Fahe changed the film. 'What if there are no records and no information because there is no one left?' he said. 'Maybe the estate is dead and deserted.'

Fahe looked at him. 'You can give that happy news to Yavi,' she said, and then added grudgingly: 'You're probably right.'

Yavi called a meeting in his room when they got back from the Town Square. Despite the dull ache behind his eyes and the overall feeling of lethargy—both from the time lag as well as the fact that he was still sleep-deprived—he couldn't help the stirrings of excitement as they exchanged information. It was quite obvious from their faces that at least Fahe and Keas were completely drawn into it as well—they were even talking to each other without Fahe biting Keas's head off.

'I spoke with one of the employees at the Kuzerazi Fresh supermarket,' said Rindan. 'Got a bit lucky, actually. I saw a delivery truck and offered to help load it. I mentioned how come a small town like Vaker had such a lot of deliveries. He replied that the goods were going to neighbouring villages. I asked him then if that included Fezar, and he gave me a strange look. Said those people were odd. Well, then I told him about your project. He had a break coming up, and he had a flask of this revolting spicy tea that he asked me to share.

'It turns out that the Fezars are exceedingly shy. He said that as far as he knew, no one had ever seen any member of the family in many years. He didn't know anything about a mill. They never come into town, and yes, they do take deliveries, but there's a drop-off point near the estate border on the highway—a wooden shack. He'd only done the delivery once. The payment was left in an envelope, so he didn't see anyone. Oh, he also said that he's pretty new up here, but he gets the impression that the townsfolk aren't too enamoured of the Fezars.'

'That's the same sense I got,' said Zurel, who repeated her curious conversation with Bross.

Fahe and Keas told the others how local information about the Fezars stopped at about thirty-eight years ago, just after Komas's death.

'We checked microfilms of newspapers for the months around Komas's death, but they seem to have just completely dropped off the face of the world after that,' finished Fahe. 'Oh, but there's something curious about his death.' She looked at Keas.

He looked a little taken aback that Fahe was giving him a chance to speak. 'Oh... he, I mean, Komas...' He cleared his throat. 'I mean, apparently Komas's body was never recovered. He was presumed dead when nobody could find him after searching for days. He left for a walk one evening, and never returned. They found his backpack, though.'

'Interesting,' said Yavi. 'I checked the land records. The estate is in the name of the Fezar Trust. They pay a significant amount of land tax and there have been no irregularities in payment. There are no records of any existing communications hook-ups that I could access.'

'But they do call the market for deliveries,' pointed out Rindan.

'Maybe they call from a public comm,' said Fahe.

There was silence as they all digested the information.

'The Fezars are definitely recluses, then,' said Yavi finally. 'There is no Infonetwork ID either. I think that leaves only one option.'

'What's that?' asked Fahe.

'We go and knock on their door.'

'But how?'

'We'd need detailed maps,' said Rindan.

'I got some maps,' Yavi said. 'I also loaded some walking maps on my GPS. They show paths for hikers to take, and rate them according to difficulty.'

'Going up there is all very well,' said Zurel. 'But they *have* kept to themselves for almost forty years. Clearly, they want as little contact as possible with the outside world, and I guess that includes visitors. You really think trooping in like this is a good idea?'

'Well, I've been thinking about that,' said Yavi slowly. 'You're right—we may not be welcome. I think I should go alone.'

Rindan snorted. 'You're not going anywhere I am not.'

'Honestly, sometimes you act like I'm still fourteen,' began Yavi, but Fahe interrupted indignantly.

'Yavi, that's just not fair! You drag us all the way up here, then you make us search around in dusty libraries, and now you want us to stay put? No way. I'm coming too.'

'And *you* are not going anywhere I'm not,' said Zurel.

# 12

There were two options to approach the Fezar estate. They could take the interstate highway to the deliveries drop-off point that Rindan had found out about, or set off in the opposite direction, skirt around Vaker and go into the interiors of the High Lands area up to where the roads ended. After that they'd have to walk almost six masaafs to reach the edge of Fezar property.

It was a unanimous decision to go for the latter. Even though the highway route was the far easier approach, it would have attracted unwarranted attention. They took the borrowed motor, and enough food and drink to last them the day, and altogether had a very pleasant morning. The sun was out, and it was cold enough to enjoy a day out in it. There was an air of a picnic outing when they started out. Everyone was in high spirits—even Keas, who relaxed palpably once they were in the wilderness.

The ground was soft—like Keas had said it would be—quite like a deep-pile carpet. It hadn't rained here for a few days, so thankfully it wasn't boggy. The trees gradually grew denser as they rounded the face of the mountain and climbed higher. When they were almost at the top, Yavi discovered that his GPS wasn't working.

Zurel pulled out her comm device. 'There's no signal here. We're out of range.'

'It doesn't matter,' said Yavi, putting the GPS receiver away in his backpack. He pulled out a map and shook it open. 'We are close. The estate borders should begin just up ahead.'

'It looks like a forest to me,' said Fahe, shading her eyes and looking up. She sniffed. 'And what's that smell?'

'What smell?' said Yavi, whose nose wasn't as sharp as Fahe's, but Keas was nodding.

'It's the pines,' he said. 'Those tall, pointy trees. They secrete a resin that has a distinctive smell.'

They carried on into the forest, and the path more or less evened out ahead. It was a relief not to have to climb any more, and the shade from the trees made for a perceptible drop in the temperature. Everyone pulled on their jackets once again. The smell Fahe had noticed was sharper now, and pleasant. They found some curious, rather pretty cones on the forest floor that Keas said came from the pines.

About half a masaaf into the pine forest, they came to the Fezar border: a wooden fence that ran as far to the right and left as they could see. Metal plates with the words 'Private Property' were nailed at intervals.

They stopped for a little conference and decided to have lunch while they were at it. Spreading a plastic sheet on the damp ground in a small clearing, they shared out the food.

'So what now?' said Fahe. 'Do we just jump over the fence?'

'They don't exactly say to keep out,' pointed out Yavi. 'But it would still be trespassing.'

'In any case,' Rindan added, 'where exactly would we go?' He was looking at the map that was spread out between him and Yavi. 'This doesn't show any details and we don't have GPS any more. No comms of any sort. In fact, we're pretty well equipped to get hopelessly lost.' He waved his arms around. 'There's been no sign of civilization as far as we've seen on this entire walk. Look at how big the Fezar lands are. Even if we do cross the fence and go inside, exactly how do you think we'll be able to cover the entire area searching for the house?'

'According to Grandfather's notes,' said Yavi, unfazed by Rindan's pessimistic summary of their situation, 'there's a lake that's more or less in the centre of the estate, and he mentions a 'Lake House', which I presume refers to the Fezar homestead on its shores. And there *is* an unnamed waterbody marked in the map here as well. As long as we travel in a north-easterly direction, we should hit upon it.'

'I have a compass,' said Zurel.

'So it's not as though we'd get lost anyway, unless we were very stupid.'

'Actually,' said Keas tentatively, 'we wouldn't. I can... er... track a little bit. There doesn't seem to have been much human traffic here, so I'm more or less sure I could bring us back the way we came.'

'More or less,' repeated Rindan under his breath. 'Great.'

They finished eating and packed up the wrappers and empty cartons, still arguing. After prolonged discussions, they came to the conclusion that it was best to look for a legitimate way in—a gate or stile. Yavi and Rindan decided to go to the right along the fence and slightly downhill. Zurel and Fahe would go left. Keas, who seemed to prefer Zurel's company the most, chose to go with them.

'Our outer time limit is half an hour,' said Yavi. 'At that point, wherever we are, we'll turn back and return here. So we meet again in an hour.'

Zurel, Fahe and Keas did come upon a stile very shortly.

'We have plenty of time,' said Fahe. 'We could go in and explore a bit.'

'Don't think that's a good idea,' said Zurel sceptically. 'Trespassing is against the law.'

'Yeah, but it doesn't say "no trespassing",' insisted Fahe.

'That's true,' said Keas. 'I've usually seen no-trespassing signs with private-property notices. Some even threaten prosecution.'

'See?' said Fahe, encouraged. 'Oh come on, you don't have to be as much of a spoilsport as your uncle.'

Zurel ignored her and appeared to think. 'All right, we go in,' she said at last. 'But we'll stay in sight of the fence.'

Even though it had been her own idea, Fahe felt inexplicably uneasy as she put her foot on Fezar property. She looked through the dizzyingly tall trees at the sky. Suddenly, for no reason, she wanted nothing more than to go back across the fence, but that would mean admitting that Zurel was right.

In any event, there was no time for her to ruminate. They had hardly taken a few steps when the sharp, unmistakeable sound of a gunshot rang out. A fraction of a second of absolute stillness followed, then the rush of a flurry of birds taking off into the air. In the middle of all that, Fahe found herself taken down by the weight of Zurel's body on hers.

'Down, down!' she hissed urgently, and they rolled unceremoniously down a slope behind them.

Fahe's fall was broken about halfway down the incline when she rolled into a tree. She groaned for a few seconds, but scrambled to rise on finding that she wasn't any worse for wear. Some way from her she saw Zurel, her arm wrapped around a tree. From the other arm dangled Keas, whose eyes were round with fear as he scrabbled frantically with his legs for balance.

Noticing that Fahe was about to get up, Zurel made violent head-shaking motions. She let Keas go and used a hand gesture they had practised during their training sessions to tell Fahe to stay down and quiet.

Fahe complied, but her heart was hammering in her chest as her mind began to piece together what had happened. She knew a shot had been fired, and now they could hear voices too. Shouts, in fact. As the bits fell into place, she realized with mind-numbing terror that it could be Yavi who had been shot. Were those shouts his voice?

If Yavi was hurt... if anything happened to him...

Fahe scrambled up, slipping on the damp, slippery ground, and, ignoring Zurel's hissed angry '*No!*', ran up the slope towards the sound of the voices.

Fahe ran blindly, screaming Yavi's name. She had no idea how far she had run when she emerged headlong into a clearing with a small knot of people. They scattered to reveal a vision out of her worst nightmare.

Yavi and Rindan were on the ground. And there was a lot of blood.

'If you kill my brother...' cried Fahe, but then stopped short.

Both Rindan and Yavi were staring at her in surprise. Rindan had a hand pressed to his right shoulder, under which was a dark, bloody patch. Yavi appeared unhurt, and was only supporting Rindan.

'That's my sister,' said Yavi. 'I'm telling you, we had no devious intentions. We're merely trying to contact the Fezars, and there seemed no other way but to come here. I'm happy to talk in detail about my reasons later, but can I have some first aid for my friend please?'

'Yes, of course,' one of the strangers said, and Fahe turned to study them. The speaker nodded at one of the others, who in turn disappeared into the woods.

There were three of them, including the one who had walked away; two were definitely men, with heavy moustaches, and the third—the speaker—she wasn't sure of. They wore curious one-piece garments that covered them from neck to ankle, with zippers down the front, and sturdy walking boots. Their heads were wrapped in a sort of turban that covered their hair, neck and face, except for the eyes, nose and mouth. The clean-shaven one was armed and appeared to be their spokesperson.

'Please accept our apologies again,' she said.

Rindan, who seemed fine apart from the bloodstain spreading around his shoulder, was breathing heavily. He raised his other hand. 'It was a mistake. Happens. We *were* trespassing.'

'We're not in the habit of shooting trespassers, I assure you.'

There was a low, rumbling sound and the man reappeared driving a very odd-looking vehicle. It was mostly like a shallow tub, attached with six wheels, and it had two rows of seats on top—rather, inside. It was completely open except for a windscreen in front. The tyres were thick and wide, and it was easy to see how it could negotiate the uneven forest floor easily. The bottom and sides of the 'tub' had dried mud spatters.

The man braked to a halt and vaulted over to the back seat. He opened a small hatch towards the back of the vehicle and pulled out a blue plastic box that he handed down to one of his companions.

Yavi held out his hand for it. 'It's all right, I'm a physician.'

Helped by one of the others, he cleaned and bandaged Rindan's wound.

'He needs to be taken to a hospital,' one of the waiting Fezars said. 'We'll transport you to the highway, where an ambulance will be waiting.' She took out something that looked like a comm handset from her pocket and pulled out a short antenna. She walked a short distance away, punching in numbers. Fahe watched, intrigued, as she talked into the device. She remembered how they had been unable to find any comm records for the Fezars.

'What can you see?' whispered Keas, unable to resist any more.

They were positioned behind a large, mossy boulder, well back from the others, and in addition, a thick cover of trees hid them safely from view. They were too far to see much, but Zurel had her binoculars, which she had trained on the little crowd out in the clearing.

'My view is obscured by the trees, but I can see more or less... They've got a vehicle of sorts... never seen anything like it... six wheels.'

'Vehicle? Are they taking them somewhere?'

'I assume—well, I hope—it's getting Rindan to a hospital.'

'Is he fine? Rindan, I mean. Will he be... he's not badly hurt?'

'Seems so,' said Zurel. 'He's conscious, walking around. He's holding his shoulder. I think... Damn it! Someone just walked across my view.'

'Do you think they've captured them?' said Keas suddenly. 'Holding them prisoner?'

Zurel lowered her binoculars and stared at Keas. 'What? Where do you get wild ideas like that from?'

'Well... it's not impossible,' said Keas, blushing.

'You read too many books,' said Zurel, going back to her binoculars. 'Now they're helping Rindan on to the motor... Fahe and Yavi are getting on too. From their body language, it doesn't look like they're being forced. Want to see for yourself?'

Keas took the binoculars. He couldn't see much because of the trees, but it was clear enough that everyone did indeed appear to be going quite voluntarily.

'Oh, they're off,' he said, and was surprised to find himself hauled up by Zurel. 'Wha...'

'Come on,' she said.

'Where?'

'You said you could track, right? Well, let's see if we find any trails and if they lead us anywhere interesting. We might as well make ourselves useful.'

'But... what about the others?'

'They don't seem to be in any danger and they didn't give away our presence either. It would be stupid not to take the chance to snoop around.'

'What brings you to Fezar?'

'I'm researching my late grandfather's life,' said Yavi. 'For a biography. I'm in the process of filling in some gaps, including a couple of visits he made here. I believe he was a good friend of Komas's and conducted some business with him.'

The odd vehicle made pretty good speed over the bumpy terrain. There was a clear path cutting through the dense forest, quite obviously made by the motor travelling through. At places, the road branched off, but the driver seemed to be certain of the way and drove without hesitation. Rindan sat in front, next to the driver. One of the others, the one Fahe had designated as the woman, was on his other side. Fahe herself, Yavi and the remaining Fezar were squeezed in at the back.

The two in front exchanged a quick look. Fahe grasped the rail in front of her seat fearfully, but their motor carried on regardless.

The woman turned towards them. 'And what was his name?'

'Avin,' said Yavi. 'Of Marik. His full name was Karis Avin.'

She didn't say anything, but continued to look at Yavi till he was compelled to continue speaking.

'I did my best to contact you from Koda,' he went on. 'That's where I live. Coming here this way, unannounced and literally breaking in, was not our intention. It was a last resort.'

'The owner of Fezar does not like to mingle with outsiders, especially not outlanders,' she said.

'The owner?' said Yavi. 'Would that be Komas's niece?'

She raised her eyebrows at him.

'Please,' persisted Yavi, 'I need to speak with her. Just once. She may be the only person able to shed light on the not inconsiderable time my grandfather spent in Kuzerazi. Without this information, my entire research—this entire project—will come to nothing.'

The two Fezars in front exchanged yet another glance across Rindan.

'I can't promise you anything, sir. But I will speak to her. If she chooses to meet you, we'll get a message to you.'

'But how will you contact...' began Yavi.

'Leave your names with us, and where you are staying.'

It was Fahe and Yavi's turn to look at each other. They didn't speak or make any other outward signals, but she could see the triumph in his face.

Western folk songs talk of the 'singing of the bamboo', but it is quite impossible to know what it means till you actually hear it. Singing is a singularly inadequate way to describe the tormented creaking of bamboo plants; it sounds more like tortured souls crying for release—at least that's what it always reminded Keas of. When he was younger, he had heard a story to that effect, and while he had forgotten the tale, the idea of souls trapped inside the interminable stems, crying for escape, had always remained with him, and it gave him the willies.

They were aware of the eerie creaking long before they came up to the wall of thickly growing bamboo. The stalks were many times their height and growing so densely that it formed a thick, solid barrier that they couldn't see past. It extended on both sides as far as they could make out, curving slightly away from them.

'That noise,' said Zurel, screwing up her face. 'What is it?'

'It's the bamboo creaking,' said Keas. It was so loud that they had to raise their voices. He shook his head. 'This is so wrong... I know bamboo is versatile, but in the middle of a pine forest? I've never heard of it.'

'I thought bamboo is a grass,' said Zurel, gazing upwards at the gently swaying stalks.

'It is.'

'That doesn't look like grass to me,' scoffed Zurel.

Keas shrugged. 'Don't look at me. It belongs to the same family. There are many, many types of bamboo in Kuzerazi, of different shapes, sizes, colour, uses.'

'How does it make this sound?'

'It's the stems, or stalks. They bend in the wind and rub against each other.'

As it turned out, it hadn't been very difficult to find a trail. They had found a couple of well-defined paths leading out from the clearing. One of them was a broad one that had an intermittent, thin strip of grass along its middle, and was obviously used mainly by the six-wheel vehicle. The other was much narrower, probably made by frequent use on foot, and well worn, which was the one they followed. Keeping well inside the cover of the trees, a walk of just under an hour had brought them to the bamboo grove, or whatever it was.

Zurel lightly punched the wall of vegetation in front of her. The track that they had been following went right up to the bamboo wall, but a close examination indicated no clues about any sort of gate. Clearly, there was a way to get through, but it was very well hidden.

'Well, this is no good,' she said. 'Let's see if we can walk around it.'

But the wall was relentlessly solid in either direction. After a fruitless session of following it on both sides, they decided to give up. What they did discover was that it definitely curved away from them.

'Like it's a boundary wall around something,' said Keas. He looked up, shading his eyes against the patches of bright sky visible through the high trees. 'Do you think it's protecting something? Keeping something in?'

Zurel kept on walking, half listening to Keas. Suddenly, she raised her hand, indicating to him to stop. He clamped his mouth shut and hurried forward to join her.

The curve of the bamboo wall was a little harder where she had been standing, and just beyond it was a broad track leading out from the forest and up to the wall. Like before, there was no sign of a door or gate among the bamboo plants, but it was certain that this path was used by something like the Fezars' six-wheel vehicle, leading straight inside.

'Get back,' she said, pushing him back. 'There might be people around. We don't want to be spotted.'

'That vehicle of theirs—do you think it's back from dropping them to wherever they took them?'

Zurel looked at her watch. 'It would depend, I suppose, on where exactly we are and where they were taken. Let's hang around for a while and see if there's any activity.'

But their vigil was in vain as well. The bamboo boundary remained distressingly inanimate except for its eerie creaking, and the vehicle track stayed empty. After a while, Zurel dusted herself up from their position behind a couple of trees.

'I'm going to risk taking a closer look at where the track meets the wall,' she said.

Keas knelt to examine the track while Zurel went towards the wall. There were definite footprints here—all mixed up, but clear enough in the damp ground. Not only did they use this for the vehicles, but people walked along here as well. Zurel was right—they could easily be spotted.

He turned to hail her, when he noticed that she had her face pressed close up to the bamboo stems. She was standing absolutely still, but somehow seemed to sense his movement, for she beckoned to him with her hand.

Keas jumped up and rushed to her side. She propelled him towards the wall where the bamboo growth had thinned enough for her to have forced a couple of stalks just wide enough apart that they could see what was beyond.

'I think we've found the Lake House.'

# 13

## A Grey Day

Fahe dreaded coming face-to-face with Zurel again, well aware that she was in big trouble. The Mariks and their personal guards were bound by a code of honour, and the first rule included not questioning the judgement of the person who had vowed to protect you even at the cost of their own lives.

So it was a relief that Keas and Zurel met her and Yavi in the Vaker Town Square. Not only was she unlikely to get a dressing-down in public, clearly the two of them had some news, with Keas almost dying from suppressed excitement.

'We found the Lake House,' Zurel informed them by way of greeting.

'And you wouldn't believe...' started Keas, but Zurel shut him up with a sharp nudge, and Yavi shook his head as well.

'Whatever it is, will have to wait,' he said. 'We shouldn't talk here.' He turned to Zurel. 'Aren't you even going to ask about Rindan?'

Zurel shrugged. 'He was walking on his own two feet, so I'm assuming he's all right. Hospital keeping him overnight just in case?'

Rindan had narrowly missed having a rather serious injury and he was going to be fine. He had been admitted to the main hospital that served Vaker and nearby towns, and he was being kept for observation. Yavi fell silent after he related all this, and it struck Fahe for the first time that Rindan's injury probably had direct bearing on the fact that there was not a scratch on Yavi himself. She looked down at her shoes.

They ate their meal quietly at a small restaurant behind Bross's teashop and trooped back to Blue Hill.

'Can we tell them now?' Keas asked Zurel as they walked in.

'Let's meet in my room in fifteen minutes,' said Yavi. 'I'd really like to wash up and change.'

The dressing-down, when it happened, was every bit as bad as Fahe had expected, and then some. Being shouted at was something she might have been able to deal with, and it might have also assuaged her guilt somewhat. But Zurel's calm diatribe left her feeling like pond scum.

'But what is done is done, and we have to get past it,' she finished. 'Learn from what happened and let go of everything else. Do you understand what I'm saying?'

'That you'll never trust me again?' said Fahe mournfully.

Zurel sighed. 'If I couldn't trust you again, I'd have to put a collar and leash on you. I admire your courage, but don't think much of your intelligence. And stupidity can get us both killed... Flames, what's that?'

Raised voices sounded from the hallway. There was a pounding on their door, and Yavi's voice. Zurel yanked the door open and he strode in.

'Grandfather's things—they're gone!'

'Gone?' said Zurel as a bewildered Keas followed Yavi in. Lily, the landlady, stood outside, looking distressed.

'The case is gone from my cupboard,' said Yavi. 'It was stolen.'

Yavi had turned his room upside down on the off chance that he might have misplaced his special case, but it was a tiny room and there was really just the cupboard to put anything valuable in. Yavi seethed with fury—mostly at his own stupidity.

'I should have never left them here,' he mumbled, showing the lock on the cupboard to Zurel as Fahe and Keas looked on. 'It's not difficult to force this.'

'The Fezars!' gasped Fahe. 'You told them about the...'

'Yes,' said Yavi. 'But hush now.' He went out into the hall to speak to Lily. 'Tell me more about this man who came to see me.'

Lily was wringing her hands together. She was speaking fast, but her Samanya was tinged with strong western inflections that the Nizrahis could scarcely understand. Finally, Keas had to interpret for them, which he did hesitantly.

'He said he was an old acquaintance of your grandfather's,' said Lily through Keas, 'and I know you're writing up his life. I told him you were out and didn't know when you'd be back, but he asked to wait, so I showed him up to the visitors' lounge. An hour or so later, he came knocking at my door, saying he'd come back another time.'

'What did he look like?' Yavi asked.

'Thin, short. A pinched sort of face. Short neck. Must have been in his late fifties. Maybe more. He had a cane and walked with a limp. He seemed completely harmless.'

'Yes, well, he seems to have picked the lock on my door and the cupboard expertly. When did you say this was?'

'Not more than a couple of hours ago.'

They all looked at each other. Yes, definitely the Fezars. The timing fit too—it must have been when Fahe and Yavi were waiting for the others at the restaurant, well after the Fezar incident.

'Robbed,' said Lily. 'Shocking! In all my life, never have I seen anything like it... Are you sure you haven't misplaced your bag?'

She tried to insist that Yavi report the loss, but he didn't want to.

'I know who took them,' he said. 'I will recover them myself.'

Across town, another outlander was intensely displeased.

'This is incomplete!' Rihal threw down a journal. 'There should be more.'

'This is all that there was, I assure you,' said Raven. 'Just the one case.' He was a small, rat-like man, with a pinched and lined face and a head of greying hair. Barely into his forties, he could pass for at least twenty years older, and that was something that he used to great advantage. 'You're lucky I got what I did. I took a bit of a chance going up there the moment I spotted the Mariks in town. The others could have been home.'

'Well, they weren't, and this is useless,' said Rihal in disgust. 'I need them all.'

'If they're so valuable, I suspect your friend keeps them on his person. He has a backpack that he takes everywhere with him.'

'Yes, I suppose so.' Rihal sighed. 'Anyway, there's nothing keeping us from proceeding anyhow.'

'Step two: make contact.'

'Correct.'

'Do you want me to?'

Rihal shook her head. 'It'll be more credible coming from me.'

Back at Blue Hill, they congregated in Fahe's room discussing what to do now. It was all a bit much to take in—being robbed on top of the discovery of the Lake House.

'This means that the journals and fabric are of some value,' mused Yavi. He fingered the half-dozen journals and two volumes of textile samples that he still had with him—whatever had been in his backpack that he had intended to show Fezar Minar if he had got the chance to meet her. 'This confirms that Grandfather was really up to something. Ironically, we've made progress.'

It was quite late when Lily came up once again and said there was another visitor for Yavi. The old woman was clearly unhappy at Yavi's insistence on not reporting the theft, but then she hadn't said much. They had discussed the option of moving out of Blue Hill among themselves, and the possibility of that happening had probably crossed Lily's mind too.

'A visitor? Now?' asked Yavi, looking at his watch, puzzled. 'Two in one day?'

There was someone standing by the bookshelf in the downstairs lounge when they entered. She turned to face them, and her face lit up.

'Yavi...' she began, and stopped in surprise as the others filed in.

'Grey!' said Yavi.

'Sareka!' said Zurel.

'Fire!' said the woman.

'Whoa,' said Fahe, taking a step back, exchanging a glance with Keas, who looked just as bewildered.

The grown-ups were sorting out the complex introductions.

'You're alive!' cried Yavi.

'I should think so!' said the stranger, looking mildly affronted.

'You two know each other?' Zurel was looking between her and Yavi.

'*You* two know each other?' shot back Yavi. 'And, er, yes... this is... er, Grey?'

'Oh,' said Zurel. 'Small world, then.' She turned to Grey. 'You're looking well, Sareka.'

'Good to see you too, Fire,' said Grey, smiling. 'No hugs for an old friend?'

Zurel and the woman Yavi called Grey exchanged a long hug until Yavi coughed.

'Fire?' said Fahe, but no one paid her any attention.

'I have some information for you,' Grey said to Yavi. 'Where can we talk in private?'

'Let's go up to my room,' said Yavi, indicating the way. 'But, hang on a minute. How did you get out of there?'

Grey smiled enigmatically. 'I got a lot more than just out.'

'Out of where?' asked Fahe, curious.

'Oh, pardon me,' said Yavi. 'This is my sister Fahe. You already know Zurel, and that's Keas. Everyone, this is Sareka, whom I've always referred to as Grey.'

'I've had nicknames in the past,' muttered Grey, loud enough for everyone to hear, 'but never such a boring one.'

They trooped upstairs to Yavi's room, and Grey raised her eyebrows as they all followed them inside the small room.

'Didn't I mention private?' she said.

'We're all in this together,' Yavi said. 'I haven't kept anything from anyone.'

'Well, it isn't so simple.' She peered at Fahe. 'How old are you? Twelve?' She turned towards Keas. 'Ten?'

'Fourteen!' said the two of them, united in outrage.

'Same difference,' said Grey, oblivious to their indignation. 'If the Academy ever found out that you knew what I know, you could say goodbye to your places there! So, I'm going to talk to Yavi first, and then he can decide if you should be told.'

'How *did* you get out?' asked Yavi curiously.

Grey smiled enigmatically. 'I didn't. I got in.'

'Well, then, how did you get out eventually?'

'Slipped out during the change of shift.' She sat down heavily on Yavi's bed and divested herself of the bag she was carrying. 'Have any water to drink?'

Yavi got her some water, but she refused anything else. She drank her fill before anyone said a word.

'Oh, Yavi, it's no surprise that you weren't able to find anything in your grandfather's things—you didn't know how to read them.'

'What do you mean?' asked Yavi, stung. 'I'm a word mage. I can read anything. Well...' He stopped when he realized that wasn't true and added ruefully: 'Anything except from my grandfather's collection, it seems. I may not be able to replicate magic in the runas I read, but I should...'

'Remember that talk we had about other forms of magic?'

Yavi sighed. Letting other people complete their sentences was not Grey's strong suit. 'Yes.'

'This is a good example. The magic is not sourced from the Flame, and if it is, it's not a way we understand.'

Yavi's mouth fell open. *Why... how... what...?* It made no sense. He touched his Flamestone ring inconsciously. It was safely tucked away around his neck on a long piece of string.

Oh, for goodness' sake—*all* magic came from the Flame.

'That's only what the Academy wants us to believe,' said Grey, making Yavi realize he had spoken out loud. 'We were talking of this only the other day.'

'But...'

'My friends and I have been researching agnostic theories for over a decade,' she said. 'There are no buts, my friend. It's a certainty. What we've been looking for for years and years, you just dropped into my lap when you gave me your grandfather's things. Do you know what this means? It's proof—undeniable proof—that the Flame is not the begin-all and end-all of magic.'

Her eyes were shining in excitement and she was completely oblivious to Yavi's discomfort.

'Then what are they?' asked Yavi gruffly. 'The diaries? The fabric?' He couldn't understand his own hostility. He had always considered himself open-minded, just like any scholar had to be. How could you close yourself off to possibilities if gaining knowledge was your primary objective?

'It was your grandfather's letter that put me on the right track,' Grey said. 'You'd said he mentioned the key being in the satin, but what he really said was, "The key is in Satin." Satin, with a capital letter. It was almost like he was talking about some *thing*, something specific. So I focused on "Satin" as a keyword, and got some interesting results.'

Yavi nodded for her to go on. He had nothing to say.

'Kuzerazi practitioners of magic—mages if you want to call them that—had been experimenting with pagan magic without the knowledge of the Pentastra. In fact, long before the Pentastra even existed to regulate magic in the eastern regions,' said Grey. 'Our history books will never tell us all this. Our Kuzerazan counterparts were always quite the mavericks. They loved to push the boundaries. And despite the fact that western society has been based on principles of social equality, my studies show that their mages were a small and tight-knit community. I doubt the common people are even aware that they have a history of magic in the region.

'There are very few documented records of the kind of studies these mages carried out, mainly because they were an exclusive group and were not too keen on sharing their secrets with the rest of the world. It's just personal diaries that are left now. Some of them are in the Hyran library.

'Now, I haven't figured all this out overnight. There have been clues, scraps of information, theories that some of us have worked together on, but your hints gave me a new angle to work from. A lot of what I have put together is speculation, and we still need to remain open to being wrong. Are you with me?'

Yavi nodded.

'Well, the Kuzerazi mages, for all intents and purposes, went and developed their own system of magic. And guess what they called it? Satin.'

Yavi listened open-mouthed. 'So... Grandfather *was* on to something.'

'He was. He and his friends probably discovered Kuzerazi's best kept secret.'

'So what do you know about this Satin?'

'As of now, not much. It is based on a completely different principle. It believes that magic is an inherent part of all humans, and that life itself is its source. They did not use a pentaster with runas; for them, magic was like a weave, a weave with four threads—of earth, fire, wind and water, held together by the source, that is, life. The Flame itself was incidental to their system.

'So, in a manner of speaking, the magic in your grandfather's things are incomprehensible to us since they are not written in a magical language that we know.'

'Do you mean to say the satin cloth samples are magical artefacts?'

'That would be my guess. And there might be some sort of hint in his journals. I went through the scans and copies you had left with me and Kariad, but I haven't been able to crack it yet, though.'

'Those patterns or errors in the weaves that we found,' said Yavi thoughtfully. 'Maybe they are significant too. But I have a question—why was this magic called Satin?'

'It's to do with the satin weave,' said Grey. 'To weave yarn into cloth, you have a set of length-wise yarns and a set of width-wise yarns that are woven through each other, right? There are different kinds of weaves. For example, a plain weave is a simple criss-cross pattern. In a satin weave, there is one horizontal thread for every four or more vertical threads. The four threads in Satin magic stand for the four elements.'

Yavi tried to visualize it and failed. 'But what does all this mean? If the Flame isn't the source of this magic, where does it come from?'

'That's what I've been trying to tell you. It comes from...' She waved her arms around. 'It's everywhere, Yavi. In nature—in the elements, in us. The weaves are just a method to tap that, give it a focus.'

'But... how... I mean, why... Is this magic viable? Powerful? Was it useable? Is it practised today? Why didn't they form their own academies?'

'I have as many questions as you do, but no more answers. And no ideas why some of your grandfather's diary entries are out of order, or whether the textile samples are indeed magical artefacts.'

Keas felt like he was in a dream—it was that unreal. Mage Yavi had travelled all the way west to Kuzerazi in search of arcane magic? And he had found it too? *I am sitting in a room with a mage and his friends, and talking about Kuzerazan magic,* he kept telling himself. *And I've seen a house on a lake inside a wall of bamboo!*

Yavi was looking a little shocked himself, which was probably why the newcomer Grey did all the talking. Keas found it hard to concentrate, but Fahe was clearly lapping it all up.

'Sorry, could you explain that again?' she said, leaning forward. 'These... weaves, you say—they do not make use of Flamestone magic? But how can that be?'

'We do magic by drawing runas, right?' said Grey with the air of a teacher of incredibly stupid children. 'The runas are inside the sacred pentaster symbol in which the five points stand for wind, water, earth, fire and life. Even though it's highly unusual for a mage to have affinity for all five, we still use the symbol in reverence to the Flame, whose power we harness. Through the enclosing pentaster, we focus the power of the Flame from five sides into the runas. And the Flamestone—usually in the form of a ring that mages wear—is our link to the primary magical source. With me so far?'

The non-mages in the room nodded.

'Now, the Kuzerazans were never bound in the study and practice of magic by the Pentastra, so they developed a way to do magic without needing the Flame.' Briefly, she told them the basic premise of Satin magic.

'So, there are Kuzerazan mages?' asked Keas eagerly.

Grey grimaced and shook her head. 'I seriously doubt they exist any more. Satin techniques appear to have been known only to a small, closed group of people, and it seems to have died out. In fact, besides text from about a hundred and fifty years ago and Avin's hints, there seems to be no documentation of Satin at all.'

'But why? Why would they give it up?'

'I have no idea. Maybe it wasn't viable. Or they couldn't control it. Or some catastrophe wiped out everyone who knew the secrets of Satin. Or perhaps it had more to do with practical matters. The indications are that performing Satin probably required four people, each one contributing a different element, and possibly a fifth mage holding it all together. Maybe it was too inconvenient to perform magic that way.'

Everyone digested that in silence. But some part of Keas wanted to jump up and dance. He felt vindicated; his ancestors had practised magic. He wanted to run to his father and thrust it at him and tell him that yes, as a Kuzerazi, he *did* have a right to learn magic—because it *was* in his blood.

'How do you know all this?' Fahe asked finally.

'Mostly from some classified documents kept at the Hyran Monastery Archives outside Koda,' said Grey, brushing an invisible speck from her sleeve. 'It wasn't easy to access. Some of it is deduction based on my own studies.' She looked up at Yavi. 'Those artefacts of yours—the weaves—they could be invaluable. I suggest you guard them very carefully.'

Yavi looked sheepish. 'I should tell you, we... er, lost them.' He told her what had happened.

Grey whistled. 'That is a sorry state of affairs. You lost everything?'

'Not everything. I had some of the journals and two cloth-sample books with me.'

'And what makes you so sure that the Fezars had something to do with the theft?'

'Who else would it be? They knew we were here in connection with Avin's visits, and they knew where we were staying.'

'You do know that your pretty Shenara friend is in town, don't you?'

'What? Who?'

'The second sister. What's her name... Rihal?'

'Rihal is in Vaker?' asked Fahe puzzled. 'Why?'

Grey looked from Yavi to Fahe and back to him. 'Please tell me Rihal doesn't know anything about this. I have had run-ins with the Shenaras, and not pleasant ones.'

'Why should she know anything about this?' It was Yavi's turn to be puzzled.

Grey blinked at him. Then she slapped her forehead dramatically. 'You really have no idea? Didn't you pay attention to your grandfather's journals?'

'Er... yes...' said Yavi, stung yet again. 'But...'

'And his travelling companion?'

'Yes. A friend from his Academy days, Varda.'

'Varda, yes. Shenara Varda. Rihal's grandmother.'

# 14

## An Invitation

Grey decided not to return to town that night. Zurel lent her some clothes and Yavi gave up his room to her, moving in to take Rindan's place in the one he had been sharing with Keas.

Nobody slept much after all the excitement. The last thing they discussed was the Lake House. It appeared that Avin really did have quite a story to tell after all. Yavi half regretted not having made more of an effort to get close to him while he had been alive. But only half, since he could never forget how badly Avin had always treated him.

He had taken fantastic secrets of Kuzerazan magic with him to the earth, secrets that he had discovered in a beautiful house built upon a lake and hidden within a giant circle of tightly growing singing bamboo. That in itself was something.

In the midst of this, the fact that Rihal and the rest of the Shenaras might be more closely connected to Avin's secrets also took some processing.

As usual, Lily served them breakfast in the lounge upstairs the next morning, and since there were no other guests, it was a private affair. Even so, they didn't say much and ploughed through the meal at top speed before retiring to Fahe and Zurel's room to talk more.

'Suddenly, what Rihal said to me the night of the Marik banquet seems a little more sinister,' said Yavi.

'What did she say?' Grey asked.

'She asked me to marry her,' said Yavi.

'*What*?' said Fahe.

'And what did *you* say?' asked Zurel curiously.

'I asked her if she knew that I was an adopted child, and that while I get all the privileges of being part of the ruling family, my children wouldn't.'

'*What*?' said Fahe again. 'What do you mean by that?'

'Exactly what I said,' said Yavi patiently. 'My children won't get a share of the family fortune, and no daughter of mine will ever inherit the title.' When Fahe opened her mouth, he pre-empted her with: 'And please don't say "what" again. That's the Marik inheritance law for you.'

The fight that Yanik had had with Mother now made much more sense to her. She bristled. 'I'm so going to change that law when I... I mean, when I can. It's completely unfair!'

'Yes,' Yavi patted her arm, 'but for now, it was enough to make Rihal back off.'

'So you think she was trying to worm Avin's secrets out of you by getting close?' said Grey. 'Interesting.'

Fahe shuddered in distaste when she worked out what Grey meant. But then a thought struck her. 'But if that's the case, it means Rihal probably doesn't really know much more than we do. She was trying to figure out what *Yavi* knew.'

Grey spread her hands.

'Do you think Grandfather Avin and Varda purposely divided up the information in such a way that neither of us would have the full story?' Yavi said.

'Why?' said Fahe. 'So you could trade information years later, figure out their big secret, become friends, get married and live happily ever after?'

'Tsk, what a wild imagination,' said Grey. She turned to Yavi. 'What's the background to the feud between the Mariks and the Shenaras?'

Yavi thought for a moment. 'There isn't a feud, really. Just that we don't trust each other. Marik and Shenara do have some business connections. And just as Grandfather left his things to me, obviously Rihal knows some stuff from her grandmother too.'

Grey exhaled loudly. 'The answers lie with the Fezars. I would stake the Flame on that.'

'The question is,' said Yavi, 'how do we find out?'

The Kuzerazi Fresh delivery truck slowed, signalled and turned into a small side road marked private. The road curved gently and then finished up in a dead end. A line of closely growing trees cut off any further progress, but nestling among them, clearly visible, was a small wooden shack. It was more of a lean-to, just three walls and a roof, with a wooden bench inside. There was an envelope on the bench.

It was an overcast day, and a light bracket in the wall of the lean-to threw a harsh white fluorescent light around the dark, plain wood. Altogether, it was odd and out of place in the forest, like an oasis in a desert.

The driver jumped down and went around to the back of the van to open the hatch. He pulled out a cardboard carton marked 'Fezar Estate' and proceeded to deposit it on the wooden bench inside the shack. He pocketed the envelope and came back for another box as Rihal slowly unbuckled her seatbelt and got down from the passenger side.

'Let me help you with that,' she called to the delivery person, but he lifted a hand to say he was all right. 'Thank you for the lift,' she went on, pulling out a packet from the inside pocket of her coat. She held it out to him. 'As promised.'

'You're welcome,' said the man, his eyes riveted on what Rihal was proffering. 'Happy to help.'

Rihal sat down to wait. No sooner had the delivery truck pulled out than she heard the low purr of another engine. The sound of heavy boots followed, and as she stood and dusted herself off, someone rounded the corner and stopped short at the sight of her.

'I thought the instructions were very clear,' the person said, not sounding pleased. 'You were to deliver the goods and clear out.'

'I'm not from Kuzerazi Fresh,' said Rihal, pressing a hand to her chest in greeting. 'You could say I'm part of the delivery too. I need to speak with El'Fezar Minar. I have an important message for her.'

The person stared back. Rihal tried to size up if it was a man or woman—a little taller than herself, the head and neck were covered with a sort of scarf or turban. There was not much of the face visible for her to pinpoint age. The padded one-piece garment that covered ankle to neck held no clues either.

'I'm sorry, that is not possible,' he said. 'Minar does not meet visitors.'

'She will see me,' said Rihal firmly. She held out an envelope. 'Give this to her, and if she still refuses to see me, I will return without argument.'

He took it hesitantly, and Rihal placed herself firmly back on the seat. 'I will wait here for your answer.' After a pause, she added: 'Or, if you prefer, I will wait out on the highway.'

The man stared at her some more. 'Wait here,' he said, and turned and walked away.

The outlanders were trying not gag on cardamom tea—except Grey, who seemed to have a stomach of concrete—and studying scans of some of the satin samples that Grey had with her.

'Did you notice that all of the fabrics have a set of numbers and letters at the corner?' Fahe pointed out. 'What do they mean?'

'Yes, I noticed that,' Grey said. 'Each one also has a defect—or perhaps an intentional pattern—in the weave. I have no idea what they might be.'

Before they could discuss this any further, Lily knocked on the door and the Nizrahis quickly stuffed everything under a pillow. The landlady poked her head inside to say that there was a message for Yavi.

'It was hand-delivered,' she said in response to Yavi's query. 'I found it when I came home from doing my shopping.'

'So no return address,' murmured Grey as Yavi tore it open.

It was a plain white envelope, sealed and with no identifying marks of any sort. Inside was a single sheet of thick, creamy paper, with a handwritten note. A logo of a an old-fashioned loom with a woman sitting at it was printed at the top, and below it the words: 'Fezar, Vaker Highway, Kuzerazi'. The note read:

To El'Marik Yavi:

You and your sister are invited to Fezar. Please be at the end of the private road approx. 3 masaaf, after the turn-off for Vaker at 15.0 this evening. You are requested to stay at Fezar, so please come equipped.

Cordially,

(Signed on behalf of)
El'Fezar Minar

Yavi whistled and then handed the note to Fahe. She read it with the others leaning over her shoulder.

'Well, well,' said Grey softly. 'What a stroke of luck.'

'Odd sort of letter,' Fahe said. 'A bit rude, don't you think?'

'Not really,' said Keas. 'It's quite Kuzerazan. A rather standard invitation.' He looked up and seemed a little taken aback that everyone was watching him. 'Um... I mean, considering they're so reclusive, this is sort of... very ordinary.'

'Quite,' said Yavi. 'Well put.'

Keas blushed.

'So, are we going?' asked Fahe hopefully.

Yavi gave her an incredulous look. 'Do you even have to ask?'

Zurel frowned. 'I don't like this. If you go in there, there's no way of contacting you.'

'Wait a minute,' said Fahe. 'The Fezars did have comms—remember? They called an ambulance for Rindan.'

'I bet they have satellite comms,' said Grey. 'That would explain it.'

'Isn't that expensive?' Zurel asked.

'Rather,' said Grey, pursing her lips. 'Clearly, the Fezars are not poor.'

# 15

# Cloak and Dagger

That light-headed euphoria of discovering a Kuzerazan connection with magic lasted only so long. As Yavi and Fahe departed for Fezar, Keas couldn't help feeling rather deflated. After all, *he* was the one who had discovered the Lake House with Zurel. It was so unfair that it was the others who were getting to visit it. He was especially jealous of Fahe. He seethed with indignation, but had to keep it to himself.

Left to his own thoughts, there was no running away now from a truth that he'd been avoiding for long—that without the help of Yavi and the kindness of the Marik family, he would have been alone and homeless in Nizrah right now. What had he been thinking of, running away like that, weeks before the Academy session got under way? What had he expected—to live under the stars in Koda? Eat the bricks off the pavements? His father was right—he was just a silly boy.

But there was a saying in Kuzerazi, that everything happened for a reason, and Keas could see the point of that too. If he hadn't run away—even if it had been foolish and reckless to do so—he would have never met Yavi and got involved in all this. His dream of remaining a mage would have remained just that—a dream, sad and unfulfilled.

And he would never have learnt about the Kuzerazan connection with magic. Yes, that had somehow made going to the Academy more important than ever, even though the Academy dealt with Flame magic and believed that that was the only way it was done. To Keas, it just proved that people were short-sighted and narrow-minded no matter where they came from.

The tall woman who had fired the shot at Rindan was called Marya. She met them and showed them to a cottage a few minutes driving distance from the road. It was small, but looked comfortable. The front door led straight into a living area, which in turn led into a kitchen. Steps went up to a loft that was converted into a bedroom. It was obviously well insulated, for it was warm inside. There was a large electronic screen in the living room, with a row of video discs and games on a shelf below, some more shelves with books and some board games. A leather-covered sofa and recliner were arranged on a fluffy brown rug in front of the screen. There was a door under the stairs, slightly ajar to reveal a bathroom, and a smaller door that could only be a cupboard.

'Make yourselves at home,' Marya said.

'Is your mistress going to meet us here?' Yavi asked.

Marya made a non-committal gesture. 'You'll be taken to her when she can see you.'

'What did she mean by "when she can see you"?' asked Fahe when Marya had left without any further explanation. 'Is this Fezar woman sick or something?'

'I have no idea,' said Yavi, strolling over to the bookshelf while Fahe went to explore the kitchen.

They waited all evening, but no one appeared. It was light till late into the night, which still felt odd to the Nizrahis, who were used to it getting dark around fifteen o'clock or so. It wasn't too long, though, that Fahe started to get fidgety, bored of exploring the cottage and playing games on the screen, and Yavi finally said they might as well make themselves at home as suggested by their mysterious host.

The refrigerator yielded fresh fruit and vegetables, bread and a variety of local processed meats that Yavi and Fahe didn't know much about. They opened one of the packets and followed the instructions to make a sort of chicken-in-gravy dish that they ate with bread. It was odd, but not bad. They finished up with a fruit salad.

'How long do you think we should hang around?' asked Fahe when they had finished clearing up.

Yavi shrugged. Fahe guessed he was beginning to get a little annoyed at whatever game the Fezars were playing. 'I don't know, but we came here to meet the Fezars and they've clearly made arrangements for us to stay the night. So we might as well.'

Up in the loft bedroom, there were four bunks, all folded against the wall. Two of them were opened and had sheets, pillows, blankets and towels. Like Yavi had said, they were clearly expected to stay the night.

'All those years ago, you never mentioned you were going to be the future Marik prefect's bodyguard.'

'It was hardly *all* those years ago,' said Zurel. 'Just five. And I hadn't known then.'

She and Sareka trudged back uphill towards Lily's after their evening out. They had tried to take Keas along too, but he had proved difficult to budge. The rain had come down hard that afternoon after Fahe and Yavi left, and it was still drizzling steadily. The two women were zipped up inside their waterproof jackets, hoods pulled up over their heads.

Normally never at a loss for words, Sareka was unnaturally quiet, and Zurel didn't really mind that. It was something in between a shock and a surprise to find her old friend here, and to realize that she was in fact Yavi's mysterious Grey. She had said as much to Sareka.

'Did you ever return to Far Darom?' Zurel asked. That was where she had met the older woman. It was just before Zurel had taken her oath of guardsmanship.

'Once or twice. You?'

'A few times, yes.'

Sareka shook her head and sighed dramatically. 'Never even missed me, did you? Didn't try to look me up?'

'Oh, ha ha,' said Zurel, sarcastic. 'Trying to find you would be like trying to catch sunlight in a bottle.'

'You should have travelled with me,' Sareka said. 'Instead of that guardsmanship thing of yours. Imagine... the places we'd have gone to.'

'Yes, I remember. You promised to take me to Kuzerazi, but here I am—I made it without your help, see.'

'So you did.'

They walked in silence for a little while.

'So, where else have you been travelling?' Zurel asked.

'Hmm... well, after I left Far Darom, I travelled in the Nizrah states, spent a few years teaching here and there. I came for a short visit to Kuzerazi, but not to these parts. I got restless here, you know. It's hard trying to hide what I am... you know what I mean?'

Zurel nodded. Eastern mages tended to lie low in Kuzerazi, and it wasn't always easy, she imagined.

'Did you find what you had been looking for?' she asked.

Sareka shook her head. 'Well, no... or maybe... I don't know. I'd been drifting along, Fire, and I've been liking it. But then, this happened—meeting Yavi and finding out Avin's secrets. For the first time, I think maybe I'm on the right track. There's a lot of theory and speculation around otherwise, but there's never been any proof we could get our hands on, nothing to indicate if we're right, if the Flame need not be the only source of magic. But now, I think we could be on to something.'

'So what happens now?'

She shrugged again. 'I wish I knew. I know the answers lie in the Fezar lands, but I'm not sure how it can be made to reveal its secrets.'

'Maybe Yavi will come back with some answers.'

'Maybe.'

'You said "we",' said Zurel. 'There are other people in this?'

'You really think I'm the only person in this wide, wide world who questions if there is something more?' asked Sareka, amused.

Zurel smiled back. 'No, what I meant was, do you have a group or something?' She turned to squint into Sareka's face. 'Knowing you, I should probably say a cult.'

Sareka threw her head back in the now-driving rain and laughed.

Zurel shook her head. 'Fahe wanted to know why you call me Fire. She said it was as unlike a nickname as any I could have.'

'What did you tell her?'

'That it's pointless asking you why you do the things you do.'

That made Sareka laugh some more. This time, Zurel found herself grinning as well.

'What is she like?' Sareka asked suddenly.

'Who?' said Zurel. 'Fahe? She's all right.'

'I hope she'll be worth it.'

Zurel didn't say anything.

In the middle of the night, Fahe woke with a jump, disoriented for a moment, her heart thumping, the moon shining directly on her face. Her blanket had slipped off to the floor and she was cold. She lay on her bunk, staring up at the sky through the window on the slanting roof above her. It was dark now, though it hadn't been when they had gone to bed. The rain had stopped and it was a clear and bright night with stars and a moon that looked full. She slowly became aware of the noises of the forest outside—leaves rustling in the wind, the creaking of the odd branch, night-time animals. She reached down to pull her blanket up when there was a sharp crack.

She stopped dead. It sounded like a twig breaking, and yet, felt different from the natural sounds around her. It probably was just an animal, she told herself. Shaking her head, she rearranged the blanket and prepared to settle down. But the second noise was different and definitely from inside—a slow, low creak, like someone tiptoeing across a wooden floor.

This time, Fahe really was scared. Wide awake, she peered into the moonlit darkness on the lower level through the metal railing of their loft bedroom. Whatever wasn't awash with the silvery light from the moon was pitch dark, and the shadows formed eerie shapes on the part of the floor and the wall that Fahe could see from her vantage point. She was frozen in place when a formless shadow moved across the wall below her.

Then, in a trice, she was shaking Yavi awake.

'Wha... what?'

'There's someone here... there's someone...'

Whoever it was, was now not making any attempts to conceal their presence. The sound of boots on the floor made Yavi jump out of bed.

'Who's that?' he called out.

Fahe was still clinging to him as Yavi reached out for the light switches. The switch clicked under his finger, but nothing happened. Yavi jabbed at it many times, but in vain.

'Whoever you are, stop!' he called. 'We are...'

A bright, glaring light from a torch blinded them.

'Hey!' cried Yavi.

'It's just me, Marya,' said her voice. 'The lights are out. Nothing to worry about, a generator failure. You need to come with us.'

'What, now?' said Yavi, clearly irritated. 'What sort of behaviour is this? Is this how you treat people you invite? We *are* guests, you know?'

'My apologies,' said Marya, not sounding the slightest bit apologetic, 'if we seem out of touch with contemporary social etiquette. The owner of Fezar keeps strange timings. If you want to see her, you'll have to come now.'

'I think we'd rather come in the morning, like civilized people.'

'In that case, you'll be going back to Vaker in the morning,' said Marya. Her shoulders rose and fell in a shrug. 'Your choice.'

She turned to go, but Yavi stopped her.

'Wait. We haven't come all this way just to go back,' he said. 'All right, take us to her.'

'There's something else,' said Marya.

'What is it?' He added, sarcastic: 'You want us to wear blindfolds so we don't see where we're being taken?'

There was a silence.

Yavi laughed humourlessly. 'You have got to be joking!'

Blindfolded securely, Fahe and Yavi sat on the back seat of the six-wheeler, clutching the rail guard in front of them, as it bumped its way expertly along the winding forest paths. It was hard to say how long they travelled, or how far, but it soon became clear that they were climbing. And then they were aware of a spine-chilling sound.

It was a sort of creaking, laboured and erratic, and it kept getting louder. Fahe felt the hairs on the back of her neck stand up before she realized that it was the bamboo wall that Keas and Zurel had talked about. The vehicle slowed to a halt. There were more creaks, this one the unmistakable sound of hinges. Then they were moving again.

The next time they stopped, Marya's voice said they had to get off. Hands helped them down and guided them forward. They were walking on rough land, which suddenly gave way to something gravelly, and then a metal surface, on which their boots clanged. A stiff breeze blew in from the side, and Fahe sniffed. She could sense the water around them.

The surface under their feet changed again. This one felt hard, like concrete, and it suddenly became warmer, like they were inside a room. The concrete floor changed to something soft, a rug or carpet maybe. They were told to stand still, and there was a low hiss of a door sliding shut and a series of soft beeps like buttons being pressed on an electronic console. The ground vibrated, and suddenly they were moving, though Fahe couldn't tell if they were going up or down. She almost stumbled, but regained her balance, by which time they had stopped moving. The hiss sounded again.

'We're here,' said Marya's voice. 'If you'll just step out'—hands guided them a few steps forward—'we'll take off your blindfolds.'

Fahe's heart was racing. Were they inside the Lake House? The house that floated on a lake? Inside the wall of bamboo that grew so thick that you couldn't see beyond it? What could make bamboo grow like that? What could make a house float on a lake?

More Kuzerazan magic?

# 16

When Keas, Zurel and Grey came down for breakfast early next morning, there was still no word from Yavi.

'You think they're all right?' asked Keas.

'No reason to imagine they're not,' Grey said. 'And I'm sure Yavi will eventually get in touch. When he gets a chance.'

'What do you plan on doing?' Zurel asked. 'Staying on?'

Grey shook her head. 'I was here to update Yavi. I need to go back and see what else I can dig up.'

She said she would head into town to find out about a bus or train back to the border, and Keas and Zurel decided to visit Rindan in the hospital. He had developed an infection the previous day and was being kept for a while longer.

## The Lake House

By breakfast time the next morning, annoyance and irritation had given way to a sense of surreality for the Mariks.

The Lake House's interior was exquisitely furnished—antique Vaker oak furniture, handwoven Nizrahi carpets, sculptures and handicrafts from all over the world, paintings and photographs, crystal light brackets that looked like lanterns and cut-glass chandeliers shaped so minutely that it hurt the eye to look at. And this was just the hallway.

Yavi and Fahe had been shown to a suite of rooms with two bedrooms, a tiny hall and a bathroom the previous night. Marya indicated the intercom to call for anything they might need, and she left without answering Yavi's question of when they were meeting Minar.

Fahe explored both her room and Yavi's, curiously examining the thick brocade material of the drapes, the satin bedsheets, the stationery in the writing table drawers, as well as each of the tiny, abstract ivory sculptures on the fake mantelpiece in her room and the miniature paintings in Yavi's. His room also had a waist-high bookshelf with a selection of well-known travel books, whereas Fahe's room had a plasma screen with an attached console to play games on.

It was only when she pulled the drapes apart to see the view from the windows that she got a shock. There were, in fact, no windows at all—just a sort of thick meshwork that they figured were air-conditioning vents.

It wasn't as though they were prisoners. The door of their suite opened out into the dazzling hallway, which split right and left. The right-hand arm led to the lifts where they had come from. The door to it was shut fast and there were no buttons to call it. On the other side of the corridor were more doors. Two of them were shut—and it was too late in the night to be accidentally sneaking into someone's room—but the third was ajar, leading to a dining space with the longest table Fahe had ever seen and more chandeliers. It was even bigger than the main dining hall at Marik. The walls were lined with glass-fronted cabinets filled with crystalware of various kinds. A swing door led on to a short corridor, beyond which was the kitchen—once again a very large and very well-appointed kitchen. It was spotless and deserted, but it showed signs of regular use.

But no windows anywhere.

The kitchen itself led out to another passage with dimmed lights. It ended in a grilled gate that opened into a courtyard. It was pitch dark outside, however, and as they couldn't find any light switches, they had to turn back. But the knowledge of the courtyard helped a bit—at least the feeling of being hemmed in was reduced.

It was Marya again who had knocked on their door around six in the morning to say that breakfast would be ready soon. It was quite late by their standards, and they had overslept. Sleep-deprived and disoriented, neither of the Mariks was prepared for the surprise that awaited them at the breakfast table.

Serving herself from the selection of fruit and cereal on the sideboard was Rihal. She nearly dropped her plate when she saw them.

'You!' said Yavi and Rihal at the same time.

'What are you doing here?' Rihal said.

'I might ask you the same question,' shot back Yavi.

'I was invited,' said Rihal, defensive.

'So was I,' said Yavi shortly.

Fahe was too shocked to feel offended at being left out.

Marya cleared her throat. 'Should you require anything, feel free to use the bell to summon the kitchen staff.'

She turned and left before anyone could recover, and there was little left to do but serve themselves. Fahe's mind worked furiously as she helped herself to scrambled eggs and squares of bread dripping with butter. If Fezar Minar had indeed invited both Rihal and themselves, did that mean she knew about Satin, about Avin and Varda... and the Flame knew what else?

*The question is*, Fahe told herself, *if she already knows everything, what are we doing here?*

Yavi and Rihal were having a heated conversation when Fahe sat down.

'Don't think I don't know what you're doing,' Rihal hissed. 'Worming your way into Minar's good books, thinking she'll tell you all her secrets.'

'You're labouring under a misapprehension here,' said Yavi, also in a hoarse whisper. 'I am researching my grandfather's history. I was bequeathed his diaries and artefacts from his travels and am merely following it up. What *you* are doing here, though, is open to speculation.'

'I find that hard to believe. Did you follow me to Kuzerazi? You are after Fezar's secrets, Marik Yavi, admit it.'

Fahe's mouth fell open at the blatant accusation. 'Excuse me,' she cut in nastily, '*you* have been following us. You Shenaras have never been up to any good!'

'Trading insults isn't going to get us anywhere,' said Rihal to Fahe coldly. 'And in my circles, children speak only when they're spoken to.'

'Lucky for me, I don't move in your circles, then.'

'That was all you wanted from me, wasn't it?' cut in Yavi, addressing Rihal. 'That night at the banquet—you were trying to get friendly to find out about Avin's secrets.'

'They're not just Avin's secrets—I need not remind you of that. Avin and Varda were friends, and they were in it together. Whatever happened here in Fezar forty years ago, both your grandfather and my grandmother had a role in it.

As did Komas. So get off your high horse and stop thinking you have some Flame-given right to them.'

Yavi opened his mouth to speak, but a sudden, disembodied voice boomed out, making them all jump. Fahe spilt her tea on the snow-white tablecloth.

'Stand by, level one sub,' it said. 'Stand by.'

Without further warning, a shuddering filled the air and everything in the room started to shiver gently. The glassware in the cabinets and dishes on the sideboard and table rattled with a little musical tinkling. There were ripples in their teacups and the chandeliers above them jingled in protest.

All three of them grabbed the edge of the table in a futile attempt to steady the vibrating room.

'What's that?' Fahe cried.

'Earthquake?' ventured Yavi.

'A planned earthquake?' said Rihal, looking a bit green.

It went on for about five minutes, then stopped without warning. They looked at each other, bewildered.

Marya appeared as they were finishing breakfast.

'Was that an earthquake?' Rihal asked before Marya could say anything.

Marya inclined her head slightly. 'My apologies for the inconvenience. It was merely some maintenance work.'

'*Maintenance*?' asked Fahe. 'It seemed like the entire house was about to collapse!'

Marya showed the barest hint of a smile. 'Quite safe, I assure you.' She paused. 'I trust your rooms are comfortable and breakfast was to your satisfaction?'

'Breakfast was perfectly fine, as were our rooms,' said Yavi coolly, 'but neither has anything to do with our purpose of being here. I would like to see your mistress immediately. I do not think that's an unreasonable request. This has gone beyond the bounds of common courtesy.'

'I am with Yavi on this,' said Rihal. 'I see no semblance of courtesy in keeping your guests virtually imprisoned.'

'Fair enough,' said Marya. 'If you will bear with this a little while longer, I will come and fetch you from your rooms for an audience with Minar.'

'Just a minute, young man,' said Rihal. 'It was a private meeting that I have requested with her.'

Marya seemed neither very young to Fahe, nor—as far as she could discern—a man, but since the former showed no reaction at being addressed as such, she was momentarily confused. Lost in thought for a while, Fahe missed some of the exchange.

'... business with her is personal as well,' Yavi was saying, 'and I am not inclined to discuss private family matters,' with a quick glance at Rihal, 'with outsiders present.'

'Neither am I,' said Rihal. 'I came here in good faith, and you've been testing my patience beyond reasonable limits.'

Marya looked from one to the other, and then nodded. 'All right, I'll see what I can do.'

Fahe and Yavi retired to their rooms to discuss the turn of events.

'How did Rihal get the Fezars to invite her too?' Fahe asked.

'I wish I knew,' said Yavi. 'Maybe she had information to trade. I wonder how much she knows about Satin.'

'I thought of something,' Fahe said.

'What?'

'You were so sure that the Fezars stole your things. But what if Grey is right and Rihal stole them?'

'And traded them for an *audience* with Minar?' said Yavi, stressing on the word that Marya had used. 'That's a possibility,' he admitted. 'It makes some perverse sense.'

'What do you think Minar wants?'

Yavi studied her for a bit. 'Interesting. Now you're talking in terms of what *she* wants from us rather than what we came for.'

'Why is that interesting?'

'Because I've been thinking on the same lines.'

Fahe was too intrigued to lash back with how condescending that statement was.

The news about Rindan wasn't good. Though his wound was healing normally, he had had an allergic reaction to some of the medication and had come out in rashes all over and was running a high fever. He was in obvious discomfort, and Zurel decided not to burden him with too much information, apart from the fact that that the Fezars had extended an invitation to Fahe and Yavi to visit them.

'You should have gone with her,' Rindan told her.

'I wasn't invited,' Zurel told him. 'Don't worry—it's all under control.

'What now?' Keas asked her when they walked to the parking area where their hired motor was parked.

'Let's see if we can find out where our friend Rihal is.'

Sareka had seen Rihal at the tourist information centre when she had gone inside to ask for directions to Lily's. Rihal had been talking to a man at the Accommodations booth, and that is where Zurel headed now.

'Good morning, how can I help you?' said the man behind the counter with a friendly grin.

Zurel smiled back. 'Good morning,' she said, affecting a sheepish air. 'I'm afraid I have a rather silly request. I was supposed to meet my friend here—she must have arrived yesterday or so—but I can't reach her comms and I have no idea where she's staying. I'm wondering if you have any way that you could look up and tell me if she's in any of the boarding lodges around here.'

'Ah, of course, that's easy. What's her name and where is she from?'

'Her name is Rihal. She's from Shenara.'

He had a touchscreen monitor in front of him which Zurel couldn't see, but after tapping around for a bit, he shook his head.

'Sorry, no records of any Rihal from Shenara.'

'You could try Koda,' said Zurel. 'That's where we made plans, so...'

'Mmm... no Koda either.'

Zurel was disappointed. 'Are you sure?'

The man shrugged apologetically.

'Well, can't be helped. Thanks for trying,' she said, turning to go.

'Oh, hang on,' the man called. 'I don't know if this will help—did your friend come alone?'

'Umm... I'm not sure,' said Zurel, thinking quickly. 'She did mention bringing some friends, but she might have come alone after all.'

'I have a Sua Raven who gave an address in Shenara. This person booked two rooms in one of the boarding houses in the Town Square.'

Zurel gripped the counter. 'Can you give me the address?'

'It's the Tara 'n' Tula. Near the north end of the Town Square—you can't miss its great big spider logo.'

'Great. Thank you a million times,' said Zurel, giving him a dazzling smile.

They followed Marya through the dining area into the passage that led to the kitchen, but instead of entering it, she ushered them through another doorway that Yavi and Fahe had missed in the dimmed lighting the previous night. They found themselves in a corridor leading towards what the Mariks had identified as a courtyard. Its grilled gate was wide open now. It was about twice the size of the dining room, but bound on four sides by high concrete walls. Similar gates blocked off passages into the various wings of the house; they were shut except for the one they had come out from and another on their left. There was a lawn on the ground, with concrete paths criss-crossing between the gates, and neat, narrow flowerbeds along them. Low stone benches were placed along the wall.

Warm-coloured light came from antique lamp posts on the path, and there were well-camouflaged light brackets in the walls as well. There seemed to be little natural illumination, given the high surrounding walls, but a strange rippling effect was fleetingly visible now and then. Fahe happened to look up and got a bit of a shock.

'Flames!' she said, grabbing Yavi's arm. 'Look, there's an aquarium on the ceiling!'

The courtyard, it appeared, was closed off from the top as well, and a giant aquarium was right above it. The water was a bright blue, the light from the sun filtering through and making it shimmer.

Yavi and Fahe stared in wonder.

'Quite beautiful,' said Yavi finally. 'I've never seen anything like this. Who designed the house?'

'It was Komas and his niece,' said Marya. 'The previous home of the Fezar family, the Old House, was badly in need of repair, and Komas decided to invest in a new building instead. He had his own ideas about the construction and decided to do it himself.'

'Then this place must be pretty new?'

'He died soon after it was completed, so about thirty-five to forty years old.'

'Where is this older house?'

'The Old House, it was called. Not far from here, but it isn't habitable any longer and, as far as I know, the Fezars haven't used it since the Lake House was complete. Perhaps Minar will be able to shed more light on its history.'

Marya was content to wait till the visitors had had their fill, and then led them to one of the closed gates, explaining that this was Minar's private wing.

'The Tara 'n' Tula?' said Keas with a shiver. 'I wouldn't stay there if you paid me.'

'You would have to pay me a lot,' said Zurel.

'What are you thinking of?' Keas asked, noticing that Zurel was pensive.

'The Suas,' said Zurel. 'They are a mercenary clan from Far Darom. Trained guards and spies who work for anyone who pays for their services. They are in great demand with Muradian families, both for security and espionage.'

'Muradian?'

'Shenara is a place in Muradia, one of the larger Nizrahi provinces,' she explained.

'The home of Rihal?'

'Exactly.'

'So that's what makes you so sure that Raven is Rihal's travelling companion?'

Zurel nodded. 'That's my guess.'

'It could be some other Muradian traveller with his or her guard,' Keas ventured carefully.

'It could,' Zurel admitted. 'It's time to pay the Tara 'n' Tula a visit.'

Fahe felt a thrill of anticipation go down her spine as a door set into the long, curving wall opened and they caught their first glimpse of Fezar Minar. Fahe had a good memory for faces, and for a moment she was sure that this was the same woman from the grainy photos some forty years ago. Then common sense kicked in—Komas's niece would be in her sixties now, and this woman was barely half that. This must be her daughter.

She was of medium height and she carried herself straight—shoulders back and chin up in perfect posture. As she came closer, they noticed her curious hair, neither cut short nor worn long. It was about shoulder length and loose, and yet not untidy. Her features were sharp and well proportioned, and again Fahe had a fleeting idea that she looked vaguely familiar, just as her mother had in the newspaper photographs. She was also quite dark-skinned for a Kuzerazan—could have easily passed for a Nizrahi.

Minar ran her fingers through her hair. She was slender to the point of thinness and walked with the long, easy stride of an athlete. She wore dark trousers tucked into thick walking boots and a plain white shirt that was buttoned instead of laced. Over her arm, she carried a heavy woollen cape that Marya took from her with a slightly admonitory look. She smiled apologetically at him before turning to her guests, placing a hand on her chest and bowing low in greeting.

'I am El'Fezar Minar,' she said, her voice slightly breathless, 'and I welcome you to the Lake House.'

She was flushed too, and Fahe had the distinct impression that she had just hurried back from somewhere. Her boots and trousers bore damp mud stains, and the cloak appeared damp too. She then turned to Marya.

'Marya, would you please bring us some tea and refreshments? We shall repair to my study.' Turning back to the Mariks, she added, 'I hope you haven't been waiting too long. If you'll prefer, Marya will show you to your rooms and you may freshen up first.'

Fahe looked to Yavi, who was just as bewildered by Minar's statement. Marya cleared his throat delicately. 'Your visitors arrived last night, Minar.'

It was Minar's turn to look surprised and mildly annoyed. 'You should have told me,' she said to Marya, and to the others, 'My apologies. I trust you are satisfied with the accommodation arrangements?'

'Satisfied is somewhat relative,' said Yavi carefully. 'I would appreciate an explanation about the way we were brought and kept here.'

'Brought and kept?' said Minar, with a disarming smile. 'You must excuse me if I'm a little out of date with social niceties, but it was my understanding that you had asked to see me. I'm merely complying with your request. I do apologize for my lateness, though—I was avoidably detained elsewhere.'

Fahe had been so intrigued with the between-the-lines drama that had just played out between Minar and Marya that she had forgotten that they were still standing in the hall. It was clear that Minar really wasn't used to having visitors, and she said as much herself as she apologized yet again and led them into her study.

# 17

To Keas, trying to trace Rihal and her companion was very exciting. He almost forgot to dwell upon the fact that the Marik siblings were inside the house on the lake and he wasn't.

'Spying, you said,' he asked Zurel. 'What if this Raven stole Yavi's things, like Sareka was suggesting?'

Zurel admitted that that was a distinct possibility. It was a bit of an anticlimax, however, to discover that Sua Raven and his companion had checked out of the Tara 'n' Tula.

'What do we do next?' Keas asked.

Zurel thought for a while. 'Let's to go the library and see if we can find some photos of Rihal and Raven. Maybe we could show them around.'

The Infonet had plenty of recent photographs of Rihal, but there was nothing about Raven. They had decided that their mysterious visitor the other day had been him after all. A description amounting to a small, bony, dark man in his middle years, with a short neck, was not much to go by, and Zurel was extremely doubtful that the limp and the cane were real, but oddly enough, they got some results, both with the photos and the description.

*Minar*

'I saw her at the breakfast counter this morning... no, yesterday,' a young tourist staying at the the Tara 'n' Tula told them after peering at Rihal's photograph. 'There was an older man with her—sort of short and thin. They ate quickly and left. I didn't see the woman again, but the man was here this morning too. Later, when I was returning to my room, he seemed to be moving out with his things.'

Zurel and Keas had gone around asking at the establishments in the Town Square, and Rihal and Raven had both been spotted at a couple of eateries and, of course, at their boarding house. The Tara 'n' Tula said that they had paid their dues and left no contact addresses. The motor hire company had no records of interest.

Minar's study was a curious circular, multilevel room, with a domed ceiling so high that they had to squint up at it. It was capped with stained glass, but was too high for anyone to make out details of the design.

The study was clean but untidy in a way that happens when you have too many things crammed in one place. The open shelves and wood-framed glass cabinets built into the walls were chock-full of books, papers and various unidentifiable artefacts placed haphazardly. The floor was bare and hard, but there was an old, worn rug on which stood a large antique Vaker oak study table, inlaid with coloured stonework, and a matching chair. The desktop was neat, with its stacks of books and papers piled towards one side, and pens, styluses and brushes collected in a giant mug. Clashing awkwardly was a modern draughtsman's table-and-stool set next to it, equipped with thick sheets of paper and instruments.

Next to the door from where they entered was a metal spiral staircase that wound its way up to the other levels. The second level of the study was an extended library of sorts, with rows and rows of shelves, while the third level was too high and dark for the visitors to discern anything. Marya brought in some stools for them to sit on and they grouped around the main table. Minar nodded to Marya, who went around the room, tidying up a few things and leaving with a tray containing used tea mugs.

'I must say,' Minar said, 'it was something of a surprise when Marya informed me that Avin's grandson was in my grounds, wanting to see me. It was an even bigger surprise when you were followed by Varda's granddaughter. And even though she has been here longer than you have—as I've been told—you asked to see me first, therefore...' She left the rest unsaid.

'I apologize for the uninvited visit and for trespassing,' said Yavi. 'I tried my best to contact you, but there are no listings for Fezar on any communications system, either on comms or the Infonet. I did think of sending a courier with a message, but it seemed quicker to come down myself.'

'Well, we Fezars haven't been much in the public eye over the past decades,' admitted Minar. 'Since we are quite self-sufficient here, it seems such a waste of resources.'

'Excuse my curiosity, but the other day, when one of our companions was shot, I saw your people using some sort of communications device.'

'Oh, that's a satellite phone. And we do have private Infonet access. By the way, how is your friend? That was a most unfortunate incident. I trust he's recovering well? I hope Marya has offered to cover his treatment expenses.'

'That will not be necessary,' said Yavi. 'And he's quite well, thank you.' He wanted to get to the point and not make polite conversation. 'Well, as your... people... might have communicated to you, I am the official biographer of Karis Avin, and my sister is assisting me. It was his dying wish that I should document his life.'

Fahe's eyes widened at this blatant lie, but she didn't say anything.

'He bequeathed me his journals from his travels,' continued Yavi, 'including some cloth samples that I believe have their antecedents here in Fezar. He spent considerable time here—he came here twice that we know of, both long-term visits, and both times accompanied by his friend Varda. Komas is frequently mentioned in his journal too...'

'Pardon me for interrupting, Yavi,' said Minar, leaning forward on her stool, one hand resting on her knee. 'You mean to say your grandfather is... no more?'

Fahe was intrigued by her use of such a quaint term. She had a keen look about her, perhaps curiosity. Once again, Fahe had a feeling that there was something uncannily familiar about her, and the thought was oddly unnerving. A strange woman in a strange house with strange companions—was it too fantastic to be real?

'My grandfather died last winter,' Yavi confirmed.

'Oh. I'm sorry to hear that. And... Varda?' Again a slight hesitation.

'Varda passed away in the spring of the previous year. Did you know them?'

Minar seemed to shake herself out of a reverie. 'I, well... no, of course not,' she said, a little sharply. 'They were here last long before I was born.'

'Of course,' said Yavi, 'how silly of me. But as I was saying, there are a lot of gaps about Avin's work in Fezar, and I sought a meeting with you in an attempt to fill in the blanks.'

'What makes you think I'd know anything? I wasn't even born when they were here.'

Fahe privately thought she was protesting too much about her age.

'Well, Avin left plenty of journals. They are nothing much apart from personal observations about travel and so on. But I was hoping you might be able to shed some light on the work they were doing—Komas, Varda and Avin—and also their friendship.'

Minar ran her fingers through her hair. She appeared to be thinking. 'They were mages, Avin and his friend,' she said finally, 'and Komas was, I suppose, a sort of manager for them. They would be gone for weeks and, sometimes, months at a time. I, of course, only heard the stories later on.'

'Was Komas a... mage too?'

She shook her head. 'He was no mage. He had other talents, but not so much the discipline for magic. I won't pretend that, as Kuzerazans, we Fezars have had no interest in magic, and Komas coveted the powers of the Flame just as much as you ever did, Mage Yavi, or your young sister does.'

Startled, Fahe shot a glance at Yavi—how did she know he was a mage?—but he only inclined his head to acknowledge the fact. 'What were these other talents of Komas that you mentioned?'

'He was eccentric, but there was method to his madness. He was a scholar in his own right, an inventor and something of an artist. He was a genius when it came to making things—

he was way ahead of his time. He designed and built this house—the one we are in, the Lake House.'

'The little that we've seen of it is quite breathtaking,' said Yavi. 'That courtyard, for instance.' He looked up. 'And this study.'

Minar nodded. 'It used to be his study. It passed on to me eventually. As for this house,' she smiled, 'you've not seen the most amazing thing about it. You will, in time.'

'My grandfather mentions the Lake House in his journals too, and Marya was telling us some of the history of the family, about how Komas built it to replace the Old House.'

'Oh yes, but the Old House itself was one of a kind. The sort of modifications Komas made were equally intriguing and outrageous. His study there was built in such a way that it was, in fact, a huge lift. It could go up and down, to any level of the house—up to his bedroom and right down to his basement workshop. Wait, I think I could show you some of his ideas.'

She sprang to her feet and went across the shelves just behind where Fahe was sitting. She knelt and struggled with one of the cabinets. The door sprang open to reveal stack upon stack of large books and files. She pulled out a large red file filled with loose sheets.

Minar riffled through the yellowing pages. 'Here. See this.' She set it on the table, and Yavi and Fahe leaned over.

There was a sketch of a six-wheel vehicle rather like the one the Fezars had.

'This was his idea for a medium of conveyance that would easily run on a variety of surfaces,' she said. 'He thought of this in his youth, many decades ago, and even built a miniature prototype. But it was only much after his death that the Tub was first seen—that same six-wheel all-terrain model we use out in the estate.'

'That's amazing,' said Fahe, truly impressed as she stared at the detailed diagram. It was labelled, with copious notes in the margins, and though she didn't understand much of the short-form notations, it was clear that whoever had drawn it had thought it out carefully rather than scribbled it on a whim.

'I thought so too,' said Minar. 'I wish he'd been around to see that he was right. Oh, I have more...'

As she turned away, Fahe was surprised to see Yavi draw a quick, invisible runa on the ageing manuscript. It glowed briefly for about a second, and Yavi frowned to himself. Minar turned back to them, and there was no scope for discussion.

'And this one,' she put down another diagram, 'was one of his last ideas—his concept of an interconnected network, like the present-day Infonetwork. The first commercial computers were being built around that time, though a worldwide network was more than ten years away. He also envisaged a technology by which different kinds of devices would complement each other; for instance, a small computer inside your motorcar giving you directions to your destination. Yes, some of his ideas were outlandish.'

'Maybe not that outlandish,' said Yavi. 'There are motors with built-in GPS systems around already.'

Minar raised an appreciative eyebrow. 'Ah, well, maybe Uncle Komas was on to something then.'

'He could have sold his ideas and made a lot of money,' observed Fahe.

'Indeed,' said Minar. There was a hint of amusement in her voice.

'*Uncle* Komas?' asked Yavi. 'But wasn't he your mother's uncle? Manara was your mother, right?'

'Correct. But I've always referred to him as Uncle Komas.'

'You seem to have kept all of his papers. Might there be a chance that there are references to the research he was helping Avin and Varda with?'

'I've been through every scrap of paper he wrote, every model he built. If you know what exactly they were working on, I could tell you if there are any references to it. But you should know, plenty of his things are quite obscure. He was secretive about his projects until he was sure he had nailed the concept. He would shut himself up in his study for weeks on end and we wouldn't see him at all—that's when his mobile study came in useful for him.'

'Was Komas interested in the history of magic? I know that Kuzerazans don't like to speak about their magical tradition, but they do have one. History was one of Avin's interests too, and it is likely that his forays into Kuzerazi were to study western magic.'

'It's a possibility,' Minar admitted. 'And as I said before, shunning magic is something we make a song and dance about, but deep down, every Kuzerazan knows that if magic can exist in one place, why not in another? There's a possibility it exists on our doorstep, even if we choose to ignore it.'

'Do you think it does, then?' Fahe asked. She couldn't imagine having the option of using magic but choosing not to. 'And do others?'

Minar shrugged. 'I don't know. Maybe some do, and some lie.' She smiled.

'Are you a practising mage, Minar?' Yavi asked.

Minar blinked, and even Fahe was taken aback by the direct question. 'I don't know how to answer that,' she said at length. 'I won't deny I have made some forays into it, but I have not received any sort of training, so cannot really give myself the epithet of a mage. And the only Flamestone I have is a rough cut that belonged to Komas.'

'Well, I'm a word mage myself, with an interest in old texts, and my studies have indicated,' he paused here, leaning forward and affecting a slightly—but not very successful, Fahe thought—conspiratorial air, 'that there are ways to do magic other than with the help of a Flamestone.'

Minar spread her hands. 'Who am I to argue with a scholar? What other ways are these?'

'As you can imagine, information to that effect isn't easy to come by. I haven't any reliable sources to quote, but history does document that the Kuzerazans have always walked their own paths, rejecting the control of the Pentastra and their ways of adherence to the Flame. Who am I to deny the possibility that they did not stumble upon different forms of magic?'

Minar's eyebrows rose a fraction. 'Are you implying that western mages defied the Flame?'

'Certainly not. Only that they were, in essence, true scholars—they would not allow an administrative body to set down restrictions to the pursuit of knowledge, and thus there are no records of Kuzerazan magic.'

Minar laughed. 'You sound like Komas,' she said, adding, 'in his journals.'

Yavi leaned forward. 'So he does talk about alternative magic then?'

'He talks about a lot of things, Yavi. Alternative magic, alternative energy, alternative lifestyle—wherever he saw a system, he wouldn't rest until he took it apart and figured out how to get to the same results with a different process.' She studied him appraisingly. 'You surprise me, Yavi. I did not think you would come in here and talk so blatantly about magic—a subject that is taboo in the west.'

'I only did because I perceived you to be open to it,' Yavi replied. 'I wonder if you would permit me to look at Komas's journals? I am particularly interested in his observations during Avin's visits—for some clue to whatever they were working on.'

Minar hesitated. 'I know he's long dead, but that doesn't give you the right to go through his personal things.'

'I understand that it is intrusive and quite presumptuous of me to even ask to go through your great-uncle's effects,' said Yavi earnestly, 'but without any answers about why Avin spent months in Fezar, my entire project is doomed to failure, and I will remain unable to fulfil my grandfather's dying wish.'

Minar didn't say anything, so Yavi pressed on.

'Avin did leave something apart from his journals—a collection of textile samples. They appear to be,' he paused here and continued carefully, 'satin.'

There was the briefest of reactions from Minar, but Fahe was either imagining it or Minar controlled herself superbly. She raised her eyebrows. 'Textiles? Are they from the Fezar Mill? You do know we had a thriving weaving mill here at one time?'

'What happened to it?'

'It was running into big losses. They had to shut down.'

'May I show you the satin pieces I have with me?' Yavi asked. 'Perhaps they mean something to you.'

'I doubt it—it was all before my time—but I am quite curious.'

'Since you're no better informed about Avin, Varda and Komas's work, perhaps pooling our resources will lead us both to some answers. Aren't you even a little curious about what they might have been doing?'

'What makes you think they were up to something?' Minar asked.

'My grandfather left a note to that effect,' said Yavi carefully. Fahe wondered if he had said too much too soon.

'I have to admit, I am curious now,' said Minar. She exhaled loudly. 'Let me think about it, Yavi. Perhaps there will be no harm done to, as you say, pool our resources.' She looked at a small clock on the shelf. 'If you'll excuse me for now, I must receive Rihal and find out why she has been so keen to meet with me. Perhaps we all have information of use to the others.'

Fahe resisted the urge to snort, but Yavi nodded.

'Certainly,' he said. 'But would it be too much to ask to keep our discussion confidential?'

'It is a private matter between you and me, rest assured. Pardon my curiosity, but it appears that relations between you and her are somewhat tense, as Marya reports. Is that correct?'

'Yes. Despite Avin and Varda's enduring friendship, relations between Marik and Shenara have been strained over the past decades.'

'That is sad,' said Minar, and she appeared genuinely upset. Then she shook herself. 'Well, if you would return to your rooms, we will meet later in the day—perhaps dine together. I wish I could see you sooner, but an estate this large needs some work.'

'If I might be so impertinent,' said Yavi, 'there's something that intrigues me. You mentioned being self-sufficient here. How does the estate sustain itself?'

Minar laughed. 'That certainly is an audacious question. Well, we grow some of our own food and our energy needs are met by hydroelectricity. In fact, we produce a surplus that we feed into the grid, which in turn generates some revenue for us. But of course, maintaining an estate of this size isn't cheap. My great-uncle made some judicious investments, and it keeps us ticking over comfortably.'

'You say "we",' persisted Yavi. 'Do I take that to mean you are not the sole surviving member of the Fezar line?'

Minar appeared amused. 'You have a scholar's curiosity. Komas was like that too.' She hesitated before saying: 'Fezar's future is secure. Does that satisfy you?'

Yavi shrugged. 'I suppose it will have to.'

Minar rose and rang a bell on her desk. Marya appeared immediately, and Fahe was sure he had been standing outside all the time, eavesdropping.

'Marya will escort you back. I trust you have everything you need? If you require anything else, ring the bell, and Marya will see to it.'

'We are most thankful for you hospitality, Minar,' said Yavi, touching a hand to his chest, 'but I fail to see why we are virtual prisoners, and why we were transported here in this mysterious way. Would it be too much to ask to have some freedom of movement?'

'I must apologize for that,' said Minar with an apologetic half-smile, 'but it's a limitation of the house. You see, it's not just you; the rest of us are just as restricted.' She raised her hands. 'If you'll bear with me just a while longer—it will be much easier to show you than attempt to explain.'

# 18

# Bad Guests

'Minar is lying!' said Fahe in an urgent whisper the moment the door closed behind them.

Yavi looked startled. 'Yes, I know, but how do you know?'

'I have brains, I figured it out. Marya said the family shifted to the Lake House before Komas's death, and Minar must have been born years later. But the way she was talking about the Old House, it's like she had lived in it. Like when Komas shut himself up in his study for days and days—she said something like "*we* wouldn't see him for weeks". I mean, if she'd heard the story from her mother, she wouldn't have said "we", would she? And the way she talks about Komas is like she knew him personally. Yet, she doesn't talk about her mother at all. I don't know, but something's not adding up.'

'That was very sharp of you,' said Yavi. 'I didn't catch that.'

'She also lied about the mill making losses. It was quite prosperous, according to news reports. Keas and I didn't find any reason why it shut down—just that it did suddenly, and all the workers were paid off well.'

'Hmm, interesting,' said Yavi.

'How did *you* know she's lying then?'

'Those diagrams she showed us. Komas didn't do them, she did them herself—I can tell things like that. We'll discuss this later. Now hush.'

'What are you doing?' asked Fahe, frowning at him.

Yavi had flattened himself against the door, head turned to one side. He put a finger to his lips. Fahe rolled her eyes and sat down on the chair to watch him. But she didn't want to watch him play silly games—she was dying to discuss what had just transpired. She said after a short while, 'Do something fun, or I want my money back.'

Yavi ignored her. Moments later, he opened the door slowly and leaned outside. He looked both ways and then disappeared into the hall. Fahe jumped up and followed him.

'What *are* you doing?' she hissed as he went towards the door they now knew was Rihal's room. 'Are you...'

Yavi nodded. 'Go into the dining room and warn me if anyone comes back.'

'Okay!' said Fahe, equally excited and appalled. 'I'll cough as a warning.'

The door was unlocked, as Yavi had expected, and he slipped inside, leaving it ajar so he could hear Fahe. Rihal had a single room with an attached bath, but it was a much bigger one than their bedrooms. The decor was also slightly different—a more spare, modern look, with straight lines and angles, and a colour scheme in black and white, yet quite vibrant.

A folding paper screen separated the sleeping area from the sitting space, but Yavi's eyes widened when he saw the state-of-the-art computer system. He went closer. The screen was blank, but a telltale light at the bottom indicated it was on. There was a keyboard and a touchpad, which he tapped. The screen lit up immediately, and he saw that it was a standard system.

He looked at his watch, followed by a quick glance at the door. He didn't know how much time he had, but he was likely safe. Pulling up a chair, he checked the logs to see if Rihal had been up to anything. If she had, it appeared she had wiped her tracks clean.

The computer had Infonet access, and that meant that they were not completely cut off from the others. A thought struck him: he could send a message to Zurel. And while there was nothing he could do to hide the fact that someone had been using the system, like every child growing up in the past decade or so, he did know how to hide his traces on the Infonet. Anyway, there would be no way to tell that it was he who had been using the system and not Rihal. The Mariks ran their own servers in Koda for secure communications, and he was sure it was perfectly safe for him to route a message to Zurel that wouldn't be easily retrievable. He composed a quick note:

> Zurel:
>
> We're in the main house of the Fezars, the Lake House, they call it, probably the one you saw. Rihal is here too. There's something mysterious about it and about the owner Minar. And there's definitely something up—we are not being allowed to leave and our movements somewhat restricted, though we're not complete prisoners, and otherwise safe and looked

after. I hope to find out more soon. Will be in touch if I can.

News of Rindan?

MY

He wiped the history and put the computer back to sleep before resuming his search, but there was no sign of his stolen things, or that they had ever been here. The bedroom area was unremarkable. There was a low bed placed against one of the walls, with a very striking wall hanging showing an abstract pattern at its head. Since the design seemed very like old lettering, Yavi was instinctively drawn towards it, and he realized it was actually a window blind, the sort that folds up in horizontal pleats if drawn open. He checked to see if there was a real window behind it, but there were just air-conditioning vents as in their own rooms. He did some quick runas to check if the lettering meant anything, but it didn't.

Obsessively neat, Yavi looked down in distaste at the unmade, rumpled bed, but he was interested to see the power cord of a portable computer on it. There was no sign of the computer itself, which made sense—Rihal obviously carried it around with her since there was no way to lock the doors from outside. There was a small walk-in wardrobe and a bathroom, both testifying to Rihal's untidiness, but there was nothing interesting in either.

Not sure what else to do, Yavi decided to make his escape. Pulling the door shut behind him, he went to retrieve Fahe, wondering if there was any way to sneak into Minar's study when she wasn't around. The thought that Grey's influence was undoubtedly rubbing off on him did not alarm him as much as he would have imagined.

Good to hear from you.

Rihal has been travelling with a Sua companion, and likely they were responsible for the theft rather than the Fezars. Record of them having checked out of lodgings, but I suspect the Sua will remain in town as long as Rihal does. Attempting to trace him.

Sareka went back east. Says will be in contact soon. Rindan had minor setback, but doing well altogether.

Stay safe.

BZ

'Aren't you going to ask them about the Lake House?' asked Keas, from over Zurel's shoulder as the woman typed out her reply.

'Ask them what? What the view is like?'

Keas blushed. 'No need to be sarcastic,' he said mildly.

'Sorry,' said Zurel, shutting down Yavi's portable computer, which he had left behind. 'I feel restless. Not used to hanging around waiting, doing nothing.'

'How could we find out where Sua Raven is?'

'I am clean out of ideas. If he's in Vaker, he needs a place to stay, but there are no signs of him having checked in anywhere.'

'Maybe he's using a made-up name,' Keas ventured.

'An alias?' said Zurel. 'Possible. I wouldn't put it past the Suas to have fake identification. Though why would he hide his identity now if he hadn't before?'

'Well, you don't necessarily need identification to check into a boarding house,' said Keas. 'Especially if you're paying cash in advance. That is quite common in the Low Lands area, and I don't see why it should be different here.'

'Hmm... if he is using an alias, it means he could be anywhere. Or...' she trailed off into silence.

'Or what?' Keas prompted.

'Or that he's followed Rihal into Fezar,' said Zurel slowly. She stood up suddenly. 'Come on.'

'Where are we going?'

'To ask some more questions and see if we have better luck.'

'I have a business proposition for you,' said Rihal, once she had settled herself on the stool recently vacated by Yavi.

'Kindly elaborate,' said Minar, crossing her legs and resting an elbow on one knee. In her hand, she held a piece of paper.

'Most of it is already explained in that note I sent along with your man Marya.'

Minar nodded, her eyes fluttering to the the note she held:

> To the Fezar Family:
>
> Greetings from Shenara.
>
> My name is Rihal, and I am a businesswoman from the family of Shenara, Muradia, in the Nizrah Union. My grandmother Varda was a close friend and confidante of your ancestor Komas.
>
> I have recently come into possession of some artefacts

belonging to Varda and of information pertaining to the same, all of which I believe might be of consequence to you. Based on our families' past acquaintance and a possible mutual interest, I seek an audience with you, and further, to discuss matters that have latterly come to my knowledge.

May the Flame protect you.

Shenara RIHAL.

'A business proposition,' said Minar, 'as I understand it, would involve you making me an offer of some sort, for which I would have to pay you back in kind.'

'That's right,' said Rihal. 'As my note explains, I have acquired some information about the very curious legacy that my grandmother Varda left me. When she died, she left me a letter that explained that she and her friends Komas and Avin—who married into the Marik ruling house—had made a discovery that could secure the future of our respective families. However, given the dangerous nature and questionable consequences of the discovery, they had decided to keep it a secret. Thus, they divided everything amongst themselves in such a way that no one party could profit from it. However, later in her life, she began to see things differently. She decided that her family should be allowed to reap the benefits of her efforts, and thus decided to leave me the letter, explaining all this. However, in order to respect her friends' wishes, in case she predeceased Avin, I would only get possession of the artefacts after Avin's death.

'Well, Avin died a few months back, at which point I was contacted by my family's lawyers and handed a case that was full of notes and items belonging to Varda. They were alien to me, but I had them evaluated, and I believe that they pertain to an arcane form of Kuzerazan magic called Satin.' Rihal paused. 'Do you know of it?'

'Yes, I am aware of Satin magic.'

Rihal nodded slowly. 'As you know, I am a businesswoman, and have recently suffered great losses in the storms that have wracked the southern coasts.'

'I am sorry to hear that,' said Minar neutrally.

'Ups and downs are a part of business, but Varda's legacy comes at an opportune time for me. Forgive me, Minar, but how aware are you of the sort of damage caused by the summer storms in the east?'

'Not much, I have to admit.'

'There has been extensive loss of life and livelihood in my part of the world, and I believe that Varda's legacy might help me regain some of that. At least I myself want for nothing, but many of my staff have lost their homes and families, and I want to help them.'

'That is certainly very commendable on your part, but I fail to see how I can help you.'

'Well, Varda doesn't go into details, but she mentions that she, Avin and Komas discovered a window to see the future. "We could see tomorrow today," were her exact words. Minar, do I even have to explain to you what this means to someone like me? If I could see the future, I would know when and where to invest. It is a foolproof business plan.'

Zurel decided to try the friendly man at the tourist office once again, and he clucked sympathetically when she told him that she hadn't been able to trace her friends.

'That is quite tragic,' he said, shaking his head. 'Anything I can do to help?'

She shrugged mournfully. 'I don't know. Is there any way you can check if they've left town?'

'Hmm, well, let me see...' He appeared to think, and then brightened. 'Perhaps we could look up to see if they purchased a train or bus ticket.'

'Could you? That would be great.'

He led her to the travel counter, behind which sat a woman eating biscuits and reading a novel with a lurid cover.

'There's been a mix-up with this woman's holiday group,' he said to her, 'and we're trying to find out if her friends have left town already. Could you check and see if there are any outgoing tickets by the name of—what was it?'

Zurel supplied the necessary details, hoping that Raven wasn't using an assumed name. The woman behind the counter reluctantly tore herself away from her colourful novel and started tapping around on her computer.

'Someone called Raven bought a bus ticket to Besnal,' she said at last. 'No other names given.'

'Raven, that's him, thanks,' said Zurel, flashing a grateful smile. 'So he went back east then.'

'You seem happy that your friend left town,' said the man, looking at her in surprise.

Zurel kicked herself mentally. 'I'm just happy to have traced them. I thank you both for your help.'

'Will you be staying, then, or will you be wanting to book a ticket yourself?' asked the woman. She'd already picked up her book, as if willing Zurel to stay on.

'I think I will stay on,' Zurel said.' There's some lovely countryside around here that I want to explore,' she added rather grimly.

'Wouldn't that be cheating?' asked Minar mildly.

Rihal smiled. 'All is fair in love, war and business. I forget who said that, but they were right.' She raised her hand to keep Minar from interrupting. 'Don't get me wrong. I don't want it all for myself. That's why I said it was a business proposition. I have a set of Satin weaves with me that Varda left me, and her accompanying notes. I am willing to share them with you in exchange for knowledge of how Satin magic operates and a glimpse into this window to the future. Whatever we find, we share.'

'What makes you think I have any idea about what Varda and the others did?' Minar asked. 'Komas has been dead almost forty years. I never even met him.'

Rihal studied Minar for a few moments. 'For decades, your estate has flourished even though your family has been all but absent from public view. Once the Fezar Weaving Mill was a prosperous source of revenue, but that shut down even before Komas's death. Apart from some income from electricity generation, you have no other source of sustenance. Your land taxes are high and you obviously live well. Come on, Minar, I'm not a fool. There is a certain window that you have obviously been taking liberal glances out of.'

'Are you implying that I'm cheating the system with prior knowledge of the future so that I may make judicious investments to secure my future?'

'You call it cheating; I see it as sound business sense.'

There was a long silence.

'And what about the Mariks? Don't they have a right to an equal share of this information?'

'For one, they are free to ask for their share. For another, I hardly think they are here for a social call.'

'Yavi is writing Avin's biography. He is after information.'

'You believe that?'

'Why should I not? My enquiries tell me he is not involved in the running of the prefecture of Marik.'

'You believe that too?' asked Rihal.

'If I already have my own access to this "window" as you call it,' said Minar, changing tack, 'what makes you think I would be interested in your artefacts?'

'I have a collection of original Satin weaves. Given how the magic works, these will make your magic far stronger than with the copies you must be using now.'

'Has it occurred to you that I might have created original Satin weaves for myself?'

'Maybe you have,' Rihal said, 'but you did agree to see me. You have been expecting something of interest.'

'Perhaps I was bored and curious.'

'What if I tell you that I know something about Komas? It is the same information that Manara was after that led to her accidental drowning.'

Minar's face was blank, but the blood drained from it. 'What sort of information?'

'I asked you first.'

Nothing in the voice or the expression changed, but Rihal could almost feel the force of Minar's rage.

'Then show me what you have for me.'

Rihal unpacked her bag and unrolled a cloth folder that was filled with curious artefacts. There were wooden tablets with intricate criss-cross patterns carved on them, a couple of crude frames with roughly woven cloth, some small stone pieces with similar cross-hatched engravings and a few sheets of yellowing paper with hand-drawn grids. Next, she displayed about half a dozen collections of fabric samples. Finally, she produced some medium-sized notebooks.

Minar studied the display for a long time. She bent to examine the artefacts. Then she counted the fabric books.

'This is incomplete,' she said at last. 'There should be more cloth pieces.'

'What?' said Rihal, aghast.

'If Varda and Avin divided everything between themselves, maybe the Mariks have the rest.'

'I...' Rihal appeared to think. 'All right, give me some time to find out. Meanwhile, I suggest you don't tell Yavi anything. After all, we don't want him to find out about Komas, do we?'

When Minar said nothing, Rihal rose, packing up her things. 'I need to return to Koda to pursue my enquiries. Will you have one of your people escort me to Vaker?'

# 19

## Deception

'Any luck?'

'No, nothing. She does have a computer in her room, though. I sent Zurel a message.'

'Why can't you just ask her?' Fahe asked. 'She has to have stolen them if Minar hasn't.'

'There's a little matter of evidence,' said Yavi.

'Well, maybe.' She fidgeted for a while. 'Yavi, I have another idea. Well, kind of.'

'Let's hear it.'

'Don't laugh, but what if... I mean, I think that Minar is, well, not who she says she is.'

'You mean she's an impersonator?'

'No, no, no. I mean, she's actually Komas's niece. She's Manara, not Manara's daughter.'

'That's ridiculous,' said Yavi. 'Manara would be in her sixties by now.'

'I know, I haven't figured it all out yet. Maybe she knows Satin ways to stop ageing?'

Yavi shook his head. 'That's jumping to a really wild conclusion. And remember, Satin takes five people—she's by herself.'

'But think about it,' Fahe persisted. 'She looks exactly like the person in the newspaper microfilms. She never talks about her mother—it's like she never existed. The name Minar could be a short form of Manara. She talks of Komas like she knew him personally. And in any case, there's no record of Manara ever having had a child. Just think about it—it is a possibility, right?'

'There could be simple explanations for each of those. Minar could be the spitting image of her mother—that's known to happen. And she could also have heard a lot about Komas from her. As for having no offspring on record—that's really no good reason to think she never had any.'

'What would you call good reason then? Not like we can ask her, "Are you really your mother?"'

'I think she's obsessed. With Komas, with his theories and ideas. Her mother probably worshipped her uncle and told her a lot of stories, till he became larger than life for her. And now she's built up an entire image of what he was like, and cut off as she is here, it's started to consume her.'

Fahe rolled her eyes. 'So you basically think she should get out more?'

Yavi grinned at her. 'Basically, yes.'

'Bah,' said Fahe, annoyed. 'I have a really strong feeling about this, Yavi. You have to believe me. At least, you have to believe that she's lying about Komas, that she's met him?'

'Well, Komas's body was never found, maybe he's still alive and has a den somewhere in this mysterious house,' suggested Yavi.

'You're just making fun of me now!'

'No, I'm serious. Yes, I do think Minar lied about never having met Komas. But I'm not sure how it all came about.'

Kuzerazi Fresh's bakery made some interesting toasted sandwiches and Keas decided that those would do nicely for their lunch, which he had been detailed to take care of while Zurel pumped her tourist centre friend for more information.

Lunch arrangements made, he found an empty bench outside the tourist office and sat down to wait for Zurel. It was a working day afternoon and there weren't many people around. In any case, the weather was dull and gloomy—not conducive to picnic plans. Behind him, in the children's park, there were a group of teenagers, fooling around in the toddlers' sandpit. Keas didn't really take any notice, but after a bit, he had an uncomfortable feeling of being watched.

Though he was no longer terrified of being hauled off to the nearest civil guards' station and packed off home to Saje, it would be stretching it to say that he was completely relaxed. With his father being who he was, that would be stupid. Keas turned around and found the youngsters, who were perhaps a few years older than him, staring. He looked away and stayed steadfastly with his back to them. So, when he felt a tap on his shoulder, he jumped, startled.

'Hey, what's your name?' He was being addressed by one of the boys in the group. His three companions stood by, watching.

'What's it to you?' Keas asked, heart thumping.

The boy shrugged. 'Just being friendly. No law against that. You seem alone. Why don't you join us? We're going for a ride.'

'No, thanks. And I'm not alone. I'm waiting for my friend.'

'My name's Tarsa,' the boy persisted. 'Go on, tell me yours.'

'Keas.' It was a common enough name. Then, inspired, he added: 'Marik Keas.'

Tarsa raised his eyebrows. 'You look and talk like a Kuzerazan, but you give your name like an outlander.'

By now, the others had come over too, and Keas was trying not to show how uneasy he was.

'Look, I have done nothing to bother you, so please leave me alone.'

But their next words made his heart leap to his mouth.

'Keas is also the name of El'Idrin Win's son, who's been missing,' one of the girls said. She reached out and touched Keas, who flinched. 'The Low Lands are full of notices about you, Keas. There's a reward too.' She turned to Tarsa. 'Maybe we should call the guards?'

Keas was standing now, and he started to back away. He was shaking. It was over. They had spotted him. He would be dragged...

He bumped into someone and nearly screamed, whirling around, but it was only Zurel, who caught his arm and pushed him behind her.

'Are you bothering my brother?' she asked casually.

'He's not your brother!' spat Tarsa. 'Look at you two—you look nothing like each other. We are calling the guards. There's a thousand ren reward for information on Win's son.'

'Speaking of looking,' said Zurel, 'take a look at this.' She opened the flap of her jacket, and Keas, who was standing behind her, had no idea what the others saw, but they gasped and backed away as one. 'As for the guards, go on, call them.

They'll be interested to hear about how you assaulted an outlander. That's a serious one, isn't it?'

'We never assaulted him!' cried Tarsa.

'You did. I saw you touch him, and that girl did too.' Zurel pointed, and the girl shrank back. 'And you threatened him.'

'They're nuts, Tarsa, let's go,' the other girl said. 'In any case, his hair is too short for him to be a real Kuzerazan.'

Tarsa glared at Zurel and Keas, but let himself be led away. Keas sat down with a bump. His legs wouldn't hold him up any longer. He mentally thanked the young guard at Marik House who had given him an embarrassingly short haircut. 'This was a mistake,' he mumbled. 'I should never have come back.'

'Get up,' said Zurel, and without exchanging another word, they returned to their motor, keeping an eye out for the kids.

'What did you show them?' Keas asked finally, unable to bear the silence.

'I'm a registered bodyguard. I'm authorized to carry firearms.'

'Oh.'

'Exactly how long were you planning on hiding your identity from us, Keas?'

'What?'

'Don't play games with me. I know who you are. I saw your birth certificate on the train the time you were mugged on the Trans-Nizrah route. We might be ignorant Nizrahis, but even we have heard of Idrin Win, the mystical blind healer of Kuzerazi.'

'There's nothing mystical about him,' said Keas glumly. 'He's as ordinary as you and me.'

Zurel looked at him. 'Is he really blind?'

'Completely.'

'Flames,' she breathed. 'Then how does he...'

'Don't ask me, I don't know! You... you won't tell anyone, will you? You *haven't* told anyone, have you? Yavi?'

'I haven't. I realized you'd run away for a reason, and Yavi is no fool—he probably guesses that you've run away too.' She shot him a smile. 'Though not that you're Win's son, I should think.'

'Please don't tell him. Anyone.'

'It's not my story to tell.'

'Thanks.'

'You're an idiot. You've been terrified of being recognized, haven't you?'

'Yes. I've been photographed many times by the press with my father. I... Zurel, where are we going? Lily's is the other way.'

'Raven has gone back east, Rihal is at Fezar. I don't like sitting and waiting and doing nothing. We're going to Fezar too.'

An eerie stillness filled the air as they got closer to the Fezar property. It made Keas uneasy because he knew what it meant. It had been getting progressively humid as the day wore on and the sun was soon obscured by a heavy layer of cloud.

'It's going to rain,' said Keas for the dozenth time.

He knew something that Zurel didn't know—couldn't know, perhaps—and he wasn't sure how to make her believe him. This was no ordinary deluge that was about to follow. It could last for days. It was the waterfen that tipped him off. It was a shrub that grew on boggy soil, and it was known to roll up its curiously pointed leaves in anticipation of heavy and prolonged rainfall.

For Keas, looking for signals among plants wasn't superstition or blind faith—he could read plants, he could understand them, and the waterfen had more or less told him that the rain that was to follow was not going to be fun. They had raincoats and things, but roads could become hard to navigate with heavy rain.

'Zurel,' he said, a little louder. 'This rain isn't going to be a little drizzle.' And prophetically, there was a low rumble of thunder.

They had found the little wooden delivery shack right next to the road that led in from the highway. There was no sign of anyone around, so they cautiously made their way inside. The trail was easy to follow—there was a well-worn path, with the double track that indicated the six-wheeler traversed here regularly. They kept inside the cover of trees—just in case.

Keas also couldn't help thinking about Rindan and how he had been shot, and that made him jumpy as well. He had no wish to know what a bullet through his shoulder felt like. They walked on, quite slowly, for about half an hour. Zurel would periodically take out her binoculars and scan the area.

'Zurel,' called Keas again, distressed. 'The rain!'

'Will you stop whining for a moment?' said Zurel. 'Look here...' She grabbed his arm and pulled him closer, handing him the binoculars. 'Through the trees right there. What do you think?'

'What? I don't see anything,' said Keas, a little sulkily. 'Oh.'

There was a small cottage visible through fine drizzle that hung in the air now.

'Come on,' said Zurel, taking her binoculars back and walking faster.

Keas followed, forgetting that he was sulking. The cottage was deserted, but when they peeped in through the windows, they were surprised to find that it was fully furnished.

'I think someone lives here,' said Zurel. 'A caretaker maybe.'

'Then they might come back any moment,' said Keas.

'So we should be quiet and careful, and keep our eyes and ears open.'

Keas followed her around apprehensively as she made a methodical search of the place. There were some surprises—the refrigerator was full of fresh food, and there were dishes on the draining board by the sink. They were all completely dry, so whoever had eaten and done the dishes hadn't done so in the very recent past.

Zurel put her foot on the pedal of the bin beneath the sink and studied its contents. She whistled softly.

'Yavi and Fahe were here.'

'How do you know?' Keas asked, peering into the bin himself.

'Those chocolate wrappers, see? We carried them from Koda—you don't get those here.'

'Oh,' said Keas impressed. Then, thinking he should contribute something intelligent, added, 'But they're not here now.'

'They're at the Lake House, as Yavi said,' said Zurel, speaking slowly, deep in thought. 'How long do we have before the rain gets bad?' It was drizzling harder now.

Keas blinked. She was asking him?

'Say, a half-hour. No more. Any longer, it'll be raining too hard to drive back.' Their motor was parked at a narrow turn-off some way ahead of the entry for Fezar—they had seen it on their road map, and since it led to a dead end, they had decided it would be okay to park there. It could be more than an hour's walk back. He suspected it was already too late to drive back, but somehow, he preferred the idea of being trapped in the motor rather than inside Fezar. On the other hand, he felt eminently safer hiding in Fezar than returning to Vaker and being in public view again.

Zurel appeared to think for a while. 'I think it would... What in the Flame is that?'

Above the soft drone of the rain, there was another sound—a loud purring sound that seemed to be getting louder. They looked at each other, panic-stricken.

'It's a motorcar!' said Zurel. She grabbed his hand. 'Someone's coming. Come on, we have to get out of here!'

Sareka was annoyed. That scrawny little man had been following her from the moment she left Vaker and he hadn't even the decency to try to conceal the fact. She had passed him on the way to the refreshment stand at the airport while waiting for her flight to Koda, and he had actually deigned to smile and nod at her. She hadn't tried to give him the slip then. Playing games was not her priority.

It wasn't exactly the first time that she had been tailed or had followed someone herself. She had engaged in enough subversive acts in her adult life to have had to learn how to spot and throw off a tail. What worried her was something else entirely. The description that Lily had given about Yavi's uninvited visitor kept running through her head. *Thin, short, pinched face, short neck, late fifties.* A cane and a limp could always be added and subtracted at will. Sareka wished she had Zurel with her. Maybe then she could have lured him into a dark alley or something and had her hit him over the head. Then they could have tied him up and questioned him or something. She dismissed the fantasy with a sigh.

She needed to contact Zurel and tell her about the man. But her handset hadn't been working in Kuzerazi for some reason, and after she had crossed the border, she found it had run out of charge. At the Koda airport, she found a vacant charging port and plugged her device in. She waited for a few minutes, till it had enough power to start up, but Zurel's comms were unreachable. She also tried Yavi in case he was back from Fezar, but in vain. Yet another try on Zurel's codes resulted in 'a connection error due to device being out of range'.

*Damn the woman! Must have followed Yavi into Fezar herself,* Sareka fumed. She composed a message for Zurel instead, so at least she would get the news whenever she came back in range:

> Am back in Koda. Being followed by a man whose description fits the one who stole Y's things. About to give him the slip. Any news of Y and F? Call me when you can. Have a hunch I'm following up. Will get in touch if I find anything.

Sareka had work to do, and for that she needed to be in Koda, where she could get in touch with her contacts who could bring her information. Thankfully, Cousin Kariad could be depended upon to provide a warm welcome and not ask too many questions. But before that, she needed to scratch an annoying little itch.

She went into the women's toilets at the airport, where she took off her ankle-length raincoat and folded it up into her bag. From it, she removed a scarlet mage's cape ('borrowed'; she had never been officially anointed as a mage, though she was for all intents and purposes a practising one) and swung it across her shoulders, buttoning it up quickly. She combed her hair, tied it back and pulled the hood of the cape up. She also slipped on a Flamestone ring. Next, she undid the little buttons in the legs of her fold-up travel trousers and let them down to her ankles. She took off her sandals and replaced them with the boots she was carrying in her capacious bag. A pair of glasses completed her ensemble, and she looked at herself in the mirror, satisfied.

The man would be on the lookout for a woman in a drab raincoat, messy hair and bare feet in sandals. She, on the other hand, was now a respectably dressed mage. As long as they didn't end up face-to-face, she was banking on getting away.

# 20

Dinner was a sombre affair, not for any sinister reason but because it was so formal. It was taken early—in fact, the Mariks were used to having a high tea followed by a late dinner, but western families seemed to eat their evening meal early. The other matter of interest was that Rihal had disappeared. When asked, Minar replied that she had been called away on business but that the Mariks were welcome to stay as long as they wanted.

Minar was dressed in Kuzerazan finery—full-length trousers and a laced silk shirt with heavy embroidery. The visitors' outfits, in contrast, were quite drab and utilitarian. Their invites had said nothing about a formal dinner. Marya also joined them. The two people from the kitchen who served them could have been the same ones who had accompanied the Tub on the day of Rindan's accident, but it was hard to tell with their peculiar headgear, which they continued to wear indoors.

Marya's presence at the dining table also indicated his hierarchy in the household. It was already clear that he was Minar's right-hand man. This was the first time they were seeing him minus his head covering, and he was quite pleasant to look at, Fahe noted with surprise. His skin was very fair—hardly surprising as he went about with most of his face covered—with unnaturally hairless cheeks. Fahe revised her inference—Marya was clearly Minar's right-hand *woman*.

As they were finishing dessert—a curious dish made of sweet, thickened milk and boiled rice, and garnished with ground almonds—Minar said she would like to show them something special about the house.

'If you recall, I mentioned that the architecture of the Lake House limits us in many ways,' she said, 'and I'm sure you've noticed the lack of windows. You're probably wondering why.'

'It did cross our minds,' said Yavi.

'Well, then, let me show you.'

Led by Minar, the visitors climbed the spiral staircase in her study, past the library level, right up to the top.

'Interesting place you have here,' Yavi called out as they crossed the library.

'Thank you,' said Minar. 'My workrooms are on the top level. That's where I conduct most of my studies and experiments, and of course, this is the library. Most of the books here are from Komas's collection, and I haven't even read many of them.'

They stepped on to bare wooden flooring on the top level. There was a narrow path along the edge, with a number of doors, leading off it. Minar reached up towards a cord hanging down from the ceiling and pulled at it. White light flooded the area.

'Come,' said Minar, leading them down a short corridor that continued on from the landing. 'Marya, would you do the honours?'

'Of course,' said Marya, and disappeared through one of the doors.

The others followed Minar, who led them to the end of the corridor, which finished in a column that curved outwards. It rose from floor to ceiling and was made of glass. It was filled with water, and there was a curious, continuous movement in it. This water was a dull greyish-blue and there was considerable rippling movement. There was also more wildlife—some small fishes and a water snake, and some bits of leaves and other unidentifiable objects.

Fahe wondered what was so wonderful about it. Was it the same giant aquarium on top of the courtyard? But before she could speculate any further, the disembodied voice that had startled them that morning rang out again.

'Stand by,' it said. 'Level one surf. Stand by.'

'What...' began Fahe, but that strange shivering started all over again.

Fahe grabbed the wall next to her, and saw Yavi doing the same. Only Minar stood still, legs apart and arms folded confidently across her chest as she stared at the column. There was a little smile on her face.

'Watch,' she said.

As they watched, a most curious thing happened. The level of the water in the column started to fall very slowly. What was even odder was that an overcast sky became visible as the water fell, and a thin drizzle that was battering down on the water and on the glass column.

Somewhat puzzled, Fahe went closer to the column. It wasn't really a column at all—it was a sort of window. Then she heard a sharp intake of breath from Yavi and turned to him, surprised.

He was staring up at the falling water level and, being the tallest person in the room, what he could see wasn't visible to Fahe yet. When the level of the water finally reached Fahe's eyes, she could only watch dumbfounded.

More and more of the sky was becoming visible, and then there were trees and high mountains, partly covered by clouds, in the distance. This was followed by the tops of the green-brown wall of closely growing bamboo, and finally stretching ahead of them, the pebbly lake shore. The shuddering movement all around continued.

They were surrounded by water—by the lake, to be precise. And the water level wasn't falling—the house was rising like a giant lift! Fahe gazed in disbelief at the lake, which was silently buffling from the falling rain on its surface.

The tub-like vehicle came to a halt outside the cottage. Hidden among the trees in the forest behind the building, Zurel and Keas had little notion of what was going on. A light came on inside; it was considerably murky, now that the sky was completely overcast and the rain was coming down hard. They could see a silhouette moving past the curtained kitchen window now and then, but not anything else.

After about a quarter of an hour, the light snapped off. They were too far—and the rain too noisy—to hear the motor now, but they saw it clearly enough when it went back the way it had come, swerving around the bend in the track. It was impossible to tell anything about the driver, who was covered from head to foot in rain gear.

Yavi listened keenly as Minar explained about the submerging and surfacing mechanism of certain parts of the Lake House. The hollow walls and a weight tank at the bottom of the house were filled with water to make it heavy and sink, and it was pumped out to make the house surface. The more elaborate technical details were, however, lost on the visitors.

'This house was one of Komas's most ambitious and successful ideas,' Minar said.

'*One* of?' said Yavi. 'You mean there are more such spectacles?'

Minar only smiled and asked if they'd like to see her main workroom. Of course, they were only too happy to, and she led them through to one of the rooms nearby. It was about twice as long as it was wide and had a plain sanded floor. A mismatched assortment of bookshelves was arranged along one wall—the tallest reaching right up to the low ceiling (that Yavi could touch if he stretched out his arms and stood on tiptoe), and the shortest about waist-high. The shelves were packed with books and notebooks. A plain table, with a couple of notebooks and a small portable computer, was set near the door.

The first third of the room was demarcated by a wooden screen, and Minar led them through beyond it, where the more interesting part was.

The first thing that caught Yavi's eye was an arrangement of some curious objects on the floor. If he had seen the collection of artefacts Rihal had displayed for Minar, he would have found these similar. But to him, they seemed to be crude handicrafts, nothing much to look at, given the repetitive grid-like patterns drawn, carved or engraved on them.

Minar leaned down and carefully picked up a stone tablet about the size of a book. 'Do you know what this is?'

Yavi and Fahe examined it. 'Er... local handicrafts?' said Fahe.

Yavi was about to reply when his eyes fell on the wooden bench against the wall. Next to it was a haphazard pile of bound books, books containing collections of fabric samples—his grandfather's fabric samples, now his.

'What's the meaning of this?' he asked, suddenly angry. She had some nerve!

'Well, you could call it an experiment, I suppose,' said Minar, looking a little surprised at his tone. 'It needs some fine-tuning.'

Yavi turned to her, angrier than ever. 'No, I mean, those... those are mine!'

'Yours? What do you mean?' She turned to look where he was pointing.

'They belonged to my grandfather. You had them stolen from me a few days back. I really hadn't expected this of you. I thought I trusted you—well, to an extent, at least.'

'Yavi, wait a moment. You're labouring under a misapprehension. These are my weave... er, things. They belonged to Komas and were passed down to me.'

Fahe went closer to examine the books. 'Yavi,' she interrupted. 'These aren't yours. Yours had those numbers written on each sample, remember?'

Yavi blinked. He walked to where Fahe was and looked down. There was one other thing that he should have noticed straight off—his own collection was also a little shabbier than this one. But, otherwise, they could have been the same. He felt slightly uneasy, but couldn't tell why.

'I... uh, I'm sorry,' said Yavi, looking very sheepish. 'Yes, I... er, as my sister points out, these cannot be mine.'

He shook himself. Maybe, just maybe, Minar had a copy herself. It was proof, after all, wasn't it, that she did know what Avin, Varda and Komas were working on. Maybe it was time to corner her.

'It's all right,' she was saying graciously. 'It was a misunderstanding.'

'I beg your pardon for the insinuation,' said Yavi, 'but I am not very well informed about... all this. Are these cloth pieces are magical artefacts used for Satin?'

Minar's face was unreadable. Then she said, 'So you know about Satin.'

'Very little,' said Yavi. 'I know the theory of Satin magic, but have no practical knowledge of it.'

'I see. And what does Rihal know?'

Yavi shrugged. 'I have no idea. But my collection of cloth bequeathed by Avin *was* stolen a couple of days ago. All except two volumes.'

'They are not ordinary pieces of cloth. They are called weaves, magical weaves,' Minar explained absently. She tilted her head to one side and was thoughtful for a few seconds. 'Are you saying what I think you are about the theft?'

Yavi gave a non-committal shrug. 'There is something that puzzles me. You clearly are aware that Komas and his friends were toying with Satin. Yet, earlier you said you didn't know anything about what they were doing. And now you brought me here to show me this?'

She hesitated, and then nodded. 'Yes, well, I wasn't certain how much you knew. I thought you were trying to drop hints the first time we met, and I wasn't sure how to respond and how to tell you about Satin magic.'

'Well, then, what exactly were they doing?' he asked.

'They were experimenting with a new kind of magic.'

Yavi was sure he looked particularly idiotic with his mouth hanging open, but he couldn't help it.

Minar motioned to them to sit, and they perched on the bench while she sat on the floor.

'You say you are aware of the basics of Satin?' she asked.

'Superficially,' said Yavi.

'Well, it was apparently Avin's idea to marry Satin and Flamestone magic. Satin takes its form from weaves. It is powered by people drawing strength from the elements of wind, water, earth and fire. The outcome depends not on the strength or skill of the mage, but on the accuracy of the weave.'

'Unlike the runas we use,' said Yavi slowly, 'which depend on the abilities of the caster.'

'And runas are individual—you can't use a runa your sister draws or vice versa. Also—correct me if I'm wrong—aren't runas temporary? Once you use them, they're just pretty designs.'

'Yes. It's in the drawing of a runa that you source the Flame.'

'It's different with weaves. They are permanent, but each time you copy it, it's efficacy decreases. Which is why what you have with you—if they are Avin's original weaves—are invaluable.'

'Is it true that Satin requires four to five mages working together?' Fahe asked.

Minar shook her head. 'Not necessarily, but traditionally it does need all four elements, to different degrees. Most individuals have more than one elemental magic inherent in them. Between Avin, Varda and Komas, they were able to source all of them.'

'What about word mages like me?' Yavi asked. 'I have no affinity to any sort of natural element.'

'You do. It's just that, over the years, you've developed your powers in such a way that you've never needed to push yourself further to find out.'

'So was Avin successful?'

'It would appear so,' said Minar. 'Do you know how Satin works?'

Yavi and Fahe both shook their heads.

'Well, as you know, it is channelled through weaves, but you don't need anything as complex as woven cloth. A magical weave can be a representation of the satin fabric weave in any form. For example,' she picked up the stone tablet, 'like this engraving, or even that object, which is simply a collection of loosely woven strings. You can make effective weaves by drawing on paper, carving on wax or wood, using pieces of thread or wire, or anything at all that can be combined to make a correct four-n satin fabric weave.'

'Sorry, but what did you mean by a "correct four-whatever satin fabric"?' Fahe interrupted.

'The weave of the satin fabric,' said Minar. She walked to her table and came back with a notebook and pencil, drawing while she spoke. 'Cloth consists of a set of vertical threads and a set of horizontal threads woven into each other. The vertical threads are collectively called the warp. This is set up first. Subsequently, the horizontal yarns—or the weft—are carried through the warp.

'Now, as you can imagine, there are different kinds of weaves. Satin is a type of weave where a warp yarn floats over at least four weft yarns before forming an interlacing. Thus, the term "four-n satin weave". In other words, one vertical yarn goes over four horizontal strands. In case of Satin magic, these four strands represent wind, water, earth and fire. The fifth strand—the interlaced one—is the life that holds it together. Here, this will make it clearer.'

They peered over the sketch she had quickly drawn for them.

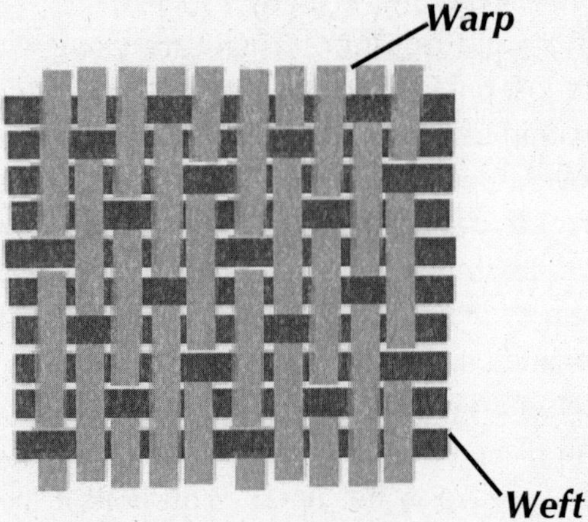


Minar's diagram of the satin weave

'The more balanced and accurate your weave construction is, the more powerful and complex the magic. Thus, by using cloth rather than a freehand drawing, you can generate more power.'

'Enough power to make a building sink and rise out of water?' asked Yavi.

'A building? Avin and Varda wanted power to move mountains and open seas—and more.' She picked up a crude weave made of strings and toyed with it. 'The thing about weaves is that they can be combined to do various things, so you can take a number of simple weaves like this one, and link them to achieve something a lot more complex. Certain things—say, if I want a light in this room—could be done with a single weave; but generating electricity for the entire house, for example, would be more complicated and need a combination of them.'

'If it's as complex as you say,' said Yavi, 'are you able to conduct your experiments all by yourself?'

'That's a valid question. There are weaves created to work with just one or two powers, and I can attempt to use a combination of them. But I won't move any mountains. I might move a pencil from the floor back to my table.' She hesitated. 'This was Avin's discovery—making weaves that took less than all four powers. This one,' she looked down at the artefact in her hand, 'needs water in three strands and air in one, and I can use it to... I'll show you.'

She went to her table again, this time to pour a glass of water. She placed the glass on the floor and sat next to it, holding the weave in her hand. 'You hold it like this, the warp vertical.'

She lapsed into silence, sitting very still. Suddenly, the crude artefact in her hand appeared to come alive. One of the strings glowed, then another, and finally a third, and the glow spread out along the length of the strings, turning them into columns of bluish fluid. Then the last string came on, but this one turned into a tube of murky air. She placed the weave carefully on the floor, and ran her fingers gently on it.

Her hand came away leading a pale white column of smoke. She directed the magical beam into the glass of water next to her. In a fraction of a second, the water was boiling madly.

Minar touched the weave again to make the magic stop. She gave a little bow to her audience. 'That's how a weave can be powered by one person.'

'Incredible,' said Yavi, but Fahe wasn't impressed.

'Why don't you just use an electric kettle?' she asked.

Minar looked a little taken aback, but then she laughed. 'I would, if I was making tea, but suppose I could generate steam to power an engine? I'm afraid I should have demonstrated with something a little more spectacular!'

'It's all right,' said Yavi. 'Fahe is as yet unaware of the basic concepts of magical practice. I've never seen anything like this before, Minar. Our brother Yanik can make water boil if he wants, but... well, it's just done so very differently. You said Avin wanted to combine Flame and Satin magic?'

'Well, Avin and Varda, being Flame mages, were at first only able to power weaves using runas—they would draw runas that directed their magic into the weave, but it wasn't a very efficient way. It took a lot of time to do even something as simple as boiling water.

'Then Varda wanted to try using woven cloth as weaves. Now, this was something that ancient Satin mages had thought of, but they never had any success with it. You see, it's easy to carve a line of water on a piece of wood focusing your affinity for water on it, but how do you imbue yarn with the power of a particular element? This was a dilemma Kuzerazi mages could not overcome, but Avin and Varda could. They simply used Flame magic.'

'You mean they created magical cloth?' asked Fahe. This sounded more exciting.

Minar shook her head. 'Oh no. They created *ordinary* cloth—weaving it together the regular way. Colours and type of yarn were found not to be important to the magic. Then, later, they imbued it with the elements using Flame magic. It was a tedious, painstaking process.'

'Was it worth it?' asked Yavi.

Minar looked from Fahe to Yavi. 'Did you notice in your grandfather's weaves that somewhere on each cloth sample there appears to be what looks like a crude design on the cloth? Almost like a mistake in the weave.'

'Yes, we did,' said Yavi eagerly.

'This was Avin's idea again, though Varda implemented it. They found that you can have a great deal of control over the effects of a weave by introducing a small localized discrepancy in the regularity of the weave. They came up with formulas to manipulate effects of a weave given its size, complexity of the discrepancy, and so on. I haven't yet understood the technicalities. All I know is that you could achieve astounding results with a modest amount of magical power.'

They digested that in silence.

Finally, Yavi said, 'Minar, you talk of Avin, Varda and even Komas like you actually knew them.'

Minar was startled. She stared at Yavi for a long time before responding. 'Sometimes,' she said, 'I feel that I do.' She stood, looking at her watch. 'If you'll excuse me, I need to see to the submerging of the house. I will see you tomorrow after breakfast, when maybe we could discuss this further.'

# 21

# Curiosity

They went back to the cottage to decide what to do next. They didn't dare switch on the lights, but did help themselves to some food—it had been a while since they had had their lunch. Keas suggested leaving money, but Zurel pointed out that it would give away the fact that someone had been there.

The Fezars appeared to be moving around in the estate despite the rain, and Rindan's accident was foremost in their minds. But a few hours later, with no other visitors to the cottage, it became imperative to take a call.

'We can either go home or we can explore further,' Zurel said, 'but there's no point sitting here like idiots.'

'Maybe we should wait till it gets dark?'

'Dusk is hours away. I don't even know when darkness falls here—midnight?'

'We could wait in the motor,' said Keas weakly, but he could see Zurel wasn't buying that.

They followed the double-track path, taking care to keep to the cover of the trees. The rain didn't let up, and they had to pull their hoods over their faces to keep the water off their eyes. Soon, Zurel had to admit that her decision to go out in the rain had been wrong, but Keas was too wet and too miserable to gloat. Fortunately, it wasn't very long after that when, following a steady but easy uphill incline, they came to a sudden dip and then face-to-face with the bamboo wall.

The place appeared deserted as before, and they went closer. It was just as they had seen it earlier—the track went right up to the wall of vegetation and disappeared inside it, but the gate remained well hidden and tightly shut.

This time, it was Keas who went up close to the bamboo as Zurel explored the area. The eerie moaning was subdued by the sounds of the rain and the fact that there wasn't much breeze just then. He put his hands on the stalks.

Keas had never really seen his gift of having a way with plants and animals as magic. He just went by instinct. This time, he simply concentrated, trying to see if the bamboo could 'tell' him anything. He felt Zurel's hand on his shoulder after a point.

'I can tell some things about it,' he said. 'It's been grown unnaturally—it can't exist here by itself. And it's been here for many years, decades... Zurel?'

But she wasn't listening. She was standing with her face close to the giant stalks, staring through. Her mouth was open. Her rain hood had fallen back and the water was dripping over her face, but she took no notice.

'Zurel?'

'Come here, look,' she whispered, gesturing to Keas.

Keas bent close to see whatever she was looking at, and muttered an oath he had never before used in his life.

Through a gap in the bamboo, they could see the lake, its surface alive with the falling rain. But of the house there was no sign. It was gone.

The third time that Fahe got up that night, the thin line of light under Yavi's door was finally gone. Excited at the prospect of her impending adventure, she darted back to her room to put on her shoes and picked up her pen torch. It wasn't very late, barely past seventeen o'clock, and she supposed it would be bright sunlight outside. Unless it was raining, of course.

The hall was lit dimly but well enough for Fahe to find her way through the dining area to the passage behind the kitchen and finally to the courtyard. The lights in the courtyard were out and it was almost pitch dark, just as it had been the first night she and Yavi had been exploring. Not wanting to switch on the torch till absolutely necessary, Fahe kept to the wall as she felt her way to the grille into Minar's section of the house.

Her heart was beating frantically as she gently pushed at the gate. If it was locked, that would be the end of that. But it yielded to her touch, and she stepped inside tentatively, suddenly very aware of the magnitude of what she had undertaken to do and with absolutely no idea how to go about it.

She stood in darkness, though a dim light from beyond the curve in the corridor threw an angled shadow at the wall and revealed the long passage ahead. From her earlier visit, she knew that Minar's study was placed much before the corridor curved away, and she slowly walked towards it, trying to gather her wits about her. She could already see the door—tightly shut and no gap underneath to tell if there was a light on inside.

Past the door of the study, Fahe kept to the side of the wall that was still in shadow. She had an unnerving feeling of being trapped from both sides now, and expected either

Minar or Marya to appear any moment. She hesitated when she realized that she could no longer hide in the shadows, but a small voice inside her head told her that since she had come this far, she might as well go on. The passage curved more sharply as she passed under the light, and suddenly she found herself facing a blind end.

It was a curious and unusual wall—uneven, with an abstract sculpture of psychedelic colours. Towards the floor, the design faded to a dull brown, till it merged with the carpet, and towards the top it gave way to black. As she peered up at it, she noticed that the blackness was, in fact, heavy drapes. Was there something up there that the drapes covered?

She noticed something else that sent her heartbeat racing like she had run a masaaf at top speed. She was standing in the middle of the passage, and on two sides of her there were two other doors.

When Yavi finished writing up his notes for the day, he was unaware of the fact that Fahe had already checked on him twice. Feeling restless and unable to sleep, he came out into the small area that connected their rooms. The idea was only half-formed in his mind, but when he saw Fahe's door tightly shut, with the sounds of a video coming from within, he decided that enough was enough. Minar was playing a game with them, that much was certain, and he wasn't going to lie around passively while she planned her next move. She might have given them significant information, but there were still a lot of holes.

In any case, what was her motive? Had she shared the same information with Rihal?

Yavi picked up his backpack, checked to see that his multipurpose knife was in his pocket, and quietly left their rooms. Snooping around in his host's house was not something he had ever expected to be doing; but then, he had done so many new things this past week that it was just simpler not to overthink anything.

When he found himself in the long, silent corridor in Minar's apartments, he didn't waste time exploring its entire length as Fahe would barely a quarter of an hour later. He turned the handle of the study door, holding his breath. When it swung open, he stepped inside gingerly, half expecting to come face-to-face with the imperturbable Marya. But the large, circular room was empty. A lamp switched on near the table cast a dim glow around.

Relieved, yet waiting to draw breath till he felt the door shut behind him with a muffled click, Yavi made a slow visual survey of the study. He didn't know what exactly he was looking for, but he was sure that this was where he would find some clues.

Feeling vulnerable standing in the middle of the study, Yavi decided that a closer look at Minar's weave arrangement would be a good place to start. He also wanted to check out the library on the second level in greater detail. Actually, the library first.

It was a relief to hide himself in the shadows of the bookshelves, even though he was on tenterhooks, expecting Minar or Marya to jump out from the shadows and challenge him. He made a careful circuit of the bookshelves before he finally convinced himself that there was no one there.

Fahe looked to her right and left, trying to muster the courage to try one of the doors. Then she looked up at the dark drapes above her. She frowned as she noticed something interesting at the corner. Going closer to the carving on the wall, she saw that it was built in such a way that there were hand- and footholds. She could easily climb up. So there *was* probably something hidden up there, and there was a way to get there too.

It didn't solve her problem, though. Where she was standing, she was completely exposed, and if anyone were to suddenly appear, there was no place to hide. The thought of that put her in a minor panic. Finding out whatever was behind the curtain was an utterly fascinating prospect, though also sort of forbidding. Doors, on the other hand, were eminently more run-of-the-mill.

Taking a deep breath and forcing down her unease, she reached for the handle to her right and pressed down very, very slowly. She held her breath as the door swung inside, and peered in through the crack.

It was dark, and at first she could see nothing. She blinked, waiting for her eyes to adjust to the darkness. She followed the thin line of light from the door as it ran across the floor of what slowly revealed itself to be a smallish room by the standards of the house. It crossed a chair that had clothes hung on its back and ran up a wall. The next thing she became aware of was a sound of coarse breathing—almost a snore, but not quite. She sucked in her own breath—there was someone inside!

By now, she could also make out a bed, and a huddled form on it. It was impossible to tell if the mound of sheets was

Minar, Marya or any of the other staff. As her vision adapted, she realized that the room was not only relatively small but also quite utilitarian. She could make out the outlines of a table and a wardrobe apart from the bed and chair. Surely this stark, basic room wasn't Minar's?

Fahe retreated, suddenly conscious of her wildly beating heart and terrified that it might even wake the sleeping person. She was now pretty sure that if it was Minar's room she needed to search, her destination was in the opposite direction. There was nothing to be gained from standing around, so she squared her shoulders and stepped across the corridor. She placed her hand on the handle and turned yet again.

There must have been over a thousand books in Minar's library, and every single one that Yavi had picked out so far was on magic and mages. Most were about regular Flame magic, and some rare volumes from before the War of Nations. They were mainly hardcover, some obscure, some well known, well thumbed, and often bookmarked, underlined and with pencilled annotations. Apart from regular published books, there were also a few handwritten manuscripts, many yellow and brittle with age.

Yavi was unsure what he was looking for, nor did he have a plan. He wondered whether it would have made better sense to search the shelves and cupboards below, where Minar had pulled out what she insisted were Komas's jottings. He ran his fingers distractedly down the spine of a few books right in front of him, and stopped in surprise. For, staring out at him was his mentor and teacher Kariad's name.

*When did Kariad write a book?* Yavi wondered as he pulled it out. *Or is it some other Kariad?* It was by no means a very unusual name.

But there it was, in bold letters, the name 'Vala Kariad'. The book was about introducing newcomers to magical theory and practice, and the dust jacket said that Vala Kariad, reputed Disciple at the Academy of the Flame in Koda, had over two decades of experience instructing initiates.

Yavi frowned. That couldn't be right. Kariad was just in her mid- to late thirties, and she had only been a Disciple for some seven or so years. Must be a mistake. He flipped the pages to see when the book had been published when a soft creak froze the blood in his veins.

For a moment or two, he stood stock-still. Then, shoving the book back into the shelf, he snapped off the light in his multipurpose knife that he'd been holding in his mouth. It was more or less completely dark, but he still burrowed his way deeper into the row of shelves, crouching with his back to the wall.

The minutes ticked by with no other sound, and Yavi began to relax. Houses often made noises by themselves, especially old houses. Though, could a forty-year-old house be called 'old'? He roused himself and resumed his exploration. Feeling his way along the wall, also curved like the main room of the study, he felt safe enough to switch on his torch again. His circuit was interrupted by a flight of stairs, at which he stopped to consider his options.

The last time Minar had taken them up to her workroom on the third level, they had used the spiral staircase on the outside. There was no telling if these stairs led up to the same place. There was only one way to find out, so Yavi went up.

At the head of the staircase, there was a small landing but no door. Puzzled, for surely a flight of stairs ought to lead somewhere, Yavi peered closer at the wall, squinting in the meagre light of his torch. There were walls on two sides, and the third side was bound by a safety rail. The ceiling was not too high, and he could easily reach up to it. To his surprise, his hand met a cold metal handle.

He turned the narrow beam from the torch upwards and could just about make out the outlines of a trapdoor. He tugged at the handle, a little tentatively, and got a bit of a shock when it slid open noiselessly. He jumped out of the way as a well-oiled mechanism pushed a small metal ladder downwards, inviting him up into the gaping hole in the ceiling.

A pale blue light illuminated a large split-level bedroom. Fahe instinctively knew that there was no one home. It had the unmistakable stillness of a room left empty for a prolonged period of time.

There was a large bed with thick, carved posts, from which hung fine silk curtains tied back with tassels. The bed itself was placed low on the floor, about the level of Fahe's calves, and a dark bedspread of some shiny material trailed carefully on the floor. The pillows had frilled edgings similar to the bed curtains. There were shelves above the headboard, but they were polished and empty. The two bedside tables had drawers on top and cabinets below with a door of a twisted metal grille. They had lace coverings, on top of which were placed electric lamps that looked like old-fashioned candlesticks. There was a sort of chest at the foot of the bed, again of the same dark wood and twisted metal. Fahe could see neat layers of folded blankets inside.

One of the walls had cupboards built in along its length, and the carvings on the edges of its doors matched the bedposts. Other furniture included a dressing table set with a triple mirror on hinges that could be adjusted and a cushioned stool pushed into the cavity underneath. A chandelier similar to the ones in the dining hall hung down from the ceiling, and a single blue light shone from somewhere within its interiors, casting that eerie glow all over the room.

The stairs leading up turned at right angles along the wall. Under it was another door that Fahe imagined was the bathroom. She walked up, deep in thought and puzzled, unsure what to make of this curious room. Upstairs was a sort of sitting and living area. There was a recliner with two tables on both sides—one that had a lamp and the other empty. There was also a roll-top writing desk, its top edged with the same metalwork as the bedside table and ottoman below, and its sides and legs carved like the bedposts.

The upper level ran the entire width of the room and about a third of its length. The long wall was covered with floor-to-ceiling drapes that fell in elegant pleats, and the shorter ones had a bookshelf each, even though they only contained a few lonely volumes and some sparse odds and ends carefully arranged.

The only illumination was from the blue light, but it was enough for Fahe to notice the cords for the drapes. Expecting to find more air-conditioning vents, she gave an experimental tug. The drapes slid open smoothly to reveal a glass wall, and Fahe had to remind herself that they were underwater.

Fascinated, she stood staring out for a long time. The water was unusually alive, and it struck her that it might still be raining outside. Peeling herself away and pulling the drapes closed, Fahe gave some thought to the fact that she was in Minar's room, and she could come back any time and catch her there.

*I need proof that Minar is Manara*, Fahe reminded herself, looking around. The desk was the nearest to her, and she went to it, pulling it open. To her surprise, it was empty. Dark, polished, spotless and completely empty.

Downstairs, in the bedroom area, it was much the same story. Except for the ottoman which had blankets, everything else was gaping and bare. There was not a speck of dust anywhere—*why would there be dust in an underwater house?* wondered Fahe—and there was also absolutely nothing to indicate that a person could live here. She even explored the bathroom, which had not so much as a toothbrush.

Puzzled, Fahe sat down in the middle of the bed and dropped her head in her hands, trying to figure this out. Marya had said that this was Minar's private wing, so this elaborate bedroom had to be hers. And just in case it wasn't, why was it there? Whom did it belong to and why was it so bare and impersonal? Also, where did Minar sleep, then?

There were just the three doors in this section of the house, Fahe recalled to herself. One was Minar's study, one was probably Marya's room, and then this one. This *had* to be Minar's bedroom.

There was one other option left yet—those curtains high on the wall. Maybe she needed another look at them.

Yavi scrambled awkwardly through the trapdoor and found himself on his hands and knees on the bare floor of a small room. He stood and automatically started to dust himself. The room was bereft of furniture or decorations and there was a door opposite him. It had a plain metal handle with no latches of any sort. Yavi stood quietly for a while, straining for any sounds that would indicate he wasn't alone up here. The floor was wood, and his limited experience of wooden floors told him that it was very easy to make a racket walking on them.

Finally, convinced that there was no one else around, he walked carefully to the door. This seemed to be Minar's workroom level, so Yavi presumed he was in one of the rooms they had seen when she had brought them to see the submerging/surfacing mechanism of the house. He peered cautiously out of the door and found himself, to his surprise, in another room, much larger and with one of the walls taken up completely by an elaborate set-up of switches, monitors, levers and so on.

The floor under his feet felt different to him, and he looked down to see carpet. The door swung automatically shut behind him as he walked towards the main console. There were no lights on, but the instruments cast an eerie glow strong enough to see. It didn't take him very long to guess what the controls were for—the sub/surf mechanism. He studied the blinking monitors with its figures and charts, wishing Grey was there with him so she could explain what this was all about in detail.

Yavi was afraid to touch anything, but he was fascinated by the display in front of him. There was a set of five small screens on one side, and a collection of keypads and buttons in the middle. On the other end was something a little more intriguing. The best way to describe it was probably a large monitor, about a metre square, but it was dark, with no sign of any backlight. On it was an eye-wateringly intricate multicoloured design that was now becoming rather familiar—a weave. He would have thought it had been made by coloured pens on a blackboard, but for the slight flickering at one corner.

His pulse quickened. This was definitely magic, and Satin—maybe some Flame magic too. There was a small pad wedged into the side of the console, with a pen tucked in its spine. When he picked it up and flicked the pages, he saw some notes. Times and dates, though no mention of year, and some odd notations that he couldn't read.

Having had his fill of the control panel, he decided he wanted to find Minar's main workroom. He peered carefully out into the corridor before stepping forth, and found himself right next to the viewing gallery where Minar had demonstrated the wonders of the Lake House.

With the torch in her mouth, Fahe had no difficulty pulling herself up towards the dark curtain. She pushed it aside to find herself at the mouth of what could best be described as a cave. It was dark and empty, so she heaved herself up inside and let the curtain fall back. She switched on her torch to look around.

It was a sort of concave room with a flat floor—very definitely not a real cave. A light bracket hung on the wall, but no lights were on. At the far end was another opening, and when Fahe stepped through, she found herself in a narrow tunnel.

There was probably just about enough space for two people to walk abreast, but it would still be a tight squeeze. Pointing her torch upwards, she saw that the ceiling was generously high, at least twice her height. A few steps ahead of her was a turn and she went ahead to see if it was leading anywhere. But there was more tunnel, an unending, dark space stretching in front of her. Feeling claustrophobic, Fahe headed back into the cave room to think.

The thought of going into the tunnel alone was frightening. But another part of her was burning with curiosity. What was it for? Where did it lead? Was it a way out into the forest? Not knowing was equally unthinkable.

She took another hesitant step inside it, trying firmly not to think of bats and spiders and rats and other things that lurked in underground tunnels. Flames, this was an *underwater* tunnel; goodness knew what those contained. She made a careful torchlight examination of the floor, walls and ceiling in front of her and found no evidence of insect, rodent or bat life. What she did find were bare fluorescent light bulbs fitted into the ceiling, though she couldn't see any switches.

Taking a deep breath, Fahe plunged in. With a final look behind her, where she could see light from the crack of the curtain in the cave room, she turned the corner.

Immediately, she wanted to go back. The narrow light beam from her torch was barely enough to see by, though it at least showed what was directly ahead of her. But it was sharp and penetrating, and she periodically pointed it upwards and around her to check for bats and spiders.

She couldn't really say what made her plod on single-mindedly. Was it only curiosity? Her heart was beating so hard and loud that she imagined it was echoing off the walls. The temptation to turn around and look behind her was one that she had to fight with all her effort, for she knew that if she looked back and saw the darkness behind her as well as in front, she would lose her nerve. While she knew very well that the darkness existed and by not looking she wasn't making it go away, it was still comforting not to see it for herself.

She lost track of how long she was in the tunnel. It could have been fifteen minutes or two hours. Then, without warning, she stumbled on an uneven bit of the floor. She shot out a hand towards the wall to steady herself, but her torch was knocked out of her grasp. It bounced on the floor and went out.

The blackness that engulfed her was complete and stifling. She found she couldn't breathe. Something invisible was pressing down all around her, smothering her. She gasped and fought for air, scrambling against the wall.

This was like the recurring nightmare from her childhood, where she had been exploring underneath a bed and suddenly found that the space was too narrow for her to crawl out. The heavy furniture was impossible for her to lift with her arms and shoulders and she was in such a panic that she couldn't even scream, and if she did, in her nightmare world, there would be no one to hear her.

She was breathing fast now, almost panting, but it was harder and harder to take in air. She felt light-headed, and it was disorienting since she couldn't see anything. Her extremities felt numb and too weak to hold her up. She couldn't see; she was blind. She couldn't even tell if her eyes were open or closed. She felt about her face, and she could feel herself blinking, but all she saw was the unending darkness. Terrified, she couldn't move. And the smothering—it was getting worse and worse.

She had no breath to scream for help. In any case, who would hear her? She thrashed against the wall and was only marginally aware when her hands made contact with a small rectangular fitting somewhere over her head. She tried to grasp it, but it sort of gave way under her fingers.

Suddenly, the tunnel was flooded with light.

# 22

# Corridors

It was dark in the narrow strip that ran in a circle along the ledge of the third level. Yavi looked down from the side of the railing, and the study beneath him was the same as he had left it, bathed in a pale yellow light. He didn't dare to turn on the bulb that Minar had earlier; anyway, his eyes had more or less adjusted, and it was all right to navigate by. He was just about to pull away from the railing when something caught his eye.

One of the cabinets that lined the study was open. He was pretty sure they had all been tightly shut when he had passed through. He felt the hairs on the back of his neck stand up, also recalling the creak he had heard earlier. He looked around, suddenly uneasy. But the study, all three levels of it, remained quiet and still except for his own breathing and his racing heart.

His adventurous streak somewhat diminished, Yavi decided not to explore needlessly any more and made a beeline for the door Minar had led them through for the workroom.

Even shrouded in near darkness as the room was, Yavi noticed something that had escaped him the last time he was here—a small, narrow door in the corner. It was ajar, and the reason he noticed it now was a pale glow coming from it, providing what little illumination there was. Curious, he crossed the workroom towards the light.

He found himself in a short, blind tunnel of a room, the door at one of its narrow ends. If he reached out with both arms, he would easily be able to touch the walls on his two sides. But much though he wanted to, he hesitated.

A large, magical weave lay arranged along the walls of the tiny box-like room, and it was activated, or powered, or whatever the correct term was. Starting from the left of the door, the glowing cloth was draped all around the room on tiny, invisible pegs, not quite touching the floor. When Yavi leaned in closer for a better look, he noticed that it was not one weave, but many. Pieces of cloth of different sizes, and arranged to cover about every bit of the wall right up to the low ceiling. The glow from the magic gave the impression of a single, continuous fabric.

The living, pulsating yarns of the cloth were too tiny to differentiate with the naked eye, but they all converged in a curious circular pattern a little off-centre on the wall opposite Yavi. A beam of yellow-white light sprouted from it and spread out to the middle of the room. Halfway across, it seemed to hit an invisible barrier to form a flimsy, translucent curtain of ghostly light.

Mesmerized, Yavi didn't know how long he stood staring. The fluid pulsations and the white curtain were almost hypnotic. As he stared into it, he was sure he saw flashes, flashes of... he couldn't really say what. They were just images, and they went even before he could register their presence. It was impossible to have turned away, so he did the only other thing. He reached out slowly to touch the curtain of light.

Fahe nearly died with relief when the light came on. Once again, there was no way of telling how long it was before she composed herself. She found herself sitting on the floor of the tunnel, now bathed in a gentle white light from a bulb directly above her. The backs of her hands were bruised and bleeding. Her torch was resting innocently by her feet.

She picked it up and tested it. It was working fine. Heart still on overdrive, she got up slowly. She licked a finger and gently dabbed saliva on her cuts. She had to take a call now, whether to go back or forward. But now that she knew there were working lights in the tunnel—she could make out the little depressions at regular intervals that were switches—she felt a little braver.

Her panic dissipating fast, she decided not to turn back. She would leave the lights on behind her as she progressed through the unending corridor.

It was almost as though it were a reward for going on, for when she turned the next corner, she found herself in another cave room. This one was more or less square, and it was furnished and inviting. It had two doorways leading out into more darkness. But there was something more interesting.

Disembodied. That was the only word Yavi could think of later on to describe what it was like. He was suspended in space and falling at the same time. He seemed to be in a dark, narrow place that extended forward and backward, up and down. But to his right and left, beyond a filmy white curtain of some indiscernible material, lines of colour whizzed by. It was like watching a video of night-time traffic go by, shot on low-speed film, where all he could see were lines of colour and sparks of light. And while he could make out buildings and trees and objects, they were only the barest perceptions. The noise was deafening. It was the high-pitched squeaking of an audio track on fast forward—of several audio tracks on fast forward, really. He thought he caught indistinct words sometimes, laughter, screams, horns, whistles, birdsong.

There was a pressure from the inside of his skull. It was inexorable and excruciating. He opened his mouth to scream, but it was no good. He closed his eyes to rid himself of the pain inside his head, but that didn't help either. It wasn't the disturbing flashing lights, but what was *inside* his head. He had only seconds, but he was suddenly aware that if he didn't get out of there very, very soon, it would kill him.

He reached out towards the barrier-like matter on one side.

Fahe had never seen a weaving loom before, but she had seen enough pictures to know one. She gingerly touched the rows of fine yarn stretched from the top down towards where the weaver must be sitting. A short length of bluish-purple cloth was already woven, and she fingered its smooth surface. She wondered if this was going to be turned into a magical weave. She examined it for the telltale 'mistake', but couldn't spot anything.

She moved away to examine the rest of the room. The rug under her feet was worn with age and she fingered the row of spines in a squat bamboo bookshelf. They were all scientific—technical volumes about construction and so on. That made sense. Whoever had designed and built this place—well, Komas, who else?—must have required a lot of study and research.

She sank down into a rocking recliner. The cushion lining it was worn and she could feel the hard wood under her shoulder blades, but it was nice to rest for a bit. She rocked gently, looking up at the light fitting on the ceiling. Her throat and mouth were dry and she could have done with a drink of water. She looked at her watch and realized that she had been in the tunnel for less than a quarter of an hour.

Feeling a little foolish about her panic attack now, Fahe heaved herself up and went to examine the last item of furniture, a table. It was piled untidily with journals, notebooks and sheets of paper, yellowing with age. There was no dust, though. She flipped through them, but they made no sense to her. There were some blueprints as well, but she didn't know how to read them. Maybe this had been Komas's secret workroom?

She caught sight of a slim journal that looked a little odd. She pulled it out. Its cover was still brightly coloured, unlike the other faded volumes. It was called *Advanced Construction*, but when she opened it, she found that it only had a single page, which was a table of contents.

Frowning, Fahe examined it closely. Maybe the pages had been torn out. But no, it didn't look like that, for the book had no spine to speak of. She opened it again and ran her fingers down the lines of text.

To her surprise, the text changed as she touched it!

It took her a moment to work it out: when she touched a particular title, the article in question was displayed on the page. It was some sort of electronic paper technology—Fahe knew it existed, she had even seen it, but she hadn't known that there were journals being printed on it.

'Amazing,' she whispered, turning back to the cover, understanding why it hadn't faded. Anyway, it couldn't be that old... she stopped short.

The issue date was about three years in the future.

Yavi had a feeling of weightlessness, like being in the downswing of a giant wheel. It lasted for barely a moment, and he staggered. To his surprise, he found himself in an open space that he recognized immediately.

He was standing on a pebbled path running along a familiar section of his family's estate by the backwaters of Marik. The curving palm trees swayed languorously in the warm breeze. The humid heat of a coastal summer beat down upon his bare head, and already prickles of sweat stood out on his face.

Yavi was shaking. The weight that had been pressing down on his head was now gone. He stared down at his trembling hands—his own body felt alien to him. The thoughts in his head, the knowledge—they felt like they didn't belong, yet he knew they did.

'Are you all right?' the voice behind him made him jump, and he whipped around.

The sight of Rindan nearly made him cry out. He looked older than when he had last seen him at the hospital in Vaker—no, wait, was that where they had last met? Most of his hair was gone, the hairline receded to the back and sides of his head. The Marik House guards' uniform he was wearing was a little different too—a buttoned shirt instead of a laced one, long trousers instead of the calf-length ones, and he was carrying a weapon of some sort Yavi didn't recognize, tucked into a small holster at his hip.

'I... Yes.' Some instinct stopped him from asking when he had been discharged from the hospital in Vaker. He tore his eyes away and turned to go on.

He knew, for some reason, where he had to go, and he walked rather unsteadily down the path that waved through the trees in his haste to get there. The footpath led him to a side gate built into a high, concrete wall. A security camera pivoted around towards him as he approached. Yavi fumbled in his pocket and found a plastic card that he swiped in a little contraption within the grille of the gate. A blue light flashed twice and a portion of the gate slid into the wall with a low whirr, giving him just enough room to pass. Rindan followed.

Yavi wanted to stop and drink it all in, but his feet led him quickly up the path. He had never seen this place in his life, yet he knew it so well. He automatically lifted a hand to acknowledge the figure that was waiting for him at the door leading inside. He couldn't help smiling broadly at the man in the doorway. The surprise of recognition was washed away by the deep, instinctive consciousness that their friendship went back years.

'Mage Yavi,' he said, returning a shy smile.

'Mage Keas,' replied Yavi, ducking into the doorway and into air-conditioned comfort.

The years had changed Keas little, though he was taller. He was still stick-thin, but he was well tanned now, which the harsh sun of Marik was responsible for. His face was almost unnaturally clear—Yavi suspected he used some sort of herbal concoction to keep it that way—but for a bare hint of stubble. The hair was the same black, curly shock, cut unfashionably short; the green gaze was careful and considering.

'Are you... there's something different about you,' said Keas slowly.

Yavi looked down at himself and got yet another shock. The clothes he was wearing—he'd never seen them before. And as for his waistline—it was significantly thicker than when he had started out!

Keas stared at him for a few moments, and then shook himself. 'Shall we go? The Prefect of Marik awaits us.'

That was yet another jolt, when he realized that the prefect they were talking about was Fahe and not Mother. But as he turned to follow Keas, he doubled up, not so much in pain but the incredibly uncomfortable sensation of someone having reached inside him, grabbed his insides and yanked him hard. The same disembodied, weightless feeling came back as he had had when he touched the light in Minar's workroom. The bright electric lights gave way to a soft glow and he felt a hand holding his arm tightly.

He lurched and banged forcefully into a wall, making the tiny room shudder. He felt another body alongside him as he bounced off the wall, clutching and grasping at whatever came to hand to break his fall and get some balance. Things came away in his grasp in that mad scramble as he was pushed and pulled. Then he finally crashed down into a hard, wooden floor.

'What the Flame were you *doing*?' cried Minar's voice, shaking with anger.

Yavi's vision cleared and he tried to sit up. They were back in the workroom, the arrangement of crude weaves scattered, presumably by his fall—his and Minar's. Minar was getting up, dusting her clothes off, spewing venom at him.

There is a fundamental fact about houses—at least, in the rational world. They cannot disappear into thin air, not overnight.

'It must be an illusion,' Keas said.

Zurel didn't have any answers. 'You are the would-be mage, you ought to figure it out,' she said. That had effectively ended the discussion, and they had since been walking around the bamboo wall.

The rain was harder than before. Keas tried hard to think of ways that an entire house could disappear to distract himself from the cold rivulets that ran down the back of his neck. They were drenched despite their rain gear, and so wet that the concept of being dry and comfortable seemed a completely alien one.

The wall curved more or less evenly, and every now and then, Zurel would attempt to find a crack to look inside and see if they could figure out how far they had come. It wasn't a very small lake—at least two masaafs all the way round—and the rain and the uneven terrain made the going harder.

'Look!' Zurel called suddenly.

Keas squinted where she pointed, away from the bamboo where all their attention had hitherto been focused. It took him some time to see what she had seen since the rain had affected visibility. When he realized what it was, Zurel was already crashing through the dense woodland. Keas ran after her, fruitlessly wiping a hand across his face.

Zurel was standing with her hands on her hips, staring up at the ruins of an old house. It was three storeys high and made of brownish stones. There was a porch that had caved in on top of an old-fashioned motor, crushing it. Wide, broken steps led up to front doors which were conspicuously shut and the windows were in considerable state of disrepair. But it would do for shelter for now.

'Time travelling!' cried Yavi, interrupting Minar's tirade. 'You have a time travel... gate? Is that what Avin and the others were working on?'

'Yes, you fool!' yelled back Minar. 'If you're clever enough to figure that out, surely you're clever enough not to jump in like that!'

'I... I didn't know!'

'Then it was even more stupid to toy with magic you don't recognize! What do you think would have happened if I hadn't found you?'

'I... I don't know,' said Yavi, intrigued. 'What?'

'You'd have been trapped—in a time and a body you are not ready for. It could have killed you. It *would* have killed you!'

'But...'

She didn't take any notice of him, but turned back towards the room where the active weaves had been. Yavi pulled himself to his feet, wincing and stepped up behind her.

Minar was standing in the doorway, perfectly still. Even watching her back, Yavi could tell she was in a state of shock.

Their banging into the walls seemed to have dislodged some of the weaves mounted there. These were lying on the floor, lifeless, some torn. The other weaves were now just limp, inert pieces of plain satin cloth. The white curtain that he had touched was gone too.

Minar was so still that she could have been a statue. Then she turned, slowly, eyes boring into Yavi, alive with an anger that made him cringe. Before he could move, she had rolled her right hand into a fist, drawn back, and connected hard and accurately with Yavi's jaw. She put her weight behind it, perfectly balanced, and Yavi found his face meeting the floor before he felt any pain.

Shocked, he lay there.

'You fool!' Minar shouted again. '*What have you done?* You destroyed the time corridor, and along with it the magic that holds this place together!'

The left side of his jaw weighed too much for him to be able to lift it and it burnt with an indescribable fire. But he managed to mutter: 'Wha...?'

'You've trapped me!' said Minar, now in a low, angry voice. 'And you've destroyed me and my home.'

Prophetically, a low moaning sound filled the air, startling Yavi.

'What's tha...' he started to say painfully, and then stopped.

Minar just stood in the middle of the floor, head hanging, defeated. Yavi stared at her, puzzled, and then the shuddering vibration of the house's surfacing and submerging mechanism started up.

It was a relief to be under the dubious shelter of the porch. As they skirted around the bashed-in motor, Keas looked up fearfully, wondering if they were safe from another roof-fall.

The front entrance must have been a sight to behold at one time. Huge double doors that were about twice Keas's height, made of solid Vaker oak, showing the typical inlay work that was native to some interior parts of Kuzerazi. It must have been painted brightly too, but all that was left were flakes peeling off.

Despite their run-down outward appearance, no amount of pushing from Zurel and Keas was able to budge the doors open. They looked at each other.

'Let's try the windows,' Zurel said, and Keas nodded as they headed back out, squinting against the rain.

The window panes were hanging on twisted rusty hinges, and they pushed them apart with some difficulty. The musty, dank, dark room that it led into didn't seem very inviting, but there was no choice. Waiting under the porch, worrying if it was going to fall on their heads, was not a very nice prospect either.

It took a while to adjust their vision to the darkness and venture to explore further. They were in what at one point might have been a small sitting room. Broken and rotting furniture was stacked haphazardly against one wall, with a rolled-up carpet balanced vertically against it. Keas kicked it experimentally and a small portion fell apart in a cloud of dust. He looked at the floor to find that they were leaving muddy footprints in the thick layer of dust.

There was a single door, not quite shut, but years of neglect and damp had swollen the wood and rusted the hinges. It took their combined strength to push it open, and they almost stumbled out into a huge hall, blinking in the sudden relative brightness of their surroundings.

Had they been aware of Minar's study in the Lake House, they would have seen the similarity of the construction. The roof of the giant hall was dizzyingly high, encompassing all three floors of the building. The ceiling was made up of a sort of stained glass, which was now paying the price for its neglect. Portions of it had disintegrated, and there was broken glass on the floor that crunched underfoot as they slowly walked towards the middle, avoiding the dripping trails of rainwater. Once-expensive furniture had also been ruined by exposure to wind, sun, rain and probably snow.

The hall was almost like an indoor courtyard, with doors opening out from it. The higher floors were edged with wide balconies, too wide for them to see anything much beyond. Directly opposite the main door were two flights of stairs going up, and the area in between was occupied by a single flight leading down into darkness.

'What is this place, do you think?' Keas said, looking up at the discoloured light pouring in from the top.

'Let's move away from under that glass ceiling,' said Zurel, taking his arm and leading him away. 'It looks iffy. I think this might be the Fezars' older home.'

'It must have been something in its time,' said Keas. He was trying to push open another door, which gave way suddenly. There was a flash of activity and a number of furry bodies scurried away. Keas screamed.

'What?' cried Zurel, startled.

'Rats,' said Keas, a hand on his chest, feeling foolish. 'Sorry... I...'

Zurel pushed past him into what seemed to have been the kitchen, but before they could explore any further, a strange, low drone filled the air.

Keas clutched Zurel's arm in fright. 'What... is that?'

'It's coming from outside,' said Zurel, eyes wide. 'Come on, let's go look!'

'Nnno...' started Keas, but Zurel was already running.

The rain had eased off a bit, leaving only a steady drizzle now. Zurel and Keas crashed through the trees towards the direction of the noise, bursting out into the clearing where the bamboo wall was, and a most curious sight met them.

The wall was gone, the bamboo was shrivelled, leaving a full view of the lake. And as they watched dumbstruck, the lake's surface erupted as a house rose out and up from its depths.

They watched devoid of thought or words as the Lake House rose with excruciating slowness. As if it wasn't enough to digest, behind them, from the direction of the old, ruined house, someone screamed. Again and again.

Screams that were indiscernible and incoherent but filled with terror and panic. They made Keas's skin crawl, for it was hard to imagine what could frighten someone like that.

Zurel jumped like she had been electrified. 'That's Fahe!' she said, and started to run back.

# 23

It didn't take Fahe long to work out the explanation behind the journal. There was nothing sinister, she decided. Inos's cousin had a publishing business and she had often seen dummy copies of future publications in their house. Of course, never one three years early, but still. Maybe, she reasoned, it was a sort of limited preview—a term Inos had taught her—to test a product before it was launched. Sometimes they tested for years, after all.

But this brought up another question: if Komas was indeed dead forty years, this couldn't have been his, could it? Maybe she was wrong—this was Minar's secret workroom.

*If this is Minar's room, she could be here any time!* The thought filled her with apprehension. And she had been leaving the lights on too. It was time to move on.

There were two tunnels leading out—one had steps leading down and the other sloped gently upwards. Fahe had no wish to go deeper into the lake's depths, so she chose the one going up. Apart from the incline, this tunnel was similar to the one before. There were lights, though some of them didn't work, but there was enough for her to see by.

Dark to Light

Fahe was frequently being chastised for having a wild imagination; in fact, that was precisely why she was where she was right now. Yavi hadn't been convinced that her opinion was worth his time, but she had begged to differ. Having an active imagination sometimes made you think of things that you normally wouldn't. And right now, she was having a very wild thought indeed.

So Minar could do Satin magic, and if the loom was hers, maybe she could create weaves too. With Avin and Varda's modifications, Satin could be made really strong—Minar had said Varda and Avin wanted to open seas and move mountains. What if they had moved something else—like time?

Therefore, thought Fahe, what if that was exactly what Minar was doing? Maybe she had hopped into the future and brought back stuff—like machines to make an underwater house go up and down and a journal printed on electronic paper. After all, she could hardly be sitting here, alone in her big house, boiling water all day.

It would also explain why it had seemed like Minar had hurried back from somewhere the day they first met her—was it only yesterday?—and she seemed to have no clue what time it was.

Deep in thought, Fahe didn't notice that when she turned a final corner, the tunnel stretched out straight ahead of her. When she noticed, she found she was unable to see the far end, where it tapered off into darkness. It was different from the rest of the passageway—which had had turns every ten or fifteen steps so far. Intrigued, she walked faster, fumbling for the light switches, but switch after switch clicked uselessly under her finger.

'Bah,' said Fahe out loud. It was dark, but not completely so because of the ambient light from round the corner. Anyway, she had her torch if required and was feeling much braver than before. Then, suddenly, one of the lights worked, and she saw the tunnel ending at a metal door. But her joy was short-lived.

At first, she thought she was feeling dizzy, but then there was a terrible groaning sound, and finally, with a little lurch of the floor, the entire tunnel started to shake.

The dull groan persisted and echoed around the tunnel with the accompanying vibration as Fahe struggled to keep her balance. She realized what must be happening—the Lake House was surfacing. A momentary horror gripped her. What if the surfacing took the tunnel well beyond the opening of its destination?

'Flames, no!' she cried, and made a dash for the door. She fell a couple of times, but scrambled back up. There was no other thought in her head apart from the fact that she had to make it through that door. She reached it, slamming against it. The dim light from the last working bulb showed a narrow bolt, which she pulled back and yanked the door open. Her momentum almost made her step through without looking, but she yelled and managed to pull back at the last second.

Right at the level of her head across the door was a thick, concrete barrier, which she had just managed to pull back from smashing her face into. And it was steadily falling lower and lower.

*The tunnel is rising!* Fahe realized despite her panic. But where was it taking her? She had seconds to make a choice—whether to squeeze herself through the gap below and go where it was originally leading, or to go up.

The thought of jumping into darkness, not knowing how far she was going to fall, was too much to contemplate. So Fahe grabbed the concrete edge, which was about chest level now, and heaved herself through. She felt cold, hard floor under her. It had the slightly rough feel of concrete. She couldn't see enough to tell where she was, how big the room was or where an exit was.

She scrambled well inside on hands and knees before she turned back to see her progress. The tunnel was now level with the floor and Fahe felt a little stupid for her panic in coming through. But it was rising relentlessly, covering the opening in the wall with a thick block of concrete, floor upwards. With the disappearing tunnel, whatever negligible light was there was also fading. Memories of the earlier smothering darkness returned and Fahe groped for her torch in her pocket. She found that her hands were shaking, and when she tried to flick the switch, it fell from her hands.

'Nooo!' she cried and fell back on her knees to pat the floor in front of her. Suddenly she spotted it—its luminous band visible in the near-darkness. She made a lunge for it, but her hand knocked the torch aside and it rolled to the edge of the floor. Fahe could sense rather than see clearly as it pitched into the gap between the floor and the tunnel and disappeared through.

For interminable seconds, Fahe remained as she was, motionless. The tunnel rose higher and higher, and the gap became smaller and smaller. When it finally closed, the darkness wrapped itself around the future Prefect of Marik again and started to squeeze inexorably.

That's when Fahe started to scream.

'Minar! What's happening?' Marya's voice met them as Yavi followed Minar through the once-underwater courtyard into a wing of the house he had never been in before.

She was running to catch up with them, haphazardly dressed and bewildered. 'You didn't say you would...'

'An accident,' said Minar shortly.

'Fahe!' said Yavi suddenly, stopping. 'I have to see if she's all right.'

'She will be fine,' said Minar. 'There are other people in the house as well. We're all fine. Marya, will you go and check on the girl?'

Marya nodded and went off without a word.

'Sorry if this is a stupid question,' said Yavi, speaking painfully through his swollen lip and jaw, 'but what has the time corridor got to do with the house?'

'It's all connected,' said Minar, staring ahead. 'The magic of the time corridor and the sub/surf mechanism. There were one thousand seven hundred and fifty-three weaves—only some were here in the present.'

*And I wrecked it*, thought Yavi, consumed with guilt. But Minar was still speaking.

'The time corridor was essential to connect them together.'

'Why did we surface when the... er... magic failed?'

'Komas had built in a safety mechanism for that. We have a lift that we use otherwise when the house is submerged if we have to go in or out, but that's not a very efficient system. Draws too much power. So he made arrangements that the house would surface if the magic failed.'

They were now standing in a sort of annexe that opened out on to a metallic bridge, which sloped down and across the lake to its shore. It was raining and dusk appeared to be close by. One of the staff had come out with them and he now went down to examine the wilted bamboo wall.

'The bamboo,' Minar whispered. 'Oh, Uncle Komas will be disappointed.'

Yavi was struck by that sentence. '*Will* be? Komas is alive then?'

Minar laughed humourlessly. 'It's hard to answer with a yes or no. But yes, he may be alive.'

'Then where is he?'

'The question isn't where, but when.'

Yavi blinked, but realization dawned almost immediately. 'You mean... he's gone through the time... thing, but you don't know where... I mean when?'

Minar didn't answer. She didn't have to.

'But he disappeared forty years ago, and you seem to know him. You can't be that old.'

Minar turned to him and faced him squarely. 'You are an intelligent person. Work it out.'

She turned and walked out on the metal walkway, down towards the lake shore, and Yavi stared after her, his mouth open, painful as that was.

*You've trapped me. You've destroyed me.* Those had been her words.

It couldn't be!

But why not? He had seen and experienced the time corridor himself.

So Fahe had been right.

'It's coming from inside the house!' Zurel yelled. She vaulted through the window, and Keas followed, running after her, aware of how much darker it was now. It wouldn't be completely dark for about an hour or so, he knew, but inside, it was much harder to see. Some light flowed in from the broken stained glass ceiling, giving them enough to go by in the main hall.

Zurel was standing in the middle of the floor, facing away from him. The screams were now louder and closer—panic-filled and utterly hopeless. It made the hairs on the back of his neck stand up.

'What do we do? What do we do?' he asked frantically.

'It's definitely Fahe,' said Zurel. She pointed in front of them to the dark flight of stairs leading down. 'Coming from the basement. Go back to the Lake House and get help. No, I don't care how you do it. Just go. We need lights at the very least. Stop staring at me. *Go!*'

Fahe couldn't scream any more. Her throat hurt and her lungs needed air. She gulped it down hungrily. She was crawling on the floor, but had no idea which direction she was going. When she banged into a wall for the third time, she gave up. She huddled into a ball on the floor and lay there, motionless, too spent even for tears.

And then she started hallucinating. She heard a voice calling her.

'Fahe! Can you hear me? Are you there? Fahe?'

A vague memory reminded her that it was lack of oxygen to the brain that made you hallucinate. So the air was bad down here. She was going to suffocate to death. She hoped she would pass out soon. That way, it would be painless.

'Fahe!'

There it was again. Louder. It sounded like Zurel.

Looked like Cousin Kedra would get to be Prefect after all.

'Fahe! ANSWER ME!'

Fahe sat up. The back of her hand scraped the wall and it hurt. 'Ow,' she said. Then she frowned.

'Fahe...'

No, not a hallucination.

'Zurel! I'm here, I'm here! Help me! HELP, HELP, *HELP*!'

'Fahe! Hang on! I'll get you out.'

Zurel. It was really her. Fahe was crying tears of relief. 'Come and get me now! I hate this darkness. ZUREL!'

Keas ran blindly through the trees in the direction of the Lake House, yelling for help. He spotted a figure near the withered bamboo, and waved and jumped to catch its attention, yelling as loudly as he could. The Lake House was now completely visible, and there was someone else walking down a metallic ramp towards the shore.

The man near the bamboo edge stared in surprise as Keas came dashing up. He grabbed his arm. 'Who the Flames are you?' he asked.

'Later... later,' panted Keas. 'She's trapped... down in the ruined house. Please... lights... We have no lights... Got to help... please... Lights... need a light...'

Another figure came running down towards them. Keas was too agitated to notice the similarity with the pictures of

Manara from the microfilm. He also failed to see Yavi, who was running down the ramp now.

Keas grabbed the arm of the woman who had joined them. 'Please... now...'

'Let's go,' the woman said, to Keas's relief. 'Lead the way.'

The big man yanked a large torch out of his belt and they started in the direction of the old house.

# 24

## Yavi's Burden

Even clad in dry clothes and warmed with sweet tea, it was a while before Keas and Zurel stopped shivering. Fahe, while shaken, was none the worse for it physically, but she was quiet. Yavi's mouth was still swollen and he glowered at anyone who tried to ask for an explanation. Minar sat still by the mantelpiece with an electric fire in the Lake House's rather grand drawing room. She stared into the glowing bars.

Keas realized that the Kuzerazans were right—dabbling in magic *was* dangerous. He had a sudden attack of homesickness. He wanted normality—a life without disappearing houses, moaning bamboo walls, ruined buildings, reclusive families, people trapped in moving tunnels. He even missed Father. He wasn't really that bad all the time. Suddenly, apprenticing to an apothecary seemed so harmless and so desirable.

But he had to give it to Fahe, even though he didn't like her. Keas didn't think he would have had the nerve to explore a dark, unfamiliar tunnel on his own. She might be a spoilt brat, but when it came to rank physical courage, she was the one to root for.

'There has to be a way,' Yavi said finally, breaking the oppressive silence, 'to realign the weaves and power them again. To fix the time corridor.'

The others looked at each other. A *time* corridor?

'We'd need the entire set of weaves and accompanying notes telling us how to arrange and power them,' said Minar.

'I have some of the weaves my grandfather left me.'

'And Rihal has the notes and the rest of the weaves you and I don't,' pointed out Minar. 'She offered to exchange them for access to the time corridor.'

So she had stolen them. Everyone turned to Minar, as Yavi asked: 'Did you let her?'

Minar shook her head. 'She didn't know I had access to an active one. I needed time to think, so I sent her home to get me a complete set, letting her think I was game. Oh, a complete set includes the ones you still have, so I dare say you should have another look at your security arrangements.'

Yavi nodded.

'But,' said Fahe, frowning deeply, puzzled, 'why would you need time to think? You already have this time corridor thing, whatever that is, so why didn't you just tell her, "No, thank you, I'm not interested"?'

Minar tilted her head and studied Fahe for some long moments. 'Simple,' she said finally. 'She had something I wanted too.'

'What was that?'

'She had information about Komas—something that I've been looking for.'

'What exactly does a time corridor do?' asked Keas tentatively, since no one else was asking.

Minar looked at him. Her eyes narrowed. 'Your name, you said, was Keas?'

He nodded.

'El'Idrin Win's son Keas?'

'Whoa,' said Fahe. 'Really? He's in our history books!'

Keas's mouth fell open in dismay. 'How did you know?' he cried plaintively.

Minar smiled. 'We've met before. Rather, I've met you, but you haven't met me yet. So, you could say, we will meet someday.'

'Pardon?' asked Keas.

'Wait a minute,' said Yavi. 'You say you will meet him in the future. So the time corridor will exist in the future. That means we *can* repair it.'

Minar shook her head. 'The time I used the corridor to enter that point in the future is already past in my lifeline. It has already happened for me.'

'Holy Flame freezing over!' said Fahe, sacrilegiously. 'You are talking about time travel!'

'Time travel?' Zurel spoke for the first time. 'Travelling through time? Is it possible?'

'It's not easy, but yes, it is, by magnifying the power of Satin using Flame magic. That's what Avin and Varda discovered.'

'So that is why the day we met you seemed confused and disoriented,' said Fahe. 'You didn't seem to know when we'd come or if we'd eaten. You'd just come here from... some other, er, time?'

'Oh, it was that obvious, was it?'

'And you *have* met Komas,' persisted Fahe. 'Yavi and I thought you had. The way you spoke about him.'

Minar grimaced. 'Yes, I have slipped up quite badly, it seems. I'm not used to communicating with outsiders, not of this current time, that is.'

'Minar, I don't understand one thing,' Yavi said. 'Why did you say time travelling would have killed me when you are clearly doing it all the time?'

'*You* time travelled?' asked Fahe, but no one answered her.

'Because,' said Minar, 'you mess things up with your system if you travel to a time when you already exist. You have to be careful to choose a time before or after your birth or death respectively.'

Yavi was silent for a few moments, not taking his eyes off Minar. 'So...'

'In a sense, I died some six years ago.'

'And where are you... at present... I mean... when do you come from?' Yavi asked haltingly. It wasn't an easy question to frame.

'When I come from, I have about twenty-one years to go before I die, if that's what you mean to ask. But with the time corridor gone, I am,' she spread her hands, 'trapped here.'

'So what happens now? You will live forever, now that you're outside your lifetime?'

'Of course not. I will age as normally as you.'

'If you aren't from here,' said Zurel, 'where... when are you from?'

'Twenty-seven years ago,' whispered Fahe to Zurel. 'I counted.'

'Correct,' said Minar.

'But... twenty-seven years ago...' said Fahe. She looked at Yavi and then back at Minar. 'You don't look *very* old. I mean to say, you must be middle-aged?'

'I suppose thirties feel middle-aged to you,' said Minar, deigning to smile faintly.

Fahe gasped. 'Then you *are* Komas's niece Manara!'

Minar raised her eyebrows. 'If that's what you want to believe.'

'Ha!' said Fahe, punching Yavi's arm. 'I was right!'

He nodded briefly. He seemed subdued.

'What I don't understand,' said Zurel, 'is that, considering you have been trapped here, you seem quite composed about it.'

Minar laughed, but it sounded a bit ironic. 'I am now because I started thinking logically again. You see, you cannot change what happens. And it's a recorded fact that Manara had an accident while swimming in the lake and drowned some years ago. So, I *will* go back. Someday, somehow. To die, if nothing else.'

'I accept my responsibility,' said Yavi guiltily, trying his best to look humble. Keas wondered if he had been behind all the recent excitement. 'And I will do everything possible to help you so you may recreate your time corridor.'

Minar stood up. 'See that you do,' she said. She walked out of the room, and the visitors didn't see her again by the time they were escorted back to Vaker by Marya.

'Pardon me, Yavi, but I have to ask this,' said Zurel. 'What have you done?'

'I was responsible for destroying the time corridor,' he said.

It was a subdued party at Lily's that packed up to go home. Yavi's repeated attempts to call Grey resulted in no response, and he was a little uneasy about the Sua man following her. But he shrugged it off—Grey was more than capable of taking care of herself and, anyway, he had a lot of worries, his adventurous friend the least of them.

The burden of what he had been responsible for was weighing down on him, but more than that was the short period when he had been transported to his life some ten years in the future. Now that he was back, he realized he still had certain memories and knowledge that should normally have taken him ten years to gather. When Keas's identity had been revealed, he had already known it, though it hadn't been foremost in his mind. He knew when and how Zurel would lose her left hand, but he didn't know if he should tell her—warn her—about it. After all, it would happen to save Fahe's life.

But ten years hence, why was it that he had had no memory of Minar and of Fezar? If he had to keep his promise to Minar, surely he should have remembered if he succeeded or failed.

He sat on the bed and dropped his head in his hands. Fleetingly, he remembered that he had yet to break the news to Fahe that, when she entered the Academy just over a week from now, he would be one of her instructors.

'Flame help me,' he said aloud and squeezed his eyes tightly shut, pressing his fingers to them.

Golden sparks and psychedelic patterns danced in the blackness of his vision. Abstract images formed and flowed in and out. And then suddenly, there was a flash of light. Yavi yelled and opened his eyes.

His heart was thumping with the knowledge of something so outlandish that he couldn't have thought it up himself. But he knew it to be true, and knew it to be part of his residual memories from that ten-year jump. So was this how it was going to be—that he would remember things every now and then? Was that why he didn't have any memory of how Minar was to be saved?

But Minar... Manara, when she had said the future of Fezar was safe, had she really meant what he thought she meant? There were other hints, so easy to see—why hadn't they seen them before? The unnerving feeling of familiarity of the facial structure, even the way she walked—Fahe had kept mentioning it. Really, he should pay her ideas more attention.

Oh, and the name, the name was always the biggest hint: *Ma*-rik and She-*nara*.

# Epilogue

## A Meeting

Sareka grimaced as she lifted a sandal-clad foot out of a pool of squelchy mud. This was singularly annoying. Was he leading her on a wild goose chase? She checked her GPS device again. It remained unchanged, just as it had about a thousand times before.

'Next time,' she mumbled to herself, delicately picking her way down an exceedingly muddy lane in an advanced state of disrepair, '*I* choose the location.'

Cousin Kariad had been uncharacteristically nosy when Sareka had turned up in her little cottage in the Academy campus. (Of course, she had taken care to remove her mage's paraphernalia well before approaching the Academy gates.) She regretted having told her cousin about her visit to Kuzerazi to deliver information to Yavi, and it was with difficulty that she had managed to stem her questions, promising to fill her in later, something she had no intention of doing. Satin magic had no place in the life of a Disciple of the Flame, Sareka thought, and if Kariad had to know, Yavi could handle it.

Anyhow, Kariad was far from her mind when she sat down to dig up her list of dubious contacts, accompanied by a large cup of tea. (She had had time to buy a generous supply of that refreshing cardamom flavouring used in Kuzerazan tea; Kariad had turned green on tasting it.) She needed to know if her hunch was right. Four hours of relentless calling and sending of messages later, she was beginning to get some answers.

The Shenaras, as she had suspected, were one of the major clandestine supporters of research into pagan magic. Or non-Flame magic, the more politically correct term. While it was impossible to find any reliable evidence, all hints pointed to the fact that they almost single-handedly funded a group that wasn't exactly famous for keeping within the limits of the law.

Called the Velvet Two, their cover was a historical research society that went by the drab title of the Nizrahi World History Society. The Shenaras' interest in non-traditional magic only pertained to its use for advantages in business, and, of course, they were never happy about sharing their knowledge. No one in their right minds would ever connect the NWHS with the V2, and even those who did know about the existence of the latter only knew of them as anti-magic fundamentalists rather than skilled mages who sought power beyond the Flame. Interestingly, however, the NWHS had a special membership to the Hyran library.

It was only an anonymous message offering information and proof about the Shenaras' involvement with the V2 that got Sareka out of bed at an unearthly hour and navigating down a dirty, disused path behind an abandoned building in the outskirts of Koda. Her informant had sent the precise location, including GPS coordinates, so Sareka had no doubt she was in the right place.

Dawn was still a while away, and there were no street lights here. Her torch was a powerful one; in fact, a special kind that could be used as a deadly weapon at short notice. There was a dead end up ahead, which was the meeting point. She squinted in the darkness and thought she could see a huddled figure. She pointed her torch at it, and it turned away, putting up hands to shield its eyes.

'Mysterious Stranger?' she called. That was the name the informant had used.

'Grey?' it called back. Why not make use of her nickname, Sareka had thought.

The voice sounded male, but as Sareka approached, she couldn't make out much because of the flowing garment with a hood that was pulled low. He also seemed about her size, maybe a little smaller.

'You said you have information,' Sareka said, coming to a halt.

'Come closer,' he said.

'No,' said Sareka.

'I have to show it to you.' He was holding something in his hand. It looked like a plastic folder.

'Then throw it to me.'

He threw it, and it landed to Sareka's right. Keeping a wary eye on the man, she bent to retrieve it.

He moved so fast that she didn't have any chance to take evasive action. He might have been small, but he was very strong. In any case, there was barely any time to struggle. She felt the warm dampness spreading all over her stomach, but there was no pain, not at first.

What puzzled her was that the man didn't get up and run. Instead, he rolled off her and grunted. She turned her head to see him.

The hood had fallen back from his head and she recognized him through a haze of slipping consciousness as Raven. He was not getting up and running off because her torch seemed to be protruding from his chest. How did that happen? Had she managed to instinctively trigger the built-in stiletto? It was in the dead centre of his chest... lucky blow...

By now, Sareka was feeling the pain with a dizzying intensity, but she grinned even as she let the darkness take her.

# Acknowledgements

This story would never have been told without the support of a number of people, including:

—Marie and Proteeti, for reading the manuscript and proffering feedback at an early stage;
—Priya and Ujjal, for help with the technical stuff about weaves;
—SV, for 'keeping' me, mostly without complaint, while I raced to finish writing;
—Davi, tea-drinker-in-arms, for putting up with the long months I spent in Delhi;
—Kate and Niklas, for being the occasional sounding board;
—Sumaira, because she threatened me;
—Karthika, for the insightful feedback that changed the story;
—and, of course, Mita.

Thank you, all. Live long and prosper.

## The Girls behind the Gunfire

Trisha Ray

**Pack up your books—it's time to kick some butt!**

Life can be hard when you're a dork. You're not pretty or popular—just intelligent and very bored with the world around you. And then you discover that one of your friends, dorkier than you and thrice as socially inept, has a major secret. One she could kill for. Literally.

Abhishikta is thrilled by the revelation that the nerdy Rikita is actually a lethal super-soldier—her geekiness belying the fact that she can kill everyone in a room, in any given situation, within five minutes, using a wooden table-leg. And Riki proceeds to induct Abhi into the Foundation, a secret organization that claims to exist only to serve human civilization. Not humanity; just civilization. Abhi takes to martial arts and guns with a bloodthirstiness previously unsuspected by anyone—even herself. What she doesn't take to, however, is the fascist control exerted by the Foundation over its soldiers. She begins to ask questions... and things start getting really messy.

An action-packed story about an ordinary girl turned reluctant assassin, *The Girls behind the Gunfire* is a tale you do not want to miss.

## The Secret Keeper

Mitali Perkins

**'I think I'll go mad living in this house... What happens to my happily-ever-after?'**

When Asha travels with her mother and sister from Delhi to her father's ancestral home in Calcutta, it is supposed to be a temporary measure only; as soon as her father finds work in distant America, they will join him. In the meantime, there's plenty to keep her busy: overcoming the conservatism of the extended family, becoming friends with her cousins, keeping her mother's depression at bay, teaching a lesson to the neighbourhood boys who don't think girls are 'good enough', fending off her sister Reet's unsuitable would-be suitors, and so on.

Overwhelmed by all that's happening around her, Asha escapes to her rooftop hideaway every day, where she pours her heart out into her diary, her secret keeper. And it is here that she encounters Jay, her reclusive neighbour, who makes her heart beat faster...

## *Extreme American Makeover*

Mitali Perkins

FIRST DAUGHTER BOOK 1

Sameera—Sparrow to her friends—is used to feeling invisible. But all that is about to change. As her father's presidential campaign heats up, Sameera trades in her summer vacation for a crash course in becoming a celebrity. Step 1: Fabulous Makeover, of course!

As it turns out, the makeover is amazing. But some of the campaign staff aren't content with a trendy haircut, stilettos and designer outfits. They've decided to package Pakistan-born, plain-speaking Sameera as 'Sammy' Righton—a giggly, carefree, all-American girl. No more wearing comfy jeans and sneakers, dancing the bhangra or blogging from the heart—in other words, Sameera must forget about being herself.

What they don't know is that Sameera has a mind of her own. And plenty to say. Not to mention a gutsy, straight-talking blog that could go live to millions...

# White House Rules

Mitali Perkins

FIRST DAUGHTER BOOK 2

Last year, Sameera helped her dad win the elections to become the President of the United States of America. Now she has an even tougher challenge ahead of her: surviving life in the White House!

There are advantages, of course, to being the First Daughter—chilling at Camp David, the White House gym, state-of-the-art kitchen and home theatre, designer clothes, and so on. But there's the bad too—her parents are busy all the time, diplomatic duties must be taken very seriously, constant Secret Service surveillance, no more school and thus no more friends and gossip. And then there is the ugly—paparazzi, and people who spew venom on her blog because she's of Pakistani origin. But the most worrisome thing is that Bobby, her sort-of boyfriend, seems to have disappeared from her life altogether!

But Sameera refuses to be beaten. Against all odds, she must find a way to reach out to her friends, silence the haters, and get Bobby back. Will she succeed? Find out in this fabulous sequel to *Extreme American Makeover*.

# Potato Chips

Anshuman Mohan

**'Students are like potatoes... Only the finest of us will get made into chips!'**

When Aman Malhotra is made to change schools, he knows that his goose is well and truly cooked. From the easygoing, friendly atmosphere of Akshar, he is thrust into the big, bad world of St. Xavier's. The reason, according to his parents: a big school prepares you much better for your future, i.e., IIT. Things, Aman realizes, are about to change and not for the better. The progress graph of his life plunges downwards in a sudden freefall—his grades suffer, his classmates snicker at him, his teachers think he is a brat.

Struggling to make sense of his new, high-pressure surroundings, Aman casts his net far and wide for friends and finds Shubho, a boy with a crafty drop-shot and a mean backhand. As Aman gets to know Shubho and tries to help him out, he also begins to get his own life back on track. A hero, he finally understands, comes in the most unlikely of guises and isn't necessarily the most popular kid in school.

An honest, in-your-face story of school life and adolescence—the highs, the lows, the pranks, the exams, the friendships, the fights—*Potato Chips* is crisp and smart, fresh and funny.

## How to Salsa in a Sari

Dona Sarkar

Issa Mazumder, a nerdy half-Indian, half-African teenage girl who lives in the US with her single mother, has just been utterly destroyed because the gorgeous Cat Morena, Latina princess, Issa's worst enemy and the most popular girl in school, has stolen Issa's equally nerdy boyfriend Adam. And there's worse to come—Issa's mother announces that she and Cat's father are getting married. And they are moving into Cat's huge mansion.

Cat has no respect for Issa's traditions and makes Issa's life hell. But Issa gets some tough advice: if she wants Cat Morena to welcome *her* traditions, Issa had better learn to salsa in a sari!

# Body Talk

## Anjali Wason

**Real girls ask real questions about life, love and everything in between.**

Sex. Girls. Boys. Bodies. Relationships. Being a young woman can be confusing, but *Body Talk* is here to offer some clarity...

Are you afraid to tell your parents about your boyfriend? Do you wish you were more confident about yourself? Or do you just want to know how to flirt?

*Body Talk* features over 400 questions that girls just like you have asked across India; it brings together real voices from the real world, in which everyone is curious about life, love and sex. Packed with advice on everything from how to use a condom to cyber dating to sexual harassment, *Body Talk* is an essential guide for any young woman interested in understanding her feelings, her body and her life.